Holy Smoke

Also by Libby Purves

Fiction
Casting Off (1995)
A Long Walk in Wintertime (1996)
Home Leave (1997)
More Lives Than One (1998)

Non-Fiction
How Not to Be a Perfect Mother (1986)
One Summer's Grace (1989, new edition 1997)

Holy Smoke

Religion and Roots:
A Personal Memoir

LIBBY PURVES

Hodder & Stoughton
LONDON SYDNEY AUCKLAND

British Library Cataloguing in Publication Data
A record for this book is available from the British Library

ISBN 0 340 72160 X

Typeset by Avon Dataset Ltd, Bidford-on-Avon, Warks

Printed and bound in Great Britain by
Clays Ltd, St Ives plc

Hodder and Stoughton Ltd
A Division of Hodder Headline PLC
338 Euston Road
London NW1 3BH

To all the good nuns

Contents

Introduction

This book is neither journalism nor fiction, but a meditative segment of autobiography: the hardest part was getting up the nerve to believe that it ought to be written at all. However, as any painter or writer — from the best to the worst — will tell you, once you start thinking about some image or idea in a certain way it is impossible to stop yourself recording it. My own upbringing, especially my religious upbringing, came so often and so forcibly to mind that it needed writing down.

This was not least because a quarter-century of journalism in an ever more agnostic world has, rather to my surprise, only gone to harden a belief — though sometimes a reluctant belief — that the religious perspective is the one which goes farthest towards making sense of the world.

This brings me to the other excuse for offering this book to a sceptical readership. I shall be fifty years old in the year 2000, with children reaching the ages of sixteen and eighteen that year. There is a pleasing symmetry about all this, and it seems a good time to write some things down. I remember childhood very well — indeed with additional intensity from having so recently watched my own children developing — but I am far enough through adulthood to be able to weigh up with hindsight the effect that early sights, sounds and beliefs have had. My children are still young enough to enforce frequent contact with a newer view of the world; on the other hand my mother is still around to lend me her family archives and amplify (or dispute) my vivid private baby memories.

Middle-age, in short, is a fine high vantage point for looking back. I have tried to do it without undue sentimentality, and to be honest about how things felt at the time. It was a strange childhood but a rich one: arid Israel and ornate Bangkok, French convent lunches with beer served to nine-year-olds after High Mass on feast days, the unease of a convent school in apartheid South Africa, and back in England the parallel universes of plainsong in chapel and Beatlemania outside it. Then the scene changed to a university generation which played at world revolution even as it turned more raptly towards its own drugged inner landscapes; and all this against the rootlessness of a life where home was forever moving – to new mountains, new seas, new cities.

The other reason for writing the book was to help with a conundrum of our time. What should be done about religious education – if anything – is a subject of constant anxious and aggressive public debate. Should children be 'indoctrinated?' How 'multicultural' should we get? Does RE teach 'right and wrong'?

It can do no harm for a few individuals to come clean about what exactly went on in their own religious education, just to provide a point of reference. Moreover, I was brought up Catholic, and Catholic childhoods of my vintage have had a stinking bad press. Every few years a fresh crop of former convent schoolgirls is rounded up on television, like the usual suspects, to bemoan the terror and bigotry of their childhood. Nuns hit them with rulers, threatened them with damnation, and made them bathe in long cotton robes. Priests hissed a horror of hellfire through the confessional grille and reinforced degrading ideas of patriarchal supremacy which only an uncritical reading of early Germaine Greer could ever purge. We convent girls vie with one another to swap stories of having to sleep with our hands outside the bedclothes, or collect fifty-day indulgences from Purgatory, or wear two pairs of knickers at all times, or eschew patent-leather shoes in case men saw your petticoat reflected in them.

Boys, meanwhile, were fed terrifying misinformation about their private parts and set unrealistic standards of behaviour towards their personal Temples of the Holy Spirit. Everyone's life, we are given to understand, was well and truly messed up by Catholicism: and this is before you even start on the child abuse. For years now Catholic childhoods have been the material of horror stories and jokes. Some of the accusations are true, some are probably not.

But the result of these childhoods, in countless members of my generation, is a general assumption that anybody with the slightest bit of nerve and intelligence discards the lot by the age of twenty, chucking the baby out with the bathwater and gobbling up fashionable agnosticism and the Pill at once. Some, of course, come back to faith as adults, to the irritation of those who don't. I remember once listening to a Northern Irish colleague at the BBC, a lapsed Catholic, who lived in a permanent and not dishonourable rage at what religious bigotry has done in her homeland. She was magnificently excoriating an interview with Mary Kenny:

'She says here,' spat my friend, waving the newspaper, 'that when she had her firstborn child she had an overwhelming desire, which she could not resist, to pray over the cradle. Well, Mary darlin', let me tell you this – *some of us* have indeed felt the same blasted desire, and we have *fought it*, *smothered it*, and *thrown it out the backdoor* for good and all!'

More mildly, dozens of my English school contemporaries just drifted away, disillusioned and bored by the very idea of religion. The Papal ruling against chemical contraception was an obvious stumbling-block, as was the Church's apparent indifference to the real plight of women in this dilemma. Religion suffered also from the prevailing current of worldly materialism and growing individualism in which we, the affluent post-war generation, swam and glittered freely for a while before the deficiencies of the age became evident.

Another thing which has not helped our feelings about religion is the recent onrush of happy-clappy evangelism, with emotional public conversions to the cause of a chummy personal Jesus. Ex-Catholics tend to be dispiritedly immune to all this, and very few get Born Again in that particular style. It is well known that the best way to stop an evangelist in full flow and send him trudging defeated from your doorstep is to say 'Look, I grew up Catholic.' Even the heroic social conscience of great Anglican bishops like the Reverend David Sheppard does not stir the lapsed Papists: 'Here's a fiver for the homeless shelter, but leave God out of it', we say. 'Been there, done that, worn the veil, carried the candle. Long ago. Sorry, no sale.'

The curiosity, for me, is that although I am no kind of good Catholic, I never really drifted very far. Best efforts never quite doused the lamp. It is years since I was a regular attender at Mass, let alone a communicant, but Christianity – a pared-down, undemonstrative core of belief, affecting everything, informing every decision – has never left me. With rare exceptions I find atheists unconvincing and slightly boring (although not, admittedly, quite as boring and unconvincing as the rainbow prophets of the New Age). Behaving like a Christian is difficult and not obviously rewarding, and I very often don't: but not for a moment do I doubt that I ought to.

Nor has it proved possible for me to doubt for long that all history and all the Universe has a shape, and a beauty, and an ultimate balance. Against all reason I find that I believe that justice and love will prevail, and that the clues to this truth are everywhere, from the furrow in the field to the South African elections. Goethe said, 'I believe in God and in Nature and in the triumph of good over evil' and the second and third parts don't work without the first. Nature alone is too cruel to be credible. Even if Faith seems shaky, there are still Hope and Charity, and without these life has neither nobility or meaning.

Or so it seems to me. I suppose I wrote this memoir of the roots of my life to try and find out why.

One other thing, when it comes to childhood memory: I have

three brothers, but you will find little of them in these pages.
This is not because they were not important, but because their
stories are their own property. I am far too experienced a sister
to try and hijack them.

1. Beginnings

I was born in 1950 on the second of February: Candlemas Day, the feast of the Purification of Our Lady. All through a childhood passed in half-a-dozen countries and a range of convent schools, the feast and the birthday were inextricably entwined. I suppose that if you belong to a big family and go to boarding-schools your birthday takes on particular importance because it is something inalienably your own. *My* birthday meant Mass on a weekday, white veils and the smell of warm wax candles.

Moreover, from as early as I can remember I was secretly stirred by the meaning of the feast. Mary and Joseph were travelling, burdened with a baby, and this was an easy image to understand. Coming from a big family which was moved on at the whim of the Foreign Office every two or thee years, from earliest infancy I knew what it was to be on the road and laden. Mary and Joseph's trip to Jerusalem, like the flight into Egypt, struck up very familiar echoes.

Our own family always seemed to be moving on with assorted carrycots and fractious infants, to turn up at some new posting exhausted and uncertain and several tea-chests short of comfort. It was not difficult to sympathise with the Holy Family arriving in Jerusalem with their significant baby, lodging temporarily with relatives and turning up humble and unpretentious in their good clothes at the temple, with a lamb or a pair of doves to add to their burdens. Expecting nothing but the ordinary rites of dedication and purification, they were met by an explosion of praise and welcome. The old priest Simeon had lived too long in expectation of this deliverance, ever since a burdensome prophecy that he would see the Messiah before dying. He took the Child in his arms and his cry of joy, from St Luke's Gospel, wove itself around the liturgy of the feast, intense and mysterious, speaking of death not with dread but as a consummation and a victory: 'Lord, now let thy servant depart in peace, according to thy word; for mine eyes have seen thy salvation.'

Sometimes, even at nine or ten, I was exalted at the idea of demanding, claiming, *earning* such a dismissal from the world. Like all children, I had momentary terrors of death. Like all children of that period who were taught to pray, I intensely disliked the little rhyme:

> Matthew Mark Luke and John
> Bless the bed that I lie on
> If I should die before I wake
> I pray the Lord my soul to take.

This notion of instant, overnight death frightened me as much as it would any child: but at the same time I nurtured a secret pleasure in the notion that there would come a day, at the end of the corridor of years, when dismissal from the world would not be a tragedy or a terror, but a matter of blazing light and revelation and relief. Candles flickered, the priest was in gold. *Lumen ad revelationem gentium* . . .

For of course, at first this song of Simeon's was in Latin, like the Mass: '*Nunc dimittis servum tuum domine, secundum verbum tuum in pace*'. Later it was in French (*Seigneur laisse aller en paix ton serviteur*). Then it was in English. Sometimes the great words were spoken, sometimes sung in harmony; best and most beautiful they came in the austerity of plainsong. They haunt me still, and I have never had a birthday without the lines running through my head for most of the day, particularly the moment when the level black diamond notes of the plain chant line release the chanting into something like a tune, something with a swing:

Holy Smoke

Lumen ad revelationem Gentium!
Et gloriam plebis tuae Israel.

A light to lighten the Gentiles, and a glory to thy people Israel.

Light and glory and a birthday: candles sacred and secular, flickering in happy unity. I was, let it be hastily said, a child of no saintly attributes whatsoever: a chubby and prosaic schoolgirl as anxious as any to rip the wrappings off toys and chocolate rabbits (and later, Beatle albums and white plastic Courrèges boots and hideous fishnet-effect tights). Yet an accident of liturgy ensured that around even the most worldly and grasping of my birthdays there has always curled like incense, like holy smoke, the high unearthly plainsong and the awestruck '*Nunc Dimittis*' of the old priest, sated with glory and ready for death.

When, much later, a haunting version of that '*Nunc Dimittis*' was used as the signature tune for a televised Le Carré spy story, my first reaction was a dowagerish outrage: the horror you get when some oik quotes your favourite books, a feeling memorably described by Stella Gibbons as 'like seeing a drunken stranger wrapped in one's dressing-gown'. But it was a good spy series and glory has to be shared around: so I forgave it.

My father would have no truck with any of this. It appalled him when he caught glimpses of the overblown yearning cloying religion into which he had made what Catholics then still called a 'mixed marriage'. The note of disapproval in that phrase did not escape our beady infant eyes: after all, in the Catechism such marriages were described as 'unlawful and pernicious' unless a dispensation was granted 'for very grave reasons, and under special conditions'. Fresh from scanning this booklet I once roared into the kitchen with my brother and demanded of my mother 'What was the *grave and special* reason why you and Dad got married?'

She had guests at the time – angular Protestant ladies who were probably suspicious enough already of the Papists who had moved in down Leveretts Lane – and was not amused. 'Because nobody else would bloody well have either of us' she snapped. I took this literally, and was quite satisfied.

From my father flowed a constant, but muted and not particularly threatening, current of anticlerical and atheist feeling. He had been brought up as a Scottish Presbyterian in the 1920s, son of Purves the Draper in Cupar, Fife, and occasionally he let drop horrifying little glimpses of a glum and joyless world of religious strictness next to which our Catholic training seemed positively bohemian. There was endless kirk on Sundays, he would tell us, and threats of hellfire for the slightest blasphemy: and blasphemy could consist of even reading a secular book on the Sabbath, let alone running or playing.

These memories of his always combined in my mind with his other anecdotes of long-ago Cupar, which frequently involved goats. He hated minding the family goats, was by his account frequently chased up trees, and derived from the rigours of this upbringing a lifelong distaste for the earthier aspects of country life and an absolute refusal to go camping, ever (when the rest of us did, he checked into a local hotel and joined us, gingerly, for cups of tea which he checked suspiciously for floating grass and beetles).

To escape goats and religion alike, Dad fled down the great Scottish highway of scholarship. He spoke lovingly of the kingdoms of secular learning, St Andrews and Freiburgim, Breisgau, where amid old stonework and learned, soothingly sceptical books he studied metaphysics and psychology in the 1930s. Coming from the austere windswept decencies of the old Lowland life he also grew a taste for great European cities, for drawing-rooms and stateliness, order and diplomacy, equestrian statues and the faint, intoxicatingly Continental whiff of drains and decadence.

Religion was left behind with all the other constrictions of his early life, dumped with triumphant gladness. Occasionally he worried that it would 'get' us children and never let us go. Once, in France, delivering me at the great creaking door of the current convent, Dad waited until my little brothers had trotted into their kindergarten line and said 'This word, religion. Re-ligio. It comes from the same root as "ligature", or the French *liens*. Fetters. Religion is something that ties you up, and ties you down.' We often had these little etymological conversations.

I was very struck by this definition of religion, imagining the nuns and priests of my daily school life nicely trussed up, bondage-style, and pegged to the ground. But I remember him hastily adding 'Don't mention this kind of thing – your *real* knowledge – to your mother, or your teachers. Better not.'

That, however, is the only time I remember this long-suffering man actively attempting subversion. For the most part he put up gracefully with the religiosity of our education, and indeed came to a grudging respect for nuns and monks. He picnicked happily in the hills above Jaffa with an Irish Franciscan nun, enjoyed learned classical chats with Greek Orthodox prelates and would often remark on the fine qualities of the religious figures my mother brought into our family life: Mère Béhagel, or Père Daillez, or Mother Wilson, or Father Rudd, or dear old Sister Catherine from West Cork who used to write to NASA asking to be sent up into space on the Shuttle to see the face of God in the stars – because 'Sure if I die at my age, where's the harm?' These, Dad would say, were fine people '*in spite* of being nuns or priests'.

In vain did my mother suggest to him that their innocent goodness and devotion to duty might be because of their vows, and not despite them. He would shake his head and return to his book.

Meanwhile his children's bedrooms were strewn with missals, rosaries, dinky little toy shrines to St Bernadette, luminous Virgins, gruesome plastic crucifixes, and holy pictures given as rewards for school performance and often featuring a long-haired, soppy-looking layabout unaccountably wearing his heart on the outside of his frock. I speak, as it were, through my father's eyes: the rest of us knew perfectly well that this was the accepted image of the Sacred Heart of Jesus.

But Dad was not one for confrontation or unpleasantness or

divided parental authority, and he put up with the evidence of our indoctrination with a forbearance which (come to think of it) was almost more than Christian. Occasionally I would see his neck muscles tighten when I thoughtlessly droned hymns in the back of the car on early school runs, particularly that rather queasy number which goes:

> Soul of my saviour, sanctify my breast
> Body of Christ, be thou my saving guest
> Blood of my saviour, bathe me in thy tide
> Wash me in waters flowing from thy side.

Now, of course, I better understand that he was suffering double discomfort, pricked on two sides at once. The rebellious, atheist side of him loathed the very idea of religion, any religion. As if that were not bad enough, at the same time the remains of old Presbyterian instincts bristled fiercely at the *kind* of religion this droning daughter represented. The ghosts of old Covenanters rose in him, horrified at the hymn's fetid atmosphere of rich Papist emotionalism, of bells and smells and bishops and swooning St Teresas with worryingly Freudian swords in their vitals and creepily hysterical metaphors. 'Deep in thy wounds, Lord, hide and shelter me', I would croon, as any child croons in the back of a car; and he would shudder. Or, sometimes, retaliate with some joke of his own, often in schoolboy pig-Latin:

> *Caesar adsum jam forte*
> *Brutus 'ad arat*
> *Caesar sic in omnibus*
> *Brutus sic in 'at.*

He was a good and forbearing man, was our father. He died in 1984 and heaven, one hopes, will have had the good taste to receive him without any embarrassment of trumpets or harp arpeggios. I like to think (in that sentimental Catholic way that made him cringe so much) that there is a corner of the place

11

reserved for the likes of him: a celestial annexe with deep leather chairs, a selection of agreeable books, all the main European newspapers and decent coffee. There would be an absolute ban on harps, a dress code that wings and robes must be left in the lobby, and blinds which can be pulled firmly down to exclude the garish blaze of Eternal Glory.

The reason for our Catholicism was our mother. Half her family was from Irish stock, actors from Dundalk. Somewhere back in time, we were often informed, my great-grandmother played Lady Isabel in an early staging of *East Lynne*, and spoke the immortal words: 'Dead, dead, and never called me mother!' This nicely set the tone for a full-blooded enjoyment of melodrama which reached its rank flowering in my maternal grandmother. To Granny (who also insisted on claiming a streak of Romany blood, and read tea-leaves unless forcibly prevented) every operation was terminal, every emotion vast and formless. 'People love me', she would say with utter confidence. 'They love to do little acts of charity for me. It's a joy to them in their lives.'

She spent most of the second half of her own life sitting back, contentedly invalidish, recovering from some minor operation around 1930 which nobody could quite remember – rumoured to be a totally unnecessary appendectomy. For a period when we were back in England she lived with us, and would sit with the tomato plants in the warmth of the greenhouse, smoking Wild Woodbines and calling out in an artfully quavering voice when she wanted a cup of tea. Once my brother called her bluff. Summoned with the usual studiedly faint request:

'Would you do an act of Christian charity for your old Granny?' he said briskly:

'Depends what it is.'

She asked him to fetch her handbag – 'my purse', as it was known – and with an authentic throwback to the bald theology of his Presbyterian ancestors my brother retorted:

'That is not an act of charity, Granny, it is an errand.' Whereon he went, dutiful but irreligious, to fetch it.

My mother, having grown up with all this dramatic exaggeration, was sometimes driven to seek (as I too have been) inspiration and consolation in the pages of Stella Gibbons's *Cold Comfort Farm*, that ultimate elegant put-down of Aunt Ada Doom emotionalism. It is a most useful book for those with our inheritance: when, like Judith, any of us feel inclined in the course of a family altercation to tear our breasts and utter a cry along the lines of 'Son, son, do you want to break your mother's heart?' we remember the reply: ' "Yes", said Seth with elemental simplicity. The porridge boiled over' and we wisely put a sock in it. Another expression has proved equally useful in the lifelong battle against the female family tendency to soupy, thrilling emotion: a remark by my husband's Yorkshire mother on seeing a young couple embracing at a railway station. Looking on in disgust, she said firmly:

'There's never been any *slop* in *our* family.'

Conscious, perhaps, that there is plenty of potential slop swilling around in ours, we seize the expression gratefully whenever the need comes to stiffen the upper lip, call up the buttoned Presbyterian in us, and defuse some dangerously un-British, spookily Papist manifestation of emotion. Never been any slop in our family!

Anyway, my mother did not reject Catholicism as she grew up but kept to it, albeit with a powerful ecumenical slant. This was eccentric, at that period, but she can date her ecumenical stance firmly from an incident when she was eleven years old and a member of her Nottingham Girl Guide troop. She and another Catholic girl were so keen that – although for Catholics to attend Anglican services was forbidden by both sides – they would polish and kit themselves up faithfully for Church Parade every Sunday and march with their comrades as far as the church door, before turning obediently aside into Papist exile.

One day a new Guide leader came, discovered the presence of Catholic interlopers in her troop, and expelled them. From that day to this my mother has bristled with fury at any attempt to harness religion to exclusion, or clubbiness, or cliqueishness.

Catholic she may be, but she has refused down the years to join a great many Holy Sisterhoods of this and that. When my father married her he moaned 'I know you're a Catholic, I can put up with that, but you aren't a *Jesuit*, are you?' She knew what he meant, and concurred.

So as infants we were never taught that Catholics were better, or truer, or more virtuous or enlightened than adherents of any other kind of religion. Just that we *were* Catholics, in the same way as, wherever we went, we *were* British. Because we were, we had to go to Mass on Sunday and Confession occasionally and learn the Catechism, and be taught by nuns and monks whenever available. And that was that.

My mother herself, as a diplomat's wife, found Catholicism a useful lingua franca in every country. Catholic churches are a way in to a community, often to the host community, and lead almost always to a fascinatingly polyglot, multicultural knot of fellow-exiles. Church gave her a far more interesting and amusing way of forging links than she could have got merely by performing her duty of trudging round the British expatriate community listening to bored women complaining about the vagaries of 'local help'. At which juncture – although it is not entirely to the point – I should correct a common belief that the lives of diplomatic families are pampered, full of soft-footed servants and deferential locals and the cushioning power of money. Most embassy and consular staff, in the nature of things, are junior. They earn modestly and their spouses' ability to work is very limited. Nor had American standards of domestic comfort spread as far round the globe in my childhood as they have now. There was dressing-up, of course, but my mother's own description of her first decades of marriage is 'around the world from sink to mink to sink'. A lot of the sinks were blocked.

Even when we did have help, it was not always restful, even when bound to us by the Catholic lingua franca. None of us will ever forget the vast furious Spaniard called Jesusa, who stubbornly pressed sideways creases into everybody's jeans and walked out for ever one Christmas Eve in Berne with the ambassador expected to dinner.

My mother's way in to this diplomatic life had been piquant: as a County Council typist in Nottingham she met Polish airmen in training from a nearby camp, and was so charmed by these men's spontaneity and spirit and emotional openness – I suppose by their general dissimilarity to sour old Anglican Girl Guide leaders – that she determined to join them. She took herself off to summer school in Oxford to learn Polish and then presented herself to the Foreign Office as just the girl they needed to translate the newspapers in the post-war Warsaw Embassy. After some time out there she married – not an emotional, gesticulating, warm-blooded Catholic Pole but my cool intellectual religionless father. Which goes to show something, but I am never sure what.

My elder brother was born in Poland, and I was conceived there. All through our other postings, wherever we went, my mother deftly managed to surround herself with exiled Poles called Staj and Kasimir and Count Somethingski. I mention this here because the Polishness of their Catholicism – or the Catholicism of their Polishness – was another stream which fed my own earliest perceptions of religion. They, and the Russians who also assembled around my mother wherever she went, were exiles, their countrymen's identity and religion crushed and reviled under Soviet rule: they spoke of this with sorrowful anger, and through them our houses became even more filled with images of the weeping Polish Christus and Our Lady of Częstochowa.

Years later, when the iron curtain was crumbling I was at the BBC and first saw the famous news photograph of the shipyard workers kneeling in prayer at Gdansk: the rightness of the gesture, its rootedness in Polish history and identity and long-crushed honour, made me gasp with amazed wonder. Momentarily, that image ripped from me all the young-adult newsroom cynicism of my normal life.

So, glimpsed through the eyes of those mournful devoted

Holy Smoke

Poles of my childhood, religion never seemed to me the smug, fat-bottomed, established, trussed-up stuffy thing that many of my contemporaries thought it. It seemed to be a force for human dignity and human freedom. Sometimes, it still does.

2. Postings

After Poland my parents had a brief interlude in London, where I was born, and then a posting to Israel. Arriving in Tel Aviv they found a nation still only four years old; a far smaller Israel than today's, divided at the Mandelbaum Gate in Jerusalem. Armed with two passports they could cross over into the Arab sector and visit the Old City, but my mother tells how when our Orthodox Christian Arab landlord Mr Lotfallah Hannah went to the gate on Easter Day he had to drive to the border and wait there while a priest carried him out a flame kindled at the holy flame in the Church of the Holy Sepulchre.

The flame's destination was the Orthodox Convent in Jaffa, where it would be received with reverent ceremony by the Abbouna. But Mr Hannah kindly dropped in with his oil-lamp on the young Purves household to light a flame before my mother's icon and have a whiskey. Fortunately he had gone before my brother, aged four, climbed up and, in a festive birthday spirit, blew it out.

It was with Mr Hannah's family too that in one of my earliest faint memories we were taken to the top of Mount Tabor, to spend a night at the monastery. In old Jerusalem we slept in a tiny Polish convent hospice: you knocked on the door with 'Blessed be Jesus Christ' to which a wizened little sister opened the door with 'For ever and ever'. My brother Patrick had been born in Tel Aviv, and has a birth certificate in Hebrew dated from the year of the Creation, some four or five thousand years (it also

17

certified him to be a girl, because my mother had not appeared for the ceremonies of circumcision eight days after his birth. I mention this to reinforce the all-pervading and slightly wacky religious diversity which was part of my childhood for as far back as I can recall). I do not remember much of Mount Tabor: only a faint memory of being very pleased later to be bought a new pot, white enamel with a blue rim from the market in Jaffa, which I recognised (and, in family legend, announced) to be 'Just like on Mount Tabor'. Even my pot had an ecclesiastical tone.

For my mother, living in Israel brought on a passion for Jewishness second only to her passion for Poles. The sympathetically inclined may imagine how difficult it was, later on, for her to tolerate a Hamburg posting. Diplomats may not become emotionally involved with the feelings of their host countries, but nobody can police the emotional reactions of their wives.

Israel was a rich stew of religions. We went – with Norah and Christina, our flighty Irish household helps – on what we children called the Clatterbang Bus into Tel Aviv, and attended a Franciscan church; my elder brother went to a nursery school run by nuns but where only two children were Christian, so that there was not even allowed to be a crucifix on the wall. Greek Orthodox priests often came to call: I just remember Father Benedictos, with a tall black chimney-pot hat and big spade beard, who whenever he came to dinner would stride into our bedroom with apples and sweets hidden in his wide cuffs for small entranced children. At some stage hereabouts my mother came by her alleged fragment of the True Cross: all through childhood we enjoyed unscrewing the little nut at the base of the crucifix and peering at the splinter of wood embedded in hardened wax at its core.

So there are confused nursery memories: black-bearded, deep-voiced priests, lamps before icons, Franciscans with rope belts, Hanukkah with branched candles, holy mountains, skullcaps in the street, synagogues, Norah and Christina in headscarves making eyes at young taxi-drivers in church. The Christmas story took on particular attraction when it was pointed out to us that

Mary was just a Jewish girl, like the ones we saw every day in the street. The Crucifixion story was similarly domesticated. The legendary 'Holy Land' of first Bible stories lay all around us: it was the prosaic, noisy, dusty, orange-grovey, babblingly Arabic world of every day. I was nearly four by the time we left.

Then it was Bangkok, and suddenly there were no more black stovepipe hats or skullcaps, but Buddhas in the temples and saffron-robed priests begging with bowls in the street; dancers in tall intricate pointed hats struck strange attitudes with bent-back fingers, and boats went gliding through the city along the brown canals, the *khlongs* that still ran between rickety houses and gleaming new Banks and gilded temples. Buddha was not lonely: there were Hindu gods and goddesses too, in gold and jade and crumbly plaster, and odd little sprites demanding odd little rites, borrowed from God knows what intricate reaches of Far Eastern animism. On every building a 'spirit house' stood out on a stalk so that no shadow should fall on it and offend the protective deity of the house. It says much for the all-embracing, self-effacing nature of my mother's Catholic belief that the word 'pagan' was unfamiliar to me until years later. We sometimes took flowers to Buddha.

Indeed, Buddhas were the first religious statues to strike me with awe and a conviction that belief – whatever form it takes – is as inevitable to human beings as eating and drinking. Sculpture, like music, has a peculiar power to start communicating at the place where logic and exposition have to stop. Great statues, like music, speak to small children with a directness not to be underestimated. The peace and assurance and vivid stillness in every line of every Buddha was – as I can feel now, looking at mere pictures – ineffably soothing and comforting.

In Bangkok, however, this dim indefinite awakening of a spiritual sense combined most pleasingly with showmanship and sensation. I loved the great Sleeping Buddha at Wat Pho, whose enormous gilded plaster feet towered high above us, the soles decorated with mother-of-pearl; the Emerald Buddha (actually jade, I now read) was pretty good, but even better was the solid gold Buddha of Wat Traimit: three times a small child's height, over five tons in weight and dazzlingly priceless. It had been plastered over, nobody knows when, to protect it from some invasion by the Burmese, and the priests who disguised it had died or been killed without revealing the secret. Its true glory had only been discovered a year or two before our arrival: standing disregarded in a shipping company's yard with other chipped cement images of the Buddha, it was prodded by a boy with a stick, who was amazed to strike gold beneath the plaster. Children need awesome stories: contemplation of marvels like these could even ease the itching misery of prickly heat in the hot months.

Lord Buddha was everywhere: a host of him, always set high, cross-legged in temples under the sweeping, prickling, intricate gold roofs; he peered from windows, and perched in the servants' quarters when, inquisitive, we crept through to spy on what Som See did in her spare time. There were sacred flames too, and sacred water: in November at the Loy Krathong festival we were taken out to see a host of tiny lotus-shaped boats set floating down the river, each with a stick of incense, a coin, and a candle flame burning in homage to the water spirits.

Like all four-year-olds, I found out about death around this time, and was duly informed about heaven. But there were vague intimations, from grown-up talk and accounts of Queen Grandmother Sirikit's funeral, that even death was different in Siam. There were firecrackers at funerals, and everybody came back as something else, so death was not so bad. Among the children of the streets and the bowed, thin rickshaw-men life was held cheap and little was done for them; yet causing death was so unthinkable that our gardener would not kill poison snakes, but drag them into the road so that they would be run over.

So once again, religion defined the landscape. The precise detail of what Buddhists believed was of no more concern to the prosaic four-year-old observer than what Jews believed, or how Greek priests with black beards were different from American priests with crew-cuts at the Bangkok Catholic cathedral. The only plain thing was that (with the possible exception of Dad) people everywhere had religions.

That God and his prophets should wear a succession of disguises seemed no more remarkable than the fact that different countries had different shaped buildings. Fussy spiky gilded turrets in Bangkok, fat pointy curved arches in Jerusalem, onion domes in pictures of Poland and Russia – here God, there Yahweh, now Buddha, now Mohammed, now some writhingly erotic Hindu goddess. All, to a four-year-old, the same sort of thing.

Reverence is easy when you are small: you take your shoes off if required, cover your head if everyone else does, keep your voice down, show proper respect to Rabbi or Iman or Abbouna, to flapping orange monk or stout purple bishop. You are small, and not much is expected of you: you hear the music and look up at the whispering beautiful spaces of temple, mosque, synagogue or cathedral in peace. You take from it what you need. But the need is yours, and is private.

Naturally, there were nuns. My brother was sent to the American School, but I, being a girl, was enrolled at Mater Dei, the Ursuline convent of Bangkok.

When I began to think back into this time, I was puzzled that I have no memory of prayers or chapel at school; but my mother enlightens me. *Of course* there weren't chapel prayers and rituals, because I was initially the only Christian child in the school. The rest were Buddhist Thais. The nuns taught us all the Our Father, in Siamese, which I seem to have forgotten; but that was as far as formal instruction went. For ordinary schoolwork I got private lessons in English, but otherwise mingled in as normal a way as possible. I even joined in Thai dancing lessons, and owned a pointy gilt hat, although it must be admitted that my stiff pink Anglo-Saxon hands never did bend back as gracefully as my classmates'.

In fact generally, language was less of a problem than physique. Being tall, white and chubby was a curse. White elephants are

21

immensely prized, almost worshipped, in Siamese folklore, and touching them is a lucky thing to do. This observance was transferred to me as the nearest thing to a white elephant the other five-year-olds had to hand. Pinching me was very fashionable. The pinches, I must admit, were fairly respectful and not intended unkindly: but I did occasionally panic when I found myself in the middle of a crowd of small, dark, intense little girls with black topknots, all hellbent on getting their day's worth of luck from my bare plump pink arms.

The nuns wore white. Indeed, the first nuns I ever saw wearing black – visiting Europeans, I suppose – threw me into shrieking terror. They were, for some reason, far more frightening than even the biggest, blackest-bearded Orthodox priests in Jaffa. I thought they were witches. Much later, in an awful convent in South Africa, the nuns used to change habits from black to white for the hot season, and I still remember how our hearts lifted when they did so.

As I say, I have no particular memory of church or Mass, and suspect that mere Catholic liturgy on Sundays was a touch boring compared to the riot of belief in the streets and along the *khlongs*. But I do have clear memories of being allowed to form the centrepiece of a peculiar school pageant, together with another tall white child, Judith, a daughter of someone in Shell. We wore hats with moons on and carried stars. Or, possibly, vice versa. It must have meant something. But none of it made as much impact as the big silent Buddhas, and the yellow-robed monks, and the lights floating down the river.

3. Home

It came to an end, as postings do: in 1956, courtesy of the liner *Oranje*, we came home from the Far East to England so my father could buy a house and settle us down before leaving alone for his next posting. There were four of us children by now, toddling and crawling and wandering: Andrew had been born in Bangkok, and for the assistance of future soothsayers was issued an even better birth certificate than his elder brother's. It affirmed his coming in the seventh hour of the thousand-and-something year of the Goat, under a waning moon.

The Foreign Office in its lordly way had decided to dispatch my father to Angola, Portugese West Africa, where at the time families were not recommended to follow. A predecessor had lost a child to sickness there, and my elder brother had already been desperately ill. There was no question of risking it. My mother, equipped with an aged square Ford Popular nicknamed 'Chick' after its CHK registration number, was duly installed on the Suffolk coast to fend for the five of us with the help of an angular, wry mother's help called Vera Wilson. She was Miss Wilson to us or, in more informal moments, Woose. At first we lived in a holiday cottage on the beach at Thorpeness, No. 1 Sandy Bar; then we bought a rambling, pleasant Edwardian village house in Walberswick with a tangled garden and a dodgy roof.

This brought about one of the few nunless interludes in my early life, between the ages of six and nine. My elder brother was sent off to boarding-school aged eight, as was the custom among diplomatic families afflicted with the dubious blessing of the Boarding School Allowance. It was up near Newark, and sounded to me like a place of impossible glamour and sophistication. The two younger ones were still free of education systems, and toddled around the garden finding their own level and attempting to domesticate the half-feral cat.

As for me, my mother's archive bundles contain a letter, with *Pax Christi* in nunly copperplate along the top, from Mother Mary of the Trinity at the Bangkok Mater Dei convent, suggesting that I would be very happy at their sister school, the Ursuline Boarding School at Westgate-on-Sea, because it had a farm and a coastal walk in its grounds. There is another letter, in the same flowing script, to 'My dear little Libby' rather sharply regretting that 'the sea has such an attraction for you and Michael that Mummy cannot get you to sit down and write a long letter to me' and telling me that Judith was now 'all by herself' in the kindergarten.

I would like to say that I felt a burning loyalty to the Ursuline order, dreamed of another convent and thought back kindly of these people – Mother Mary, and poor Judith left alone to play the lucky white elephant for the little brown pinching fingers of Mater Dei. In fact, I do not remember thinking of them at all. The free winds and wild pebble beaches, the hideout pillboxes and crumbling wartime dragons' teeth and marshy paths of the Suffolk coastline were too new and thrilling. The air was too sharp and delicious, and I too young to waste time looking backwards.

Nor was I sent to Westgate-on-Sea. For a few months while my parents hunted for a house and a prep school for Mike we were both tipped into the Parents' Union School at Thorpeness, where I learnt the story of Abraham and Isaac, the steps of the sailors' hornpipe, how to make a plasticine model of 'a village in Bengal', and draw pictures of such plants as 'Jack-go-to-bed-at noon' and the Yellow Horned Poppy.

I know this not because I have the faintest idea of what Jack-go-to-bed-at-noon is (although I remember the clay bowls we made and can still do some hornpipe steps) but because my report is in front of me, adorned with a comment from one Dr Allan saying: 'Elizabeth (6yrs 5 months) has travelled extensively with her Parents. She was at school in Siam before coming to us . . . She likes playing with dolls and painting and enjoys collecting specimens for the Nature Table at school.'

Which just goes to show how wrong teachers can be. I detested dolls, and had done so ever since an awful betrayal on the voyage out to Bangkok three years earlier. My elder brother told me that if I pushed all my dolls out through the porthole in the cabin they would swim to Siam, and the exercise would do them good. So I did, and they didn't, and after that I had no time for the damn things.

But I digress. When we finally settled in Walberswick, with no Catholic school at hand, I walked down the lane each morning to the tiny village school (still visible, but now converted into a rather chi-chi bungalow).

There were two classes of about twenty each – Big Ones and Little Ones. Mrs Hargreaves did the former (she had dyed golden hair with dark roots, which we thought unspeakably fast and glamorous) and Mrs Brown taught the little ones (she had a greyish bun, which was less exciting). The age of transfer was eight. I was there for nearly three years. At first I walked home up the lane for lunch, but when I progressed to the Big Ones we all stayed in all day. There was no third room: at lunchtime we pulled desks together and were served amazingly good school dinners, often with treacle tart, dished out by the oldest children and the kitchen ladies.

Here the hornpipe and yellow horned poppy rapidly faded from memory; academically, I chiefly remember the pleasure I took in deliberately dismaying gentle Mrs Brown by writing bloodthirsty essays about murder and mayhem. Interestingly my own daughter, at the same age, did exactly the same thing: she was spurred like me by the spontaneous and glorious realisation that you can twist a primary school essay subject to say anything at all – revolting, angry, lurid or subversive – and as long as the grammar and spelling are right, Teacher's hands are tied. I also remember, in maths, never quite being able to understand the concept of 'area' because I had got it into my head that an area was a place where you parked aeroplanes. It didn't seem to matter. Everything was very free and easy, and I have few memories of anything actually being marked, let alone graded.

The school – where my middle brother eventually joined me – was the usual eclectic mix of village children, from the local solicitor's nicely-spoken offspring to the dread Alfie from the council houses, who chased us girls in the lane and threatened to pull our knickers down if we did not hand over any sixpences in our possession. My good friend Janet and I once managed to trip him up and push him right into a ditchful of nettles, which was satisfying. Not that Mrs Brown and Mrs Hargreaves did not make strenuous efforts at discipline – faint cries of 'Frogs on toast! Stop that this instant, Alfred!' would follow this mayhem down the lane after school. But somehow, they never carried quite the moral authority of the sweeping, mysterious white-robed Bangkok nuns who were receding gently into memory.

More important than maths or mayhem, in the long run, was assembly. Here, with the piano pounding, we daily sang our morning hymn: it was my first introduction to the robust hymn-ody of the Anglican Church, and thrilled me to the toes of my Clarks leather sandals. This was the first poetry I cared about: *Our shield and defender, the Ancient of Days . . . Lo he comes with clouds descending . . . Dark is his path on the wings of the storm . . . Change and decay in all around I see . . . The purple-headed mountain . . .*

The best days were when – all forty-odd pupils together – we sang:

> Hills of the North rejoice!
> Rivers and mountain spring
> Hark to the advent voice;
> Valley and lowland sing!

Home

Each verse brought new geographical excitement: *Isles of the southern seas, deep in your coral caves . . . Lands of the east awake . . . Shores of the utmost west . . .* I was quite as romantically swayed by these notions as if I had not already crossed half the world's oceans on great liners. I had *seen* eastern desert and southern jungle, and on visits north to my mother's family or to Mike's prep school had glimpsed what I firmly identifed as the Hills of the North; but somehow the evocation of them in rising song was infinitely better. I was, as I suspect that many children are, an instinctive Platonist. I knew that the idea is always greater than the reality and the story more important than the daily fact. From here it is a short distance to believing that there is something else, something that is big and beyond it all: whose corners and reflections alone can be glimpsed. All these things – the lift of a hymn, the sweep of a coast, the glitter of a temple – tantalisingly remind us of that Something which we can never see with eyes.

Far later, when in sixth-form philosophy we were told the idea of Plato's cave and the theory of a set of eternal archetypes which are only poorly and dimly reflected on this earth, I took the idea enthusiastically to heart.

Ride on, ride on in Majesty . . . Casting down their golden crowns around the glassy sea . . . Ransomed, healed, restored, forgiven . . . Fragments of heaven fell around our grubby infancy in the words of those hymns. One of the worst cultural crimes of the modern churches is their imposition of flat banality on liturgy and sacred song. This was, unfortunately, already happening in the Catholic church we attended just across the river in Southwold. It would have been disloyal to say so, but the hymns we sang there rarely measured up to the towering Wesley, Watts and Oakley verses of school assembly. Only one verse stayed, lodged like the song of Simeon in ragged ineradicable words that became part of my brain. It was in the hymn about Jerusalem the city of everlasting peace:

> How mighty are the Sabbaths
> How mighty and how deep

Holy Smoke

The high courts of Heaven
Do everlasting keep
Where find the dreamer waking
The truth beyond dreaming far
Nor is the heart's possessing
Less than the heart's desire.

On the other hand, the Mass was still in Latin. As surely as medieval children before us, we picked up dog-Latin every Sunday from the translation in the parallel column. *Dona nobis pacem . . . Libera nos a malo . . . Ite, Missa Est* were as familiar as 'Evening all' and 'Mind how you go' on *Dixon of Dock Green*. The sermons, usually quite dull forgettable exhortations, never meant much compared to liturgy and hymns, the statues and the saints. They could not take us closer to the heart's desire, the dreamer waking, the glassy sea, the shafts of brightness that poured down sometimes between leaden clouds in the wide, lonely Suffolk skies while we cycled home. I do see merit in the discipline of regular church-going – the quiet, the reflection, the acceptance of ritual and slight boredom and the need to control one's irritation and force oneself to think fraternally of fellow-worshippers who sniff, or sing too piercingly, or squash you into the hard corner of the pew. But Sunday church-going had nothing to do with theology and mystery. Those came by other routes entirely.

4. Catechism

Thinking back, I was puzzled as to why I have no memory of priestly classes in Suffolk leading to First Confession and Communion. On asking my mother, it transpires that this is because I never went to any.

Father McBride, on being offered me as a pupil, evasively said that having been abroad I might 'not be up to it' with his existing group. When he was told that I had been at a convent school he amended this to 'Ah, now, she'd be beyond it, then.' So my mother did the job herself by correspondence course, and I acquired a copy of *A Catechism of Christian Doctrine*, the famous 'penny Catechism' remembered with such horror by so many cradle Catholics of this century.

I would like to dwell for a while on this little red book (our original copy turned up in a box the other day: it was, I see, given its *nihil obstat* and *imprimatur* in 1921 and reprinted in the war, in July 1940. It certainly has a dour utility look about it). This Catechism is central to any Catholic upbringing of the century, at least before the 1960s: each of us has, to some extent, needed to make our peace with it before moving on. Opening the little red booklet forty years after I first sat down to learn the answers, I found a surprising number of them still firmly lodged in my head:

> 1 *Who made you?*
> *God made me.*

2 Why did God make you?
To know Him, love Him and serve Him in this world, and to be
happy with Him for ever in the next.

Everyone remembers those. But theological complexity follows
breathtakingly fast: no religious educator today would confront
a seven-year-old with definitions of faith as a supernatural gift of
God, with the nature of revelation, omipotence, omniscience,
the Trinity, the Three Powers of the Soul (I remembered those –
memory, understanding and will), the Incarnation, the Three
Chief Sufferings of Christ, the precise nature of Limbo, the Souls
of the Just, the Resurrection, Papal infallibility – all within the
first hundred terse questions of the 370. Nor would modern RE
teachers be smiled upon by curriculum authorities if they spiced
up their washy teaching with such startling memorable phrases
as:

74 What will Christ say to the wicked?
Christ will say to the wicked, 'Depart from Me, ye cursed, into
everlasting fire, which was prepared for the devil and his angels.'

or

125 Where will they go who die in mortal sin?
They who die in mortal sin will go to hell for all eternity.

or

343 Why are we bound to deny ourselves?
We are bound to deny ourselves because our natural inclinations are
prone to evil from our very childhood; and, if not corrected by self-
denial, they will certainly carry us to hell.

That's telling us. Lapsed Catholic writers of my generation almost
invariably make a great song and dance about the penny
Cathechism, claiming to have been traumatised and stunted by

it. And it is true that putting two and two together, any child taking it literally is liable to conclude that one missed Mass or impure thought, followed by a car crash, could do no otherwise than doom you to eternal flames. It is not an educational document likely to fit into the world of modern childrearing.

However, I was obviously a child of shamingly phlegmatic humour, because I cannot remember a moment's real unease. The question and answer format was meat and drink to a bright bookworm with a taste for tests and competitions. The intermittently grisly tone of the content was morbidly attractive, and so were certain juxtapositions which even in 1958 and even to a reasonably worldly child of eight, were beginning to look downright wacky:

327 Which are the four sins crying to heaven for vengeance?
The four sins crying to heaven for vengeance are:
   1. Wilful murder
   2. The sin of Sodom
   3. Oppression of the poor
   4. Defrauding labourers of their wages.

Turning that page now, adult and amused, I can summon back an echo of what I felt when fingers and eyes were forty years younger. I knew about the sin of Sodom, albeit not in grisly detail – we were a diplomatic family, for heaven's sake – and I understood a little about riches and poverty. There had been beggars enough in Bangkok. So even then I was aware that between these four sins there were certain qualitative differences not being fully explored by the adults who had lumped them together and set them crying out to heaven for vengeance.

From such reflections I dimly appreciated that the book was indeed written by adults – people like the elderly, stout, rather pompous bishop who came to visit our church – and not by the New Testament Jesus who had cautioned so strongly against throwing the first stone.

However, the ferocious little Catechism has a certain bleak

honest virtue which is not unattractive even now. It may be unduly harsh on 'immodest plays and dances, songs, books and pictures' and the performing of 'servile works' on Sunday (we children used that to try and get out of the washing up) but it is equally harsh on silly superstition, envy, not paying your debts, social injustice and malicious tale-bearing. It states, much more robustly than some modern born-agains might like, that cosy personal piety is not enough: '*Faith alone will not save us without good works; we must also have hope and charity.*'

It makes us liable for the sins of others if we have supported them '*by counsel, by command, by consent, by provocation, by praise or flattery, by concealment, by silence, by defending the ill-done*'.

That is high moral ground indeed. It is tough on the sins against hope – *despair and presumption* – and as for charity, I still recite with admiring pleasure the little Catechism's list of the Seven Corporal Works of Mercy: '*To feed the hungry. To give drink to the thirsty. To clothe the naked. The harbour the harbourless. To visit the sick. To visit the imprisoned. To bury the dead.*'

The Spiritual Works of Mercy are not so bad, either: '*To convert the sinner. To instruct the ignorant. To counsel the doubtful. To comfort the sorrowful. To bear wrongs patiently. To forgive injuries. To pray for the living and the Dead.*'

Maybe I was just a natural cherry-picker, but I can recreate without effort the mental mechanism whereby, from the very beginning, I let some of the Catechism flow past me leaving no mark, while dipping with pleasure and inspiration to keep other phrases of it with me for life.

To feed the hungry, visit the imprisoned, bear wrongs patiently, pay fair wages, avoid despair and accept your share of guilt when you have encouraged or provoked a crime – these were ideals which went perfectly well with the 'Hills of the North' and the mysterious rider on the wings of the storm. God, it was plain, was not a natural enemy. Even if He did allow himself to be surrounded by a thicket of extraordinarily bossy and nit-picking amanuenses. I thought I could probably do better. Inspired partly by the Catechism and partly by a dog-eared copy of Baden Powell's *Scouting for Boys*, I had a go at writing down my own rule of life in a penny notebook from Winyard's shop, naming my sect the Lone Wolves. The original is mercifully lost, but I remember it was full of echoes from the Catechism: 'A Lone Wolf bears injustice but does none' went along with the more practical 'A Lone Wolf carries a sharp knife at all times'.

Anyway, it stood to reason that there had to be some leeway in the little red book. There was my mother, perfectly friendly with Father McBride and going to the communion rail every Sunday while all the time she was without *grave reason* married to a lapsed Presbyterian. There was Granny staying again, as Catholic as they came but still prone to reading one's palm in the greenhouse with much portentous muttering even though the Catechism question 182 specifically forbade '*all dealing with the devil and superstitious practices, such as consulting spiritualists and fortune-tellers, and trusting to charms, omens, dreams and such like fooleries*'.

And there was I at Walberswick school singing Protestant hymns without Father McBride seeming bothered at all, while on the page was the thundering warning: '*We expose ourselves to the danger of losing our Faith by neglecting our spiritual duties, reading bad books, going to non-Catholic schools and taking part in the services or prayers of a false religion.*'

My mother's dislike of clique religion, and my father's disregard of all religion, protected us at this period from the isolation felt by some Catholic children in rural Protestant England. There was never any ban, for instance, on my roaring round the village with the rest of my gang doing penny-for-the-Guy and burning poor Papist Fawkes in effigy; much later, at my English convent school, I was surprised to find how fiercely banned such practices had been to some of the other Catholic girls for all their lives.

So I toed the line and kept my thoughts to myself, and dutifully learnt the Catechism word for word, right up to question 370:

Holy Smoke

After your night prayers what should you do?
After my night prayers I should observe due modesty in going to bed;
occupy myself with the thoughts of death; and endeavour to compose
myself to rest at the foot of the Cross, and give my last thoughts to my
crucified Saviour.

At the age of eight I was, admittedly, a bit puzzled about what
constituted '*due modesty*' in the bedtime process. But the old house
was so bitterly cold and draughty that for most of the Suffolk
year we all undressed and dressed in the cramped pitch dark of
the airing-cupboard anyway. So I dare say that counted.

5. The Lion, the Witch and the Wafer

I was judged fit for sacraments now, and made a First Confession and Communion with due solemnity. Again, these things impinged less than they might have done on any inner life that was growing up. Terror and mystery were muted: it says a lot for my mother's sang-froid over the whole business – and for the temporary nunlessness of my life – that my initiation into eating the Body and Blood was entirely free from trauma.

The only moment of full-blown terror came when one Sunday shortly after my First Communion I inadvertently ate a piece of bread on the way through the kitchen to Mass. I only realised at the altar-rail that my fast was broken and my Communion illegal (Question 271 stipulates '*a state of Grace and fasting from midnight*'). Having insufficient moral courage to extricate myself from the shuffling queue of communicants and duck back into the pew, I committed a technical mortal sin at the age of eight with outward insouciance and inward guilt.

Guilt, however, even Catholic guilt, needs more than mere doctrine and instruction to feed it. It needs hellfire eccentrics with a real intention of terrifying children with threats of damnation. Nothing of the sort happened to me. The priest, a sensible Irishman, seemed quite unmoved by this particular sin at the next Saturday's confession. He mildly observed that God was beyond worrying about silly mistakes; so I privately decided that digestion and religion were, after all, perhaps two separate kinds of thing.

As for Confession itself – the other staple terror of Catholic memoirs – I am slightly ashamed to say that I always rather enjoyed it. Children of big families develop a taste for the luxury of talking uninterruptedly about themselves, and any embarrassment surrounding confession was easy to alleviate with the help of the good old standard phrases. '*Bless me father, for I have sinned, it is six weeks since my last confession, since then I have been – er – disobedient, missed my prayers, harboured bad thoughts, and been – um – angry. For these and all other sins which I may have forgotten I am truly sorry.*'

And that was it. Sorted: done and dusted; sins washed away, a clean slate. I do not for a moment underestimate the harm inflicted on children to whom Catholic doctrine was presented by ignorant and brutal priests or neurotic parents; but I do feel a certain impatience when those of my own generation, from normally affectionate families, whine about the harm they believe these observances did to their general development.

What, after all, could be pleasanter than to have all your misdeeds washed away for the price of a catch-all phrase like 'for these and all other sins which I may have forgotten'? You didn't even have to swear that you *had* forgotten them, which meant that any really embarrassing ones did not even have to go through the grille to the shadowy, patient ear of the priest beyond. Traditional Catholic doctrine may place a lot of stress on eternal punishment for those who absolutely and deliberately reject God; but it has the merit of being willing to let you off on the slightest pretext. I cannot remember a time when I did not know that even the wickedest person could repent and be saved, even at the very last second, without a priest in sight. As the seventeenth-century epitaph had it,

> Betwixt the stirrup and the ground,
> Mercy I asked, mercy I found.

The really significant religious occurrence of those Suffolk years, though, had nothing to do with the catechism or the church pew but was linked very closely and intensely with 'Hills of the North', with the dark-winged God on the storm and certain distant chiming infant memories of bearded prelates, cruel deserts, temple bells and Buddhas. It came through books, one set in particular. C. S. Lewis' *The Lion, the Witch and the Wardrobe* had been published in 1950, and with its six successors in the Narnia series was becoming widely appreciated by parents in search of literate adventure fiction for their children. These stories came our way at about the same time as the Catechism, but from an entirely opposite direction.

They were much needed. Coming home from years of foreign postings to live in a rural area with limited libraries and four small children to organise (and, as yet, no television), my mother must have wondered what to do about our reading; mine in particular, since I already belonged to that common type among small girls, the constant reader. When *Little Women* and *What Katy Did* and other staples ran out and I had tired of the Famous Five and raced through my easy library books on the same night we fetched them, I used to spell my way more laboriously through anything on the parental bookshelves, from the *Encyclopaedia Britannica* to Thor Heyerdahl's Kon-Tiki expedition and a strange volume called *Memoirs of a Sword-Swallower*, in which I much appreciated the description of the moment when the rapier touches the very bottom of the author's stomach. Another book I vividly remember from that time was a collection of short stories about the Holocaust, particularly the tale of a young girl with a hare-lip who is driven in terror to the gas chamber and in the moment of greatest fear, suddenly released into a smiling open landscape where her disfigurement is cured and her loved ones returned to her, laughing and singing. I read it twice before it occurred to me that the author meant she was dead; but I still remember the shock of working it out. The idea was perfectly familiar once you thought about it: it was in a school hymn, after all: *Heaven's morning breaks, and earth's vain shadows flee.* Death as reward, death as release: it was just as old Simeon said every year on my birthday.

My mother had better things to do than notice what I was reading: she just let me get on with it.

Dad, however, was far from his children in West Africa, reading the airmail editions of the newspapers and keeping up with intelligent magazines via the Diplomatic Bag, as a leisured quasi-bachelor may gracefully do. So it was he who first read that a respected Oxford don called C. S. Lewis was writing highly regarded children's fiction. He was always concerned for our cultural education, and wrote home recommending these books. My mother duly bought them in hardback one by one and gave them to us.

It was beautifully ironic. Poor Dad: he was not to know that this recommended don Lewis was also one of the foremost Christian apologists and populists of the age, a questing convert, a romantic medievalist, friend of J. R. R. Tolkien and author not only of the didactic texts *The Screwtape Letters*, and *Pilgrim's Regress*, but of three science fantasy novels for adults in which he made powerful poetic fiction out of theological allegory, took a fierce line on the impossibility of human virtue without obedience to God, and gave in his *eldila* the best and most thrilling account of the nature of angels that anybody had attempted for centuries.

Lewis's Narnia stories came out of this literate and profound faith, and drew their imaginative and emotional power from the shy, cussed, childlike bachelordom of a lonely boy who lost his mother young. I reread them all through, between the first and second drafts of this chapter, and was shocked to find how short they are and how simply told: every bit as accessible as the Famous Five. I had thought that they were longer, because there is so much in them: but it is the images and ideas, which flower in the months and years after the first reading, which create this illusion.

They are an astonishing achievement: with a vivid, direct, unashamedly romantic imagination Lewis built in those seven adventure stories a whole moral and theological universe, which mirrored and clarified a Christian construct stretching back long before the English Reformation. He dealt with creation, sin, redemption, and the end of the world; he did it with jokes and grotesques and poetry and child heroes who – though intermittently a bit annoying – were as easy for the child reader to identify with as any of the Secret Seven. There were more answers in the Narnia books than in all 370 questions of the Catechism.

Moreover words already mattered to me, and Lewis was a philologist: the very names in the books were thrilling. Kings of Narnia were Caspian, Rilian, Tirian; there was Roonwit the Centaur, Puzzle the Donkey, Shift the evil Ape, Tumnus the Faun, Trumpkin the Dwarf, Reepicheep the gallant Mouse. From my dreams during 'Hills of the North', geography mattered too, and Narnia had maps. They showed the Eastern Seas which stretched to a mystical eternity, the Southern Desert, the northern moors and marshes where giants and witches stalk, and the Western Waste. Imagination was set free, as in six direct, fast-moving adventure stories he laid out demandingly absolute concepts of beauty, chivalry, civilisation, and individual moral duty in the face of death itself.

Against these Narnian ideals Lewis sets, without compunction, shuddery images of corruption and cruelty; all the more striking to a child because they come not only in the form of nightmare horrors but of all-too recognisable betrayals and petulant outbursts between the children themselves. The moralist Lewis – though far better disguised here than in his adult works – makes it as clear as any Catechism that evil is not something outside; that you have only to give in to your own worst impulses, even briefly, in order to create a chink in your armour and a foothold for unimaginable forces of ugliness.

The good, whether talking beasts or 'sons of Adam', prosper in a wide and lovely country peopled by creatures from homely talking hedgehogs to saints and knights as thrilling as Bayard. The Narnian virtues are gaiety and gallantry, mercy and justice and a simplicity which accepts life with joy and death with dignity and hope. Narnia's enemies – always led by variants on the same enemy, the Witch brought in by human folly at the dawn of time – are mean-spirited, proud, wicked and narrow. Without eternal vigilance and the strengh of the Great Lion, Aslan, evil will prevail.

In the last apocalyptic book, where a whole world ends, the enemies do prevail, until eternity overtakes good and evil alike. On the other side of the barrier of death those who have constantly turned away from Aslan into delusions of their own high worth and cleverness are shown as wilfully blind and crippled. There is a peculiarly troubling scene at the end of *The Last Battle* when the heroes have stepped through a stable door expecting to meet death and a demon, and found instead a new, green, lovely country. But a group of rebel Dwarves who have sceptically refused to believe in Aslan sit on the grass in the sun with good food before them; they cannot see it, and think themselves trapped in filth and darkness.

'They are so determined not to be taken in', says Aslan, 'that they cannot be taken *out*.' This, during one of my readings of the books over the next few childhood years, slowly answered a puzzle in my mind about the business of last-minute repentance 'between the stirrup and the ground'. We used to argue at school over whether this rule meant that you could get the best of both worlds and go around sinning all through your life on purpose, while sneakily intending to make a deathbed confession and go straight to heaven. I doubt there is any religiously brought-up child who has not wondered about this tantalising possibility. But the cynical dwarfs answered this question perfectly: they have coarsened themselves and wilfully made themselves blind, and so they cannot be saved even by the God who gave them free will in the first place.

Lewis mixes his mythologies with the reckless confidence of a scholar. In Narnia's terrible battles every figure of myth and horror is called up on Hell's side: Were-wolves, Spectres, Ogres, 'Cruels and Hags and Incubuses, Wraiths, Horrors, Efreets, Sprites, Orknies, Wooses and Ettins'. On Aslan's side are the talking beasts and fauns, the noble Centaurs and the Dryads and Naiads of

Baby years: with the Abbouna
on Mount Tabor, Israel 1951/2.

On the road again: leaving for Bangkok, 1953.

Mater Dei school photo, Bangkok 1955.

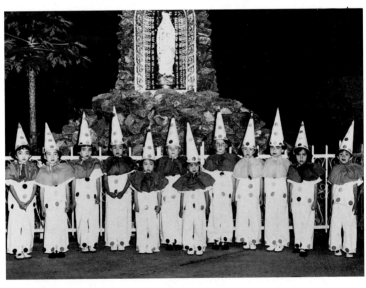

Inexplicable convent play with Madonna in background,
Bangkok 1955. Libby in centre amid Siamese
schoolmates and Judith from Shell.

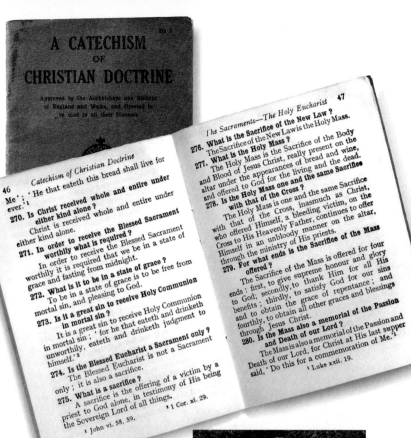

46

Me'; 'He that eateth this bread shall live for ever.'

270. Is Christ received whole and entire under either kind alone?
Christ is received whole and entire under either kind alone.

271. In order to receive the Blessed Sacrament worthily what is required?
In order to receive the Blessed Sacrament worthily it is required that we be in a state of grace and fasting from midnight.

272. What is it to be in a state of grace?
To be in a state of grace is to be free from mortal sin, and pleasing to God.

273. Is it a great sin to receive Holy Communion in mortal sin?
It is a great sin to receive Holy Communion in mortal sin; 'for he that eateth and drinketh unworthily, eateth and drinketh judgment to himself.'[2]

274. Is the Blessed Eucharist a Sacrament only?
The Blessed Eucharist is not a Sacrament only; it is also a sacrifice.

275. What is a sacrifice?
A sacrifice is the offering of a victim by a priest to God alone, in testimony of His being the Sovereign Lord of all things.

1 John vi. 58, 59.
2 1 Cor. xi. 29.

The Sacraments—The Holy Eucharist   47

276. What is the Sacrifice of the New Law?
The Sacrifice of the New Law is the Holy Mass.

277. What is the Holy Mass?
The Holy Mass is the Sacrifice of the Body and Blood of Jesus Christ, really present on the altar under the appearances of bread and wine, and offered to God for the living and the dead.

278. Is the Holy Mass one and the same Sacrifice with that of the Cross?
The Holy Mass is one and the same Sacrifice with that of the Cross, inasmuch as Christ, who offered Himself, a bleeding victim, on the Cross to His Heavenly Father, continues to offer Himself in an unbloody manner on the altar, through the ministry of His priests.

279. For what ends is the Sacrifice of the Mass offered?
The Sacrifice of the Mass is offered for four ends: first, to give supreme honour and glory to God; secondly, to thank Him for all His benefits; thirdly, to satisfy God for our sins and to obtain the grace of repentance; and fourthly, to obtain all other graces and blessings through Jesus Christ.

280. Is the Mass also a memorial of the Passion and Death of our Lord?
The Mass is also a memorial of the Passion and Death of our Lord, for Christ at His last supper said, 'Do this for a commemoration of Me.'[1]

1 Luke xxii. 19.

A Catechism of Christian Doctrine (the famous 'penny Catechism').

First Communion day, 1957.

A sample page from the author's
exercise book of preparation for *Communion Solennelle*,
and meticulous French school report: 1959–1960.

The courtyard with stone lions at 1, rue du Lombard.

Leaving for South Africa on board the
RMS Pendennis Castle, 1961.

Mother Wilson in the
pre-Vatican II black habit
with frilled wimple.

Nun in the simpler
post-Vatican II habit with
girls at 'T.W.'.

Music in the garden at 'T.W.' (author playing the flute).

Suffering the part of the perfect diplomatic daughter at a
dull reception: Hamburg, 1966.

Author (right) and friend, 1967.

Grant Purves, the author's father, putting up with religion
(note Polish Szopka shrine on television).

University: cast photo from 'Hotel Paradiso', 1970
(author on left).

wood and spring. Humans, dwarfs and giants come both good and bad; in the case of humans, sometimes starting out bad and repenting. Lewis deals also, lightly and vividly, with the matter of decadence and tyranny. Rereading *The Magician's Nephew* after a gap of decades while I was thinking about this memoir, I was startled to find his description of the row of kings and queens in the dead world of Charn:

> Both the men and the women looked kind and wise, and they seemed to come of a handsome race. But after the children had gone a few steps down the room they came to faces that looked a little different. They were very solemn faces . . . when they had gone a little further, they found themselves among faces they didn't like . . . strong and proud and happy, but they looked cruel. A little further on they looked crueller. Further on again, they were still cruel but they no longer looked happy. They were even despairing faces, as if the people they belonged to had done dreadful things and also suffered dreadful things.

I was shocked because I realised – as one sometimes does looking back at childhood reading – that I had forgotten the passage in the book at a conscious level, while unconsciously absorbing it whole. That scale of faces, from innocence to despair, is in my mind to this day as a kind of measuring-scale. I doubt I have ever looked into the face of a politician or statesman without immediately placing him or her somewhere on that scale.

At the heart of that particular book lies original sin: Digory, the boy who has stumbled in to Charn, strikes the bell and wakes the Witch. From this moment of petulant human self-will all the griefs and dangers of a whole world arise. Rereading it now I find it an untypically misjudged incident: the boy's act is fuelled as much by intellectual curiosity as by wilfulness, which creates a troubling idea of Lewis's idea of good and evil.

But what the author meant us child readers to see is valid enough. It is the Christian concept of evil arising not from any intention of God's, but from our misuse of free will. It is a very tough message. Decades later, BBC dramatisations squeamishly left that central, pivotal point out entirely, reducing the whole to a mere adventure story. Any child can see that there is no point in Digory's brave journey on the flying horse to find the magic fruit, unless we understand that he is doing it to lessen and expiate the evil he has himself brought into a newborn world.

Lewis's carefree inclusion of Fauns and Dryads – and even Bacchus and the Maenads – in his Christian myth had a particular appeal to me, and still to some extent does. After the Bangkok interlude it was never easy to accept prim Catechism strictures on false gods and paganism; I far preferred to see every kind of devotion as part of a greater one, and every supernatural or faerie creature as part of a vast, coherent, spiritual kingdom. In Lewis's vision, there are only two sides, and you have to be on one or the other. When the Last Battle comes at the end of Narnia's world, a false god is set up: the cruel Tash who rules the vaguely Arabic realm of Calormen beyond the Southern Desert. Tash is a grey, smoky figure, a man with the head of a vulture, with four arms with long predatory claws, floating across grass which withers beneath his horrible feet. He is the Devil, as obviously as Aslan is God. Yet Emeth, a good and valiant Calormene soldier who has spent his life honouring Tash, is taken as his own by the God-lion Aslan:

> Child, all the service done to Tash I count as service done to me . . . no service which is vile can be done to me, and none which is not vile can be done to him. Therefore if a man swear by Tash and keep his oath for the oath's sake, it is by me that he has truly sworn. And if any man do a cruelty in my name, though he says the name Aslan it is Tash whom he serves and by Tash his deed is accepted.

Which, for a child, wraps the whole theological thing up pretty tidily. Never mind the names: God is good, and is the source and also the destination of all good things and good people. Satan is evil and can deal only with evil. At the end of the world, God wins. Don't fret about comparative religions, and what is pagan: there is room enough in the moral universe for Vishnu and guardian angels, Bacchus and St Bernadette. There are many roads up the holy mountain.

At the very end of *The Last Battle*, it is revealed in a world of Platonic archetypes that this time, the children will not go back through a wardrobe to everyday life. They are indeed dead in their own world, but have come alive again in a place where more beautiful, archetypal, essential versions of all the worlds are only 'spurs jutting out from the great mountains of Aslan'. We note also that Peter, the eldest, is back – even though Aslan in a previous book marked the end of his childhood by telling him that he was now too old to return to Narnia. The message is quite clear: only death and heaven will bring back the full wonderment of childhood again.

I suppose it is because these books were well into my blood five years or so before puberty (and ten years before *The Female Eunuch*) that I never noticed the less comfortable aspects of Lewis. I missed the petulant dismissal of all things 'progressive' in education, the nervousness about the female principle, the intermittently patronising attitude to women and girls and the fact that Susan, the elder girl, is barred from Narnia (and not even allowed to die along with her whole family and go to its heaven) simply because she gets interested in 'clothes and make-up and parties'. There is also – even for a nine-year-old – something a little bit gushingly embarrassing about some aspects of Aslan.

But none of this mattered, and hardly matters even to the jaded adult of forty years on. The books gave echoes and foreshadowings of deeper thought, and did it nimbly and lightly. Nobody else has so blended comic dwarfs, rattling adventures and serious theological coherence; and he did it in stories less portentous than Tolkien's, and far deeper-rooted than any of the fantasy literature that has followed since. It is not necessary to be blind to Lewis's flaws in order to honour the Narnia achievement;

I know really that these flaws only annoy because the books once overwhelmed me. It is easier to forgive books that went less deep – I feel more tolerant of really preachy ones like George MacDonald's *At the Back of the North Wind*, which I read at the same period. Narnia's deficiency only hurt because Narnia had such a strong part in forming me in the years from eight to thirteen or so. Ever afterwards, all the central theories of religion seemed perfectly familiar.

And immensely romantic, too. To this day, when confronted with scientific atheism, I feel a rising rebellion against its utilitarian reasonableness. For all its human shortcomings, Christianity still has the best story and offers the most coherent, noblest ideal of life. Come to think of it, Lewis covered that quite explicitly too. Remember the moment in *The Silver Chair* when the children questing for the lost Prince Rilian are trapped in an underground kingdom by the Witch, and enchanted with sweet incense and music to believe that there is no such thing as the outer world, no sun, no God, no higher freedom? She rationalises their invention of the 'sun' by saying it is just a version of her lamp, of a 'lion' by saying they must be thinking of her cat.

> 'Tis a pretty make-believe . . . though, to say truth, it would suit you all better if you were younger. And look how you can put nothing into your make-believe without copying it from the real world, this world of mine which is the only world! Put away these childish tricks. I have work for you all in the real world. There is no Narnia, no Overworld, no sun, no Aslan. And now, to bed all. And let us begin a wiser life tomorrow.

They nearly succumb; then the Marsh-wiggle, Puddleglum, grinds his foot into the fire and makes a far from enchanting smell. His mind is cleared by the pain ('There is nothing like a good shock of pain for dissolving certain kinds of magic', says Lewis – a boy soldier himself in the trenches of 1917, he had seen pain make men pray). Puddleglum then makes a magnificent speech, possibly the best affirmation of faith ever made by a web-footed creature in a children's adventure story:

> Suppose we *have* only dreamed or made up all those things – trees and grass and sun and moon and stars and Aslan himself. Suppose we have. Then all I can say is that, in that case, the made-up things seem a good deal more important than the real ones. Suppose this black pit of a kingdom of yours is the only world. Well, it strikes me as a pretty poor one. We're just babies making up a game, if you're right. But four babies playing a game can make a play-world which licks your real world hollow.
>
> That's why I'm going to stand by the play-world. I'm on Aslan's side even if there isn't any Aslan to lead it. I'm going to live as like a Narnian as I can, even if there isn't any Narnia.

Whereon the Witch, defeated, turns into a hissing green serpent.

Walking alone once along the Walberswick riverbank – a reedy waste, treacherous with marsh puddles and highly suitable for lonely brooding in an autumn dusk – I saw that snake. It cannot have been big, nor more threatening than any other grass-snake, but it rose hissing ahead of me, glistening greeny-brown in the mud, embodying evil. I ran all the way home.

6. France

Flippantly, early in his diplomatic career, my father expressed a preference for postings to wine-growing countries. He felt that like the grape, he would thrive in places with a warm climate, a long history and a civilised outlook. The Foreign Office responded with typical dour humour by sending him to Israel, Bangkok and Angola; then seemed to relent by giving him France. But it turned out to be neither viticultural France nor Paris: he was sent as consul to Lille, an industrial sprawl in the Northern Pas-de-Calais region.

Now, the city is becoming better known to Britons as a stop on the Eurostar train route. In 1959 nobody seemed at all sure where it was. My mother, on being told by telephone that we were off to Lille, looked up Lyon in the atlas by mistake. But then, she had a lot to think of: schools, packing, reacclimatising to a long-absent husband, and the need to deliver her three youngest children a crash course in French from a dreary little book called *Madame Souris*.

Still, we would all be reunited as a family. During our single-mother phase I had taken to attaching myself with passionate enthusiasm to the fathers of various schoolfriends, rather to their alarm; as for the little boys, they barely knew their father. And although the years of freedom in the village by the sea had been good (and sown a maritime fascination which none of us would ever shake off), our fickle childish hearts rejoiced at the idea of a city, *even bigger than Lowestoft*, with cinemas. So, bag and baggage, we hit the road again and emerged dusty and weary onto the *crotte*-stained cobblestones of the old quartier of Lille.

Our new house, rented to the FO by a dour old landlady called Madame Six, was at 1, rue du Lombard, part of an imposing merchant mansion set around a cobbled courtyard (*Défense de courir ou de pousser des cris*) with a fountain (long defunct) and some crumbling stone lions (*Défense de toucher*). The big front door was made of wrought-iron backed with glass, and within lay dusty, peeling *haut-bourgeois* grandeur such as we had never seen.

Every wall had curved gilded panelling and ancient clanking radiators with sharp edges; the floors were of freezing marble and in the dining room was a florid painted ceiling in the pastoral style, depicting some mythical beribboned girl on a picnic. Chopin had once played in the *grand salon*, a room which was used only for parties and for me to do my homework on the corner of a marble table in the dustsheeted quiet. There were two sets of stairs, and a vast attic with little unused rooms to play in. The whole building is now a branch of the Ministry of Culture, but in our day it was the domain of successive British consuls, and dotted with nasty curly gilt-edged furniture in the style known as Ministry of Works Louis Quinze.

I have been back since, wheedling my way past ministry officials for a look round the old place. Memories crowded in: there are the banisters through which we used to drop torn-up paper and smuggled food onto the heads of guests at grand receptions (I once got Sir Keith Joseph with a vol-au-vent). There are the dusty double doors to the *petit salon*, and double windows too, with ingenious convex edges to fit the concave channels in the frame. There is the great staircase going up to the bedrooms, and the back stairs near the kitchen door where we children sat during grand official dinners, hoping that the cook-butler Monsieur Fleury-Cousin, hired for the evening to add French credibility to my mother's entertaining, would slip us some grapes and pastries.

At the age of nine I found this all very satisfactory indeed.

Michael was already at prep school in England, and I could well have been sent back myself this time, to some bland Ursuline foundation as recomended by Mother Mary of the Trinity. But girls got off more lightly in the 1950s, and it was decided instead to put me into a French convent just a few short blocks away from the Consulate, and see what developed.

The convent has long gone now – though Lille locals still nod towards the great wooden doors and reminiscently say '*Ah oui, les bonnes sœurs!*' – but then it was flourishing, with fifty-odd boarders in creaking iron beds within curtained cubicles, and a horde of little bourgeoises like me flocking in daily from all over the untidy conurbation. Its nuns were from the teaching sisterhood of the Sacred Heart of Jesus, founded by St Madeleine Sophie Barat in 1800 in France as a refuge for religious and children in the aftermath of the French Revolution. By the early 1960s the order was at its peak, with eight thousand nuns worldwide in schools which were run on principles very close to the academically ambitious Jesuit colleges for boys.

I was duly enrolled in the *classe de 9ᵉ* (they count down, not up, from the eminence of the *classe de philosophie*) and then accelerated after a term to join my proper age group in the *classe de 8ᵉ*. I was dressed in a blue skirt, pale blue blouse, white socks, and all-enveloping *tablier* – a coat-shaped overall in pale blue with sharp striped cuffs. The small boys, not yet quite old enough to be handed to the Jesuits round the corner, were enrolled in its *Jardin d'Enfants*, and looked like little baffled bluebirds in their cotton overalls.

Despite the rushed sessions with Madame Souris, none of us really spoke French at all. This was not considered to be a problem. The little boys picked it up rather mysteriously, with a bit of help and lots of repetitious nursery songs beginning '*Chine chine chine, les Chinois*' and '*Malbrouk s'en va't'en guerre*'. I was settled down in a tiny cell-like room with an elderly nun and a French grammar book, rejoining my nominal classmates for progressively longer periods. After a few months these extra lessons tailed off and I was a Sacré-Cœur girl like any of the others.

There were a few sticky moments, particularly in history lessons which dwelt on Joan of Arc being tortured by the wicked English, but on the whole I did what all uprooted children do. I soaked in everything, and sank far enough into the surrounding culture so as to be virtually invisible and therefore perfectly comfortable. Half a year in, I was as French by day as any of them. I even came first in French Grammar, once.

Before long I stopped missing Janet and Julie and Lucy and Keith back in Walberswick and acquired friends: proper friends who asked me home to tea. But in that northern bourgeoisie, such invitations were proper indeed: a long way away from the casual droppings-in of village life back home. They came in flowing italics, on engraved At Home cards: *Véronique souhaite avoir le plaisir d' inviter Elisabeth, pour le goûter.* Or, if the tea-party were of serious intent, celebrating our biology lessons and my recent acquisition of a Little Scientist kit it might read (I swear it) . . . *pour le goûter et pour disséquer un ver de terre. RSVP. Prière d'apporter le microscope.* Less formally Véronique and I would meet at the skating-rink on a Sunday morning to glide around together to the strains of the Blue Danube or (better!) Edith Piaf singing *Je ne regrette rien.* The idea of regretting nothing is *vieux jeu* today, but was extraordinarily thrilling to children whose whole lives revolved around examining consciences, confessing sins and making a Firm Purpose of Amendment.

School days were decorous. The day began with a hymn and a homily; classes were serious, in Lycée style, encompassing Latin, French, English (in which I got more wrong than I did in French) Mathematics, Needlework, Recitation, History, Geography, Religious Instruction and Logic. This last was part of the Jesuit system adopted by the Sacred Heart nuns; from twelve you study Logic, from fourteen Psychology, and in the sixth form, Philosophy. We did symbolic Logic, but I never quite got the hang of it; or not until my father introduced us to Lewis Carroll's logical games and he and I could spend evenings on the floor of the *grand salon* chortling over such puzzles as:

> 'My hat is green
> All cabbage is green
> therefore
> My hat is a cabbage.'   What is wrong?

School reports also marked us out of ten on such matters as *Coupe, Ordre, Santé,* and *Maintien* – deportment. I never got better than a grudging *Bien,* and sometimes the accusing nunly pen would write *Elisabeth se tient très mal.* Marks were precise in academic subjects, always out of twenty and always measured in quarters, even for essays. Years later, reading Charlotte Brontë's *Villette,* in which she contrasts the habit of trust and autonomy in the education of English schoolgirls with the obsessive 'surveillance' of French ones, I knew instantly what she meant. We were watched and concentrated upon at all times; not unkindly, but with an intensity I have never seen in any English school. The slightest slippage in marks or conduct was noted instantly. When we read of the constant beatings and scoldings in that hideous classic of French childhood, *Les Malheurs de Sophie,* we recognised that too: we were not beaten, but there was a constant sense that we would not get away with anything too original, not for a moment. Occasional strange proscriptions were put on us: at one prize day Mère Béhagel solemnly addressed leavers on the rules of life, concluding 'And for your health and your morality both, my daughters, remember one most important thing, one rule of life –' A pause, and a long breath, for effect, then the rule: '*Ne lisez jamais dans votre lit!*' To this day this memory adds a little additional pleasure to the fusty joy of reading under a duvet.

Effort was demanded in every area from maths to *maintien*: yet on the front of the programme for Prize Day were always printed the words HONNEUR ET GLOIRE A DIEU SEUL.

Moreover, if by chance all your marks were as good as they could possibly be, you would find yourself warned against the terrible sin of Pride. And warned, moreover, that if you should sidestep this one and then find yourself reflecting happily on the fact that you were *not* being proud, that was even worse: it could be a sign that your sin was at that very moment mutating into an even worse one, Spiritual Pride. In either case, it behoved you to pray for help.

Convent life in a Sacred Heart school of this era did not divide the sacred from the secular (as, later, many convents have had to do in order to attract the fees of non-Catholic children). We were normal schoolchildren leading a normal strenuous French school day, yet forever made aware of the religious hand which cupped our lives. Even some of the lay teachers would unself-consciously hand back bad work with '*Psha! Mademoiselle – vous croyez vraiment qu'un tel ouvrage peut faire plaisir au Bon Dieu?*' We curtsied not only to Reverend Mother and the headmistress (*Maîtresse Générale*) but every time we passed a portrait of Our Lady in the corridor. We were brought to order, nun-fashion, by the clear loud click! of a wooden device dating back probably four or five hundred years: a hinged wooden castanet affair which every starched and wimpled nun bore in her pocket.

At playtime we queued for pieces of baguette with a stick of dark chocolate thrust down the middle, and shrieked in mock disgust when the bread had more than one or two weevils in it; we played wild games of *ballon prisonnier* with a football in the permitted part of the Convent gardens. But in Lent we each ceremonially handed back the stick of chocolate 'for the poor' (who presumably did not mind fingerprints) and ate the bread plain. And always we took extra care not to send the football soaring high enough to bounce off – or, horrors! topple or crack – the white patronal statue of Jesus which loomed over our games, eerily showing his flaming, thorn-crowned Sacred Heart outside his robe. We did gymnastics in dark blue tunics and solid blue cotton bloomers, and eurhythmic dancing in white tunics and white cotton bloomers; but were sent out of the room if our costumes were too short or too tight, with the brisk information that a *jeune fille* thus clothed would make the Blessed Virgin cry.

On every ordinary day we put on black veils for Chapel –

nets soft with age, retained by sagging rings of elastic – and on every feast day wore stiffer, newer white veils with murderously tight elastic. Sometimes – always, naturally, on my Purification birthday – we carried candles in procession along the broad smooth parquet of the upper landing and into the dim chapel.

Perhaps the oddest thing, looking back across the yawning chasm of 1960s educational liberalism, was the ceremony of Notes. This was the quintessence of surveillance and constant judgment. Every Saturday morning, in immaculate white shirts and white gloves, we assembled in the hall – it must have been the ballroom of the original grand house – and sat in a great semicircle, balanced on stepped benches according to age. Reverend Mother – the religious head of the House, who outranked the *Maîtresse Générale* and her sidekick the Mistress of Discipline – sat alone on a tall chair at the open end of the horseshoe of pupils. After a brief preamble, each name in the school was called individually, and with the name a formulaic verdict upon the week's conduct. Then, one by one, we walked forward, curtsied to Reverend Mother, and received a card.

There were five grades: *Très Bien* (pale blue card), *Bien* (dark blue), *Assez Bien* (yellow), *Médiocre* (white) and – unthinkable horror – *Pas de note*. If you had been wicked enough to merit this last disgrace, you had to rise, walk up to Reverend Mother, curtsy, receive a cold stare, curtsy again and walk back under the eyes of your two hundred fellows. I only saw it done once in those three years at Rue Royale, but can feel the thrill of horror still. Normally, most of us got *Très Bien* or *Bien*, with *Assez Bien* reserved for palpable misdeeds and *Médiocre* very rare indeed.

In fact, in spite of all this, the school was not particularly strict. The faces of the nuns were kind, within the pointed oval of their white wimples, and they laughed a great deal, and the young ones would tuck up their outer skirts and join our ball games. And after High Mass on feast days we had a splendid breakfast, with buttered lumps of baguette to dunk in our wide milky bowls of coffee. At lunchtime, every day, even the smallest of us were issued a litre of beer between each table of eight, to set us up for afternoon school.

So 8^e became 7^e, and 6^e; it seemed that I had been a French schoolgirl for ever. I was confirmed at the great parochial church of Saint-Maurice by a bishop in all his purple magnificence, and presented with the customary box of pale pastel sugared almonds (French Catholicism has always had the good sense to mark its rites of passage with delicious food). After the confirmation, we were at a party given by a French friend of my parents', and two boys who had been done alongside me were fighting and kicking, still in their white shirts and immaculate little bow ties. When my mother pointed out this shocking comedown, the father shook his head ruefully and said '*Ah oui, madame, le Saint-Esprit est très fugace*' – very elusive, the Holy Ghost.

At Confirmation I got my first big missal: the coveted 'Feder', in maroon leather binding. This, for all my contemporaries, marked a serious stage of growing-up. No more childish little white books with soppy pictures of lambs and angels; this was a missal for adult life. I have it still, and can see what a remarkable piece of work it is.

The general editor, R. P. J. Feder, was a Jesuit priest of the Lille diocese. Surrounding the actual words of the Mass in Latin and French lie great tracts of scholarly, theologically rigorous French prose. The gospels and epistles of the liturgical year are all newly translated with a fresh demotic brightness for the late 1950s. Here too is an account of every saint's day and feast of the Church, with a note on its significance; also a slew of prayers and litanies new and old, and a painstaking analysis of every commandment, vice and virtue for the assistance of sinners approaching confession. If you were to go into the desert with nothing else, you could reconstruct the whole Catholic year from no more than its 1,846 film-thin pages.

I loved my Feder. I know this because of the feelings it arouses in me now, when after years of never looking at it I pick it up and turn its flimsy pages with their faded gold edges. I was not, I say again, a particularly devout child; but I did quite like the huge gloomy splendour of Saint-Maurice on Sundays, and singing hymns in a big congregation (one of them went to the tune of Clementine) with the promise of a *pain au chocolat* on the way home afterwards. The high seriousness and rigour of the great missal gripped me, and conveyed the majesty and romance of the liturgical year which we lived in the Continental way, the months marked out in festivals and symbols, food and parties.

There were Epiphany teas with paper crowns. Easter with its chocolate fish and rabbits, the season of Confirmations and Solemn Communions with their snowfall of pale sugared almonds. Here in the missal I had it all beneath my hand: the great turning of the seasons, the changing priestly vestments and the swelling and ebbing moods of the liturgy. In church and school chapel we trod the well-marked path from the Alleluias of Advent to the glow of Christmas, through to the dullness of Septuagesima and Sexagesima and dark Lenten vestments to the ironic palms of Palm Sunday, the black terror of the Tenebrae service on Good Friday and the explosion of white and gold at Easter. Then on to Ascension and Pentecost and Corpus Christi flowers; then downhill, dully again, to Advent and a new beginning.

Children live the seasons more intensely than adults, their lives ruled by longing and anticipation, their ideas of life and death formed by the rise and fall of the sun. The liturgy, yearning and expressive, downcast and rejoicing in turns, suited something in me very well. From *Resurrexit!* to *Dies Irae* the whole universe of feeling was here; and all captured in the Feder missal, conveniently at my fingertips to riffle through during dull sermons (and in my experience, few are not dull). Fingermarks show that I spent a lot of time with the saints and martyrs: Clare of Assisi living in '*pauvreté complète*', St Hyacinth of Silesia, the holy Curé d'Ars who would sit sixteen hours unrefreshed in the confessional, St Louis King of France, St Ignatius Loyola the converted libertine, and countless virgin martyrs, butchered priests, hermits, nuns and holy children. Thus, between the ages of nine and twelve, liturgy and feasts ran as a constant undercurrent beneath my ordinary life. Snap your fingers at me now, any time, and I will be able to tell you where we are in the cycle.

The other well-thumbed section of my Feder is the Examination of Conscience prescribed for those approaching the confessional. I know why, and the reason is far from saintly. I have noticed that children of the television age watch soap operas in order to clarify their idea of the adult world and its rules ('Mum, who's right? Should Ken give evidence against Deirdre if he thinks she's guilty? Is it wrong for Sally to sleep with Chris if Kevin's walked out on her anyway?' etc.). Deprived of any such easy dramatisation of the adult moral adventure, I frowned my way through Father Feder's methodical notes on examination of conscience ('For young girls . . . for young men . . . for parents . . . for businesspeople . . . for citizens'). Here are some excerpts, to give a flavour of the self-surveillance of that culture. As well as checking up on the obvious religious observances, it delves deep into daily life:

> Do I pray . . . even on days of headache, sulking, reprimands, sin? . . . Have I been simple and natural with everybody? or allowed pride to grow in me? Do I always want to be in the right? Do I accept criticism? Do I use lies to hide my failings? Am I disinterested in wealth? . . . Have I a good temperament? Am I master of my nerves? Am I energetic and brave, do I organise my time and not waste it? Do I look after my body? Do I work for the peace and health of others, or do I close myself to their suffering?
>
> As a young man, have I respected girls and women? Refrained from trying to trouble their feelings? played with love? As a young girl, have I been the cause of temptation to men by my bearing and clothes? and dancing? Have I nourished dreams of encounters which could never end in marriage?
>
> As a parent, do I give my adolescent children enough liberty, and talk seriously with them? Do I control their reading and their company wisely? Do I respect the autonomy of my

married children and avoid jealousy of my sons and daughters in law?

As a citizen, do I sincerely further the good of my country? Do I do my duty by voting, paying tax? Do I accept public responsibilities? Refrain from seeking political advantage to escape from communal laws? Do I offer favours to the powerful?

As a worker, do I bring conscientiousness and good will to my employment? Am I amiable with my colleagues? Do I exploit others? Do I give a good example? Do I promote progress and social peace within the solidarity of workers?

As an employer, do I pay wages which are just, legal, and humane? Do I try to know my workers individually, as human beings, their homes and family situations? Do I put myself in their part? Do they respect me and if not, why not? Do I give them enough rest? In my professional organisation do I take my place, active, loyal, working for progress and social peace? Do I think of my workers as my brothers? Am I polite? Am I careful of the health, religious and moral life of my domestic staff, especially the young? Do I offer them a family life?

That is not the quarter of it: no risk there of running out of sins, not in this world of serious duties. Religion, in that ethos, was not just something beautiful and musical and nebulously comforting. Being human did not confer only rights, but an illimitable coal-face of heavy duties. Recently, back in 1998, I noticed a proposal that in the 'Spirit Zone' of the Millennium Dome the soul would be represented by 'images projected onto clouds'. To the stern Father Feder and his colleagues the soul was far less vague and dreamy. It was a bright possession, certainly, but a troublesome one: something to be constantly monitored and maintained, polished and exercised and protected from the million corrosions of sin; something which needed to be fed by the sacraments and washed clean by Confession of even its tiniest, pettiest, most private and human imperfections.

Do I try to make my wife or husband happy? To understand, to know her tastes, desires, health? Do I let her know that I love her? Take an interest in her profession and activities . . . Do I affirm my authority over my children in order to calm my own nerves? Do I distinguish, in punishment, between their sillinesses and their real moral faults? . . . Have I wasted money entrusted to me in my work? Am I willing to lend things to others?

No wonder we girls in the playground were all so fascinated with martyrdom. It was the ultimate short cut to sanctity. One blow of the axe, one snap of the lion's jaws in the amphitheatre, and all this exhausting maintenance of the soul's integrity was over for good. You went straight to heaven, all sins wiped out. We thought a lot about exotic martyrdom, and relished *le supplice* with a morbid, rather masochistic private thrill. We fed on stories of Christian priests martyred in Japan, and the Congo martyrs, and the blessed Maximilan Kolbe who offered his life to the Nazi camp guards in another man's place; I revelled in the biblical epics then showing in the Rue de Bethune cinemas, in *Ben Hur* and *Quo Vadis?* and *Spartacus*.

My parents, for some reason, had a whole set of records dramatising the complete trial of Joan of Arc, and I listened endlessly to these, loving Joan's smart answers all the more for the comfortable knowledge that they would get her nowhere except to the pyre. I wondered how I would do, under torture, but failed to apply the idea of torture to any actual experience of pain. Indeed, when lying in bed for several weeks with jaundice I read my martyr books without once thinking to contrast their exotic sufferings and fortitude with my own furious resistance when confronted with the French doctor's damn great brown suppositories and insistence on drinking unsweetened lemonade. And the warning in Feder: 'Do I hold unhealthy conversations?' was certainly not applied by us schoolgirls to any of the games, speculations, or grisly recountings of the sufferings of the holy martyrs. I had a sawdust doll which I used to flog and crucify on quite a regular basis.

But no such dubious feelings polluted our restrainedly English weekend pilgrimages to the war graves of surrounding Flanders. A good friend of the family was in charge of the Commonwealth War Graves Commission office in Arras, and with him we often went to the old poppy-field sites of battle, heard the bugle at the Menin Gate at Ypres and contemplated the rows of plain, pure, unemphatic graves where boys fell in two wars, boys only a few years older than my elder brother.

No promises here of florid martyrs' crowns, no domed wax flowers, no angel wings or robes or Sacred Hearts: only the grimly faithful, sorrowfully serious promise that their name should live. I remember stooping to one of these graves once, to the few inches at the bottom where an epitaph was always carved according to the choice grieving families had made. This one – on the grave of a seventeen-year-old – just said *For your tomorrow, we gave our today*.

It all fitted together: whatever you had, whatever power or wealth or freedom, you might be called quite suddenly to renounce it for a greater cause. The nonsensical fantasies about martyrdom fell into place. I could see perfectly well that these poor boys had not wanted to be saints and martyrs, not one bit; nor had they had any chance to make fine speeches at the stake. They had been herded to war, seen their likely end coming, and still with dull, desperate simple courage had obeyed orders, and died.

And only religion – only the plain cross on the grave – could begin to make proper sense of that. My deliberately godless father, I noted, stood as quiet and still as anybody at Remembrance Sunday service.

At the very end of our life in Lille, I was elevated to the *classe de 5e*, and began to be prepared for the French ceremony of *Communion Solennelle*. This was presented to us as an important *étape* – a stage, a lap – between childhood and adolescence. We were told to make a more mature reaffirmation of our faith than we had been able to manage as small ignorant children at our first Communions. Even so, spirituality was not allowed to exclude social imperatives. It was apparent that the *Solennelle* was also a God-given occasion for affluent bourgeois families to dress up their thirteen-year-old daughters in elaborate long white dresses and veils, and to hold grand lunches at which the sons of equally suitable families wore smart suits and bow ties. It was a sort of premature pretend wedding, and I was always a bit equivocal about it.

But I see from the exercise book, kept by my mother, that I wrote out all the preparatory exercises tidily and underlined key words in red.

Now that my personality is awakening, God consults me. *Do you believe that the invisible divine life is the most important life? Do you want to live in the light of Faith and follow Me?* Or do you prefer passing pleasures and lies? Are you ready for combat and sacrifice, to cast off selfishness and be transformed and drawn towards the Father?

It is a personal response which I must now make. I shall make it at the end of the year.

But I never did. By the end of the year we were posted to Johannesburg. Lille, France and Europe – nuns, friends and language – fell away and crumbled almost instantly into memory.

My mother corresponded hastily with a Sacred Heart convent back in England, which got as far as sending me a set of Common Entrance papers to sit. But what the hell: France had been, educationally, a howling success, so why not try the same trick again? Instead of being sent home to school like poor Mike, I boarded the *Pendennis Castle* for Cape Town, and set off once again with my younger brothers for a fresh *étape* of alien education.

7. Johannesburg

Rotten, rotten, rotten to the core! It is almost impossible to explain the South Africa of 1962 to anybody who was not there. I was only twelve and well-sheltered, but even so (and despite the great beauty of the land itself) the rottenness breathed through the air, as rich as the smell of the pomegranates in the garden. Every distant veld-fire on the road to Krugersdorp conveyed, even to a child's mind, the image of a revolution which had to be coming, with fire and the sword.

Behind the beauty and sprawling ease of the Northern Suburbs of Johannesburg, behind our fine detached villa with a stoep and a swimming-pool, behind the towering downtown banks and offices, there was an atmosphere of primitive threat. Violence hung on the air. It was not that we particularly feared violence towards us, and certainly not from the respectful, smiling, affable black domestic servants who (by law) lived in separate quarters across our garden. It was just a general inchoate violence: a sense that something had to give eventually, because the whole apartheid society was founded on such breathtaking injustice.

There were still benches in the park, bus stops and lavatories all marked 'WHITES ONLY' and 'BLACKS ONLY'. Just a few miles from the rich, gentle suburbs and golf clubs which made Jo'burg's Northern Suburbs into an exile's idealised dream of Surrey, there were shanty townships where half-naked children wandered hungry in the streets and tried to suck from straying goats. To keep these two worlds in their artificial places there were armed police everywhere. The newspapers often gave brief, bald accounts of young men and women arrested for 'immorality' – meaning even the most honourable courtship across race barriers. Cape Coloured families were split up when one child appeared white, for a white skin must not be seen to be reared among darker ones.

Once, our smiling young gardener inadvertently went out without his identity card and had to be picked up from the police station, where he had been roughed up. I heard the grown-ups saying that it was the *black* police who got him: that particular corruption haunted me for weeks. The gardener Fred used to put his wages into a pool with a group of other local servants, so that between them they could afford to educate one boy. Our servant Elizabeth had a servant of her own, thirteen-year-old Martha, whose job was to mind Elizabeth's baby while Elizabeth attended to the needs of her Baas and Madam. We gave Martha a costume and taught her to swim in our little pool, for she was close to my age. The neighbours just about put up with this, but when Fred's son of seventeen came briefly to stay in the servants' quarters and we lent him trunks to go swimming, we were put for ever beyond the pale, and communication between the houses ceased. A little black girl in the pool was one thing; a 'buck nigger' quite another. It is interesting to speculate how much, among these people, racial mistrust was underpinned by sexual terror. I suppose that the terror of rape has always been a powerful propaganda weapon, persuading women to hate the enemy underclass even more than their men do, and to pass on that hatred down the generations. Keep them *down*, lady, we gotta keep them *down*, or it'll be the worse for you . . .

My parents did their best to make sure that all of us – especially me, as the eldest fully resident child – understood that this way of carrying on was not only wrong but ridiculous. On the ship coming over we all had to fill in our immigration forms, which contained a box for RACE. My father had put 'Protestant', my mother 'Human'. Encouraged by this example Miss Wilson put

'Ladies Breast-stroke 300 metres', and I put '3.30 Kempton Park'. Once settled, my mother immediately involved herself with Bishop Trevor Huddleston's African Children's Feeding Scheme, and took me almost every week during the holidays down to Alexandra Township to help put peanut-butter on lumps of bread and mix up powdered skim milk for distribution to the hot, patient lines of mothers and children who queued up in the sun.

But we lived in comfort, and revelled as other whites did in the beauty of this stolen country, its game parks and the wide spaces of the Transvaal. Our daily lives were supported by cooks and cleaners, miners and labourers and a million invisible semi-slaves who could never live as comfortably as we did, or vote, or sit on Whites Only benches in the park. I do not think it would have been possible not to feel guilty about this. Much later on, at University in the revolutionary year 1968, I came across certain slogans: *If you're not part of the solution, you're part of the problem . . . For evil to triumph it is only necessary that good men do nothing*. Such slogans always bit where it hurts, and they still do. But how can you do anything, when you are only twelve?

Catholic schools were found. Here, at least, should be a respite from the violent unfairness of this new world. The small boys were sent to the Marist Brothers in Johannesburg as day pupils, and I was dispatched to board in St Ursula's Convent, Krugersdorp; some fifty miles away across the high veld. Ursuline nuns were familiar from Bangkok, and I quite liked the idea of boarding. It would be lonely, being the only girl at home, missing my French and Suffolk friends. I had read a great many school stories and imagined a world of dormitory frolics and hockey.

This expectation was heightened by the business of going down into Jo'burg and buying the school winter uniform: a brown-green-and-silver striped blazer and tie, brown box-pleated gymslip, and both felt and straw hats, each with school ribbon and the brim turned up at the back and down at the front so as to be vaguely duck-shaped. We also had a khaki 'drill tunic' for marching in formation each morning before Assembly. Where France had taught me to curtsy, South Africa taught me to right-about-face and left wheel. Indeed all the appurtenances and clothes of St Ursula's could have been borrowed from Malory Towers or St Clare's in the 1940s, with a piquant edging of Sandhurst.

What none of us fully understood at the time was that the whole charade was only another symptom of the sickness of old, white South Africa. It was the same sickness which made lifelong residents of Johannesburg talk colonially of 'home', meaning England; the sickness which helped to prevent any emotional rapprochement or basic compassion between black and white. In a curious, spooky sense these bankers and industrialists and clerks and lunching-ladies were *not really there at all*. They were in denial. They did not want to be in Africa, except that it was the only place where their limited talents could make them rich and comfortable. So they disguised bits of Africa as bits of the old Home Counties.

At least the farming Afrikaners, rough crude countrymen, felt a strong emotional stake in the country, and managed to entertain brief flashes of realism about the humanity of their black workers. Their children, on remote farms out of sight of the world, were allowed to run and play with black children. This, I found years later to my delight, led to a curious friendship between Nelson Mandela and one of his white jailers, who on an impulse remembered a long-lost black farm playfellow from his child-hood and addressed the prisoner of Robben Island in his own language. Much brutality came out of Afrikanerdom, but some humanity as well. What you saw was what you got: beef-fed Boers, in a Dutch reformed Church which openly and robustly talked of lesser races.

Whereas the white-collar Anglophone South Africans were hell: ersatz Home Counties snobs, focused on an imaginary 'home' of striped blazers and golf clubs, needing always to be Baas and Madam yet contemptuous and fearful of the black Jeeveses who served them. For them the euphemism 'separate development' was a lifeline. 'They have their culture and we have ours' they would say; and with blazers and gymslips, gin-and-tonics and chintz sofas, they huddled round the pale sickly flame of their own 'culture' in terror of ever accidentally letting in the earthy vitality of the Dark Continent.

Nuns should not have been part of this culture, let alone its distilled essence. I did not think they would be. I was faintly apprehensive on the first day at St Ursula's: the habits were different, for one thing. Sacred Heart nuns had wimples pulled under the chin, creating long thin faces even for the fattest; this lot had rectangular white coifs retaining black veils, which made their faces look round. But I went in through the big front door quite willingly. I trusted nuns. They *had* to be kind and good, didn't they? It was in the rules.

But the rottenness pervaded the convent too. Inside the high walls the stench of hypocrisy and evasion was stronger, if possible, than outside. There was a furious decadent state of denial, a refusal to accept the self-evident truth that whatever the ambitions of its foundation, everything about this actual school – like everything about the white society it fed on – was built on injustice and brutality. The only black faces we saw were the cleaners, and the white nuns snapped orders at them as haughtily as any Madam in the whole benighted country. I once heard the headmistress nun say, with real memsahib contempt: 'Those Kaffirs don't clean the chapel floor properly'. She had an extraordinary, strangled, mock-posh accent – native Irish and Afrikaner crushed to a semblance of 1930s Cheltenham, so that 'horse' came out as 'hearse'. All she had said to my mother before I came was 'Elizabeth will find things very different here'. We did not know that this meant a tacit but firm endorsement of apartheid.

In odd ways the physical brutality of the wider South Africa broke in, too: that convent was not a relaxed or contemplative place, but one humming with suppressed rage and a sense of bad things never spoken of. Crude sarcasm was the weapon of choice for most of the nuns, but sometimes violence would break in, in rare but disturbing outbursts of neurotic fury. A peppery old nun like Mother Rita would lash out at our knees and calves with long rulers, purple-faced, taken out of herself by rage. Later we would see the furious little figure kneeling in the choir, still scowling.

Of course, I did not analyse any of this at first. I just perceived it as a bleak and horrible school. We slept in long dormitories of thirty or forty beds, separated by curtains on rails like an old-fashioned hospital ward. We undressed with proper modesty behind these curtains but before we slept a nun would come down the room opening them and checking that our hands were outside the bedclothes, crossed on our breasts. It was years before I worked out why. I was young for my age, by modern standards.

By each bed was a tin ewer of cold water and a basin, for our morning ablutions at six o'clock: it was sometimes so cold in the Transvaal winter that the water had a thin skim of ice on it. In chapel we did not wear veils, but little brown felt 'chapel caps' like acorn-cups: this small detail added to my bewildered sense that even Mass here was not the same as the Mass I knew, any more than the behaviour and values of the nuns related to anything I had ever seen of religion and religious orders. My schoolmates seemed to think chapel was nonsense; soon, so did I.

The food was filthy: mealie-meal porridge, thin and glutinous, and chokingly hard bread. Only on grand feast days did breakfast include a few limp slices of liver sausage. Other meals were little better. The rule in the refectory was that all kept silence after grace and stood rigid behind the chairs until told 'You may sit'. Then we sat, food untouched, and still kept silent, until a little bell was tinkled by the supervising nun who then said disdainfully: 'You may begin'.

Sometimes, if there was suppressed giggling or scraping of chairs, she would not ring the second bell for as much as five minutes, while the mealie porridge grew cold and nauseating in front of us. During breakfast letters were given out, and punishments too: Mother Rita once called out some felon and bent her, gripping the girl's head between her knees, to beat her bottom viciously with a stick while we sat silent and sickened over our porridge. It was not an encouraging start to the day.

The majority of physical punishments, however, were more

dignified: you just held out your hand – the left one, unless you were a left-hander – and were dealt stinging blows across it with the flat of a ruler. Only once did I see a nun use the edge of the ruler instead. Mostly it happened in class: there were some pitiable dunces among my contemporaries, and their inability to follow the teaching was punished as severely as if it were deliberate. Not that classes were difficult. After the rigours of France I had to be 'accelerated' in order to learn anything at all in Krugersdorp. A childish twelve, I found myself sitting next to fourteen-year-olds who had already discovered boys, make-up, and Cliff Richard (Elvis Presley records were banned in school: he danced in a 'dirty, native' way, said the nuns, whereas Cliff's pelvis moved in a more decently restrained, *white* sort of way).

The syllabus was odd. History formed no part of it, presumably because history is full of things which could embarrass 1960s white South Africans – such as revolutions which work, and crusades for justice. I was allowed, however, to miss Afrikaans lessons and read some history on my own at my father's insistence. In fact, I hardly bothered, preferring to use the periods to go up to the typewriter room and practise. We all did typing and shorthand: it was our assumed destiny to be secretaries. I enjoyed it, and in this keyboard era have never regretted learning to touch-type. The happiest moments of Krugersdorp life were spent pecking away on an old upright Remington with a cloth over my fingers and a diagram of the letters on the wall, copying out specimen business letters. It was a simple, understandable, unchallengeable achievement in a baffling world; like completing the mini-marathon round the running-track on Sports Day.

Beyond that, the narrowness and dullness was stifling. South Africa was not like the other New Worlds, America and Australia. It was not a melting-pot. Its white denizens lived in hunched, sullen terror of dilution or invasion by the vivid burning exoticism of the dark continent. Our botany books were about English wildflowers, not the teeming life of Africa. The yellow horned poppy came back into my life. Even our set-books were deliberately chosen to be as un-African as possible. All year we read Dinah Maria Mulock's *John Halifax, Gentleman* and Hammond Innes's *The Wreck of the 'Mary Deare'*. I grew very fond of them both, but it seems perverse to have travelled the length of Africa in order to read Dinah Maria Mulock.

Again, there were friends: Linda and Lesley and Colleen, and dear Thelma who brought us in extra Marmite sandwiches in her lunchbox to assuage our gnawing hunger. These girls put up with me very well, albeit with a certain condescension towards my young age and laughable innocence. They did their best to jolly me out of my state of frozen misery. I wrote home constantly demanding to be taken away; my parents are not really to blame for not responding, because they can have had no real idea at all of the worthlessness of the school. These, after all, were nuns. Nuns, surely, were civilised? Sort of European? Their mother house was in Rome, their leader the Pope. Even Dad thought that they would be all right. I still do not really know why they were not.

This was the first period when I had crushes on older girls, the ones at the very top of the school. They were usually brief, these adorations, but none the less intense: around Flora, Denise or Marika there would hover for days or weeks a light that never was on land or sea. It made up for the fact that for the first time in my life, there was no intimation of holiness anywhere in sight. All through childhood I had fed on moments of transcendence, but no gleam of it touched Krugersdorp life. Not even in the chapel or the choir. The only moment in St Ursula's when I remember glimpsing something beyond the glum absurdity of everyday life was when – rather against my inclination – we had to sing 'I vow to thee, my country' at assembly. I had little wish to vow any kind of love to the Republic of South Africa, even though the hymn was written by Sir Cecil Spring Rice who was a distant relation of my friend Thelma Rice who brought in the Marmite sandwiches. But there in that dull hall, under the bitter little eye of Mother Rita, I found myself in verse two and was without warning transported to another place: 'another country I heard of long ago':

Her fortress is a faithful heart, her pride is suffering
And soul by soul and silently her shining bounds increase
And all her ways are gentleness and all her paths are peace.

It had the same effect, an instant stunning emotional catharsis, as
the Kipling poems I had lately found. Partly, I think, it was the
excitement of coming back to my own language after three years
of total immersion in French literature, liturgy and phraseology.
By the time I left Lille I had been thinking in French, sometimes
even at home, and reading more French than English for
recreation. The thoroughly English muscularity of Kipling
thrilled me to the core: *Hark to the big drum calling – follow me,
follow me 'ome! . . . Lord of our far-flung battle line . . . look on triumph
and disaster . . .* Sir Cecil Spring Rice struck that same chord, and
for a few moments I was out of prison.

But really we sang very little sacred music: to the Schools'
Eisteddfodd we took 'Come Gentle Spring', 'It was a lover and
his lass', and 'Did you not hear my Lady?', and also a unison
recitation of 'The Wee Cooper of Fife'. To this day I can recite it
with a thick Afrikaans accent:

There was a wee cooper who lived in Fife
Nickety, nackety, noo noo noo
And he has gotten a gentle wife
Hey Willie Wackely, Ho, John Dougall, Alane quo' Rushety,
  roo roo roo

Decades later, after the political revolution in South Africa, I read
with grim amusement about the whites of Potgietersrus trying to
keep black children out of their school because it would
dilute white 'culture'. What culture? The wee cooper o'Fife and
Hammond Innes? They also spoke of 'Christian values' which
would be endangered by the arrival of black infants. Apart from
the strict prohibition on putting your hands under the bedclothes,
I discerned no Christian values in Krugersdorp at all.

Our religious instruction – from books with Bible stories

involving suspiciously white-skinned characters – was infantile after the subtle theology of France. Once a week there was a question session, when we were allowed to put anonymous queries into a cardboard shoebox. I assume that this was in order to flush out any worries about heavy petting, but in effect the questions ranged from 'Do rabbits have souls?' to 'What did they cut their hair with in the old days?' Once, the question was raised about whether the souls of Kaffirs – I apologise for the word, but only by using it can I convey the tone of that life – were the same as 'our' souls. The answer, if I remember it correctly, was that God weighed them in his wisdom, but that separate development was the best for all of us here on earth. As for our school song, it had a chorus which was remarkable even by the high standards of lunacy set by girls' school songs down the decades. The chorus went:

> Who knows the school?
> Who knows St Ursula's schoo-ool?
> Shout it over Africa – back comes the call from
> Teachers, nurses, mothers wives –
> Nuns and nurses, old girls all!

I used to imagine the shout going out over the great dark Continent, as puzzled kudu and lonely Xhosa herdsmen pricked their ears and wondered what the hell St Ursula's school might be.

Once, in a careers talk, sixth-form girls sang out their ambitions 'Mother, I want to be a teacher . . . a nurse . . . a *sickeretary*'. One said, flippantly 'I want to be a Zulu'. I heard of this in whispers later in the dormitory corridor: the word was that she was to be sent home, she was to be beaten, she was a Bad Influence. Her joke had all the horror of incest or murder.

I dare say it did me some good, in the long run. It is a kind of weird privilege to have encountered, before the age of thirteen, a white supremacist Reverend Mother. There is some kind of lesson for life in being hit with a ruler, not calmly but in a rage, by a woman whose pectoral cross swung wildly with the vigour of her assault. At least it stopped me ever again having too much reverence and respect for the outward clothing of religion.

They did not put me off religion. I found it reasonably easy to comprehend that the fault lay with *these* nuns rather than *all* nuns (or worse, all Christians). This conscious mental adjustment was assisted by the benevolent sweetness of the genuinely Christian workers we met down in the Township – stalwart Anglican followers of Bishop Huddleston. It was also assisted a little by the continuing memory of C. S. Lewis's Narnia books . . . *No service which is vile can be done to me, and none which is not vile can be done to him . . . if any man do a cruelty in my name, though he says the name Aslan it is Tash whom he serves and by Tash his deed is accepted.*

The shallow, prim vileness of one Christian community did not, I decided privately, prove anything against Christianity itself. It just meant that they were doing it wrong. Perhaps it was even harder to do than the Feder missal had suggested? Anyway, I told myself that the damn nuns were an aberration: they had less claim to Christianity than a kind, tolerant pagan would have had. So they hardly mattered. But by luck I was twelve years old before I met them. It is not difficult to see how younger survivors of brutal priestly upbringings or Magdalene Asylums usually come to quite opposite conclusions.

South Africa did leave me with odd, unresolved pockets of rage deep below the surface. To this day I will suddenly grow unreasonably angry with a petulant bishop, or a sneering archdeacon, or a bigot who stirs up hatred while dubbing himself The Reverend. Once I was in Belfast doing an interview for the Radio 4 *Sunday* programme with some hard-line Protestant clergy on the subject of Orange marches. I asked what I had always wanted to ask those people (on both sides of that disgraceful conflict) who disguise their angry politics in a religious garb. You can ask questions on a religious affairs programme which would be taboo on *Today* or *PM*. So I did. 'What about Blessed are the meek? What about Turn the other Cheek? Love thy neighbour? How does that square with banging the big drum?'

As they replied with haughty self-justification, a sudden hot wave of rage swam over me and I recognised it as a childish rage connected directly to St Ursula's. *How dare you wear that cross?*

Eventually, my parents accepted that Krugersdorp was educationally useless as well as making me miserable. At the same time they had suddenly lost confidence in the order of monks who were educating the little boys at a Johannesburg day-school. This followed a few canings and a report of a rather odd lesson, an explicit lecture on modes of capital punishment up to and including the garrotte.

So my mother loaded us all aboard the S.S. *Braemar Castle* to sail back and find some English schools. My father stayed on for six months or so. I remember looking at him on the dock at Durban and wondering whether we would see him again. It felt to me as if this extraordinary country could not possibly get through even a few months more without the bloodiest, angriest of revolutions. The fact that it lasted decades, and killed relatively few in its eventual transition, still feels like a miracle.

Or perhaps the great and continuing patience of the black people of South Africa has a sadder root. Perhaps it is connected with the humble diffidence which their long subjugation brought them to. Once my mother heard Paul Robeson on the kitchen radio and saw that Elizabeth the maid was moved by the music.

'Isn't that beautiful?' said my mother. 'Paul Robeson. He's black, you know.'

'Oh madam!' said Elizabeth reverently. 'But he sings – like a white man!'

8. Homeward

If you have to switch cultures and lives, it is best to do it slowly and by ship. We could have flown – my elder brother did, every holiday – but it was decided that a five-week voyage up the East coast on the little *Braemar Castle* would be more educational. We would cast off Africa slowly and thoughtfully, and blend back into Europe by easy stages. We would stop at Mombasa, Zanzibar, Suez, Aden, Genoa and Gibraltar; walk the deck, watch the cargoes swinging in and out of the hold, smell the cinnamon wafting on the salt air from spice islands. We would ride a camel to the Pyramids while the ship went through the Suez Canal, rescue my mother from insistent *cicisbeos* in Genoa and dodge missiles thrown by Barbary Apes on Gib.

And so we did; the voyage is with me still, a folded treasure in the bottom of the deepest mental drawer. Not only could I indulge serial crushes on most of the officers (I was by now thirteen) but the sea, then as always, provided me with abundant glimpses of transcendence, and a sternly satisfying mental library of metaphors for life and eternity.

I revelled in ocean sunsets and sunrises, the creaking of gales, the quiet lonely vigilance of the officer on the bridge at dusk, the slow rising of distant land and the nervous thrill of each new departure. It was primarily a cargo ship, unlike the *Pendennis Castle* we had come on, which was a faster mailship; the rhythm of cargo was always with us as in each exotic port we heard crashing and yelling, and watched the bales and boxes, cars and lorries, swung by crane across our familiar foredeck. The crew, far from their own families, treated us children as pets, inviting us through forbidden doors and up barred staircases. They showed us the bridge and the kitchens, blowing me cheeky kisses when they looked up from coiling some great rope to see me peering at them from some higher rail, plump and solemn and owl-eyed in my gold-rimmed glasses. We went on excursions ashore – a rickety speeding bus in Kenya stays in my mind, and an extrovert taxi-driver on Zanzibar who stopped to snap off cloves and squeeze pepper-pods and rip cinnamon-bark from the trees. I still have my magic sliver of cinnamon bark in a box of childhood treasures. We took a bus to Cairo and on the way home from the Pyramids raced the *Braemar Castle* along the Suez Canal, craning out of the windows to see the extraordinary sight of its familiar lilac flanks moving, like the ghost of a ship on a long-dry seabed, seamlessly over the sand.

So, once again in a limbo between lives, I saw the breadth of the world, the danger and the strangeness. Memories of earlier ships haunted the voyage, all the way back to the journey home from Israel when I was three and was terrified by the lava people in the ruins of Pompeii. It seemed that always, between new schools and new nuns and new friends, there was this time on a ship. Everything ended in a voyage, so that the voyage itself became a kind of home.

On the high boat deck in the evening, kicking shuffleboard counters around when everybody else had drifted down to dress for dinner, there was a melancholy kind of excitement in seeing that our cosy lamplit floating world was only a speck on the uneasy ocean. Few though we passengers were, the usual social rites of liners were observed: Neptune appeared in a green wig and First Officer's stripes when we Crossed the Line, and on fancy-dress party night, in a rising gale, the ship swayed and creaked with a cargo of dancing, squealing, garish, balloon-waving revellers slithering to and fro across the big saloon floor while rain and spray lashed against the windows.

There were elements of the Ark about this life, too: in France we had bought a little African finch who went by the name of Birdie, and inhabited a vast hanging cage of green wire. Incredibly, Birdie had come with us to South Africa aboard the *Pendennis Castle*, hanging in the chain-locker on the boat deck. Even more incredibly, he had survived Johannesburg and now travelled back with us, totally unconcerned by salt and motion alike, pecking at his cuttlefish and chirruping over his millet. I went up to see him every morning and evening, and was sometimes joined by officers, who marvelled at his chirpy survival and were willing to exchange a few kind words with a bashful four-eyed worshipper. More dramatically once, early in the voyage and still far south, a wandering albatross landed on the deck: it looked like an enormous, barrel-chested, impossible giant seagull and smelt overpoweringly of rotting fish and its own feather-oil. Sometimes there were dolphins, once a whale.

In the library was a Psalter, its cover misted with shippy mould but its text the Oxford Authorized-Revised, free from banal modernisation. On long dull afternoons I would sometimes turn its filmy pages in the library, enjoying the cadences and the images. The flaw of a predominantly Catholic upbringing is (or certainly used to be) that there was very little of the Old Testament in it. For the recipient of a fairly heavy-duty religious education in three continents, I was surprisingly unfamiliar with it. I might be able to recite the Four Sins Crying Out to Heaven for Vengeance, but was a stranger among the rivers of Babylon and the tents of Kedar.

The Psalms suited me well; plenty of weepings by rivers and wanderings in the wilderness and pits of affliction and persecution by Princes. I was, remember, thirteen years old, and a sense of affliction and persecution came easily. By accident, I swear it, somewhere off the Horn of Africa I came for the first time upon Psalm 107:

> THEY that go down to the sea in ships,
> That do business in great waters;
> These see the works of the LORD

And his wonders in the deep.
For he commandeth, and raiseth the stormy wind,
Which lifteth up the waves thereof.
They mount up to the heaven, they go down again to the
depths:
Their soul melteth away because of trouble.
They reel to and fro, and stagger like a drunken man,
And are at their wits' end,
Then they cry unto the LORD in their trouble,
And he bringeth them out of their distresses.
He maketh the storm a calm,
So that the waves thereof are still.
Then are they glad because they be quiet;
So he bringeth them unto the haven where they would be.

God, plainly, still had all the best tunes.

By the time we got to Walberswick to regroup, meet Mike from
his school and prepare for the next assault on yet another education system, we were in high spirits. The bewilderments and fears
of South Africa were forgotten and I was perfectly ready to try
out another boarding-school, sight unseen. Dad, we eventually
knew, had been posted as second-in-command at the Berne
embassy in Switzerland. Back to Europe and old stonework, back
to civilization and comfortingly drizzling rain, far from the lurid
sun and crazy paranoia of Johannesburg. 'Full circle,' he said
wonderingly; Berne had been his first ever posting, far further
down the hierarchy, and when he went back to the restaurant
where he used to eat twenty years earlier, an elderly waiter
shuffled across to his table and said 'The *Wiener Schnitzel*, as usual,
Mein Herr?'

But this time there was no question of any more exotic
overseas education. The small boys were dispatched to prep
school, and I to Tunbridge Wells.

9. T.W.

It was another Sacred Heart convent, sister to the one in Lille. Colloquially it was distinguished from the more famous and socially upmarket Sacred Heart school at Woldingham, and a slightly ailing one at Hove, by the nickname 'T.W.' – Tunbridge Wells.

Unusually for an English girls' boarding-school it stood on the edge of the town rather than remote among fields. But the garden was big, landscaped into lawns and walks and planted with rare and lovely trees by an Edwardian private owner who had, the legend said, 'very good contacts at Kew'.

There were red cloaks and sweaters instead of blazers, and gymslips were replaced by rather horrible – but at least reasonably contemporary – brown nylon skirts with fiddly inverted pleats which had to be sewn up before you washed them. The only long dormitory which could have been used in Krugersdorp barracks style had been converted into Upper Fifth study-bedrooms with gaily coloured doors, and we younger ones were accommodated in rooms of four or five, too domestic to be thought of as dormitories. Most were grouped around a Victorian gallery and named for shrines: Montserrat, Guadalupe, Fatima, Lourdes.

On the first night in Guadalupe I climbed into bed, looked around, and lay back with a sigh of relief. I was a little nervous of my peers, but this would be all right. I knew it. I was back among my own age group, more or less; the academic advances of Lille had been counteracted by the duncery of Krugersdorp. I was normal and English again and could join the Lower Fifth with confidence.

I was also, once again, in a wholehearted convent. Although lay teachers came in by day for a great many subjects, our basic care was entirely with the nuns – the Community, who lived their life by the monastic Rule in mysterious regions of the big house where no lay person except a doctor might ever set foot. In chapel they had stalls, enclosing our pews, and we saw them at prayer; in the house there were particular doors behind which we could never follow them.

First thing in the morning there was no rising-bell. Instead, a soft-footed, black-robed figure came into each dormitory bearing a small china cup with a sponge soaked in Holy Water. The figure stood by your bed, and said:

'Sacred Heart of Jesus, Immaculate Heart of Mary –'
to which you drowsily replied
'I give you my heart'
and reached out, dipped a finger in the holy water and made the sign of the cross. Sometimes you would miss the china stoup and flail your drowsy fist against a flat nunly chest; sometimes knock it from her hand entirely; sometimes the nun would have to repeat three or four times, at rising volume and with a touch of unsanctified irritation:

'SACRED HEART OF JESUS, IMMACULATE HEART OF MARY!'
before achieving any movement from beneath the blankets. Sometimes a sixth-former would be deputed to wake a junior dormitory, and the whole thing would become a garble: 'SakeheartJeezer-MaclatheartMary' – 'Gizhmyharr'. Sometimes on early Mass days we succeeded in rolling under the bed once the nun had gone, and sleeping on until breakfast-time undetected beneath the stripped bedclothes.

But I still maintain that it was a more civilised, more personal way to wake up boarding-school children than a clanging bell. And if you were ill, you could say 'Mother, I'm ill'; if you were sad, some duty nuns at least would be capable of rapidly registering the problem.

Holy Smoke

When I think of the T.W. nuns, and how their religiousness impinged on everyday life under their rule, the brightest thread in the bundle of memory is a sense of their dedication. However much at odds one might be with a particular nun, however generally rebellious and fed-up with school, it was impossible to be unaware of their total commitment. They accepted us whole-heartedly as their responsibility: caring for us was as much part of their vocation as chanting divine office. I sometimes thought that it must be very odd to be at a lay school, and to know that teachers and housemistresses only looked after you because they were *paid* to. It seemed a faintly indecent idea. Nuns were more like universal parents. Or, at least, aunts.

In those days before the full effect of the Vatican II reforms, there were still two grades of nun in the order of the Sacred Heart. The division ran straight back to medieval times, when different status was given to dowered and undowered nuns, the learned ones who illuminated manuscripts and the unlettered ones who scrubbed floors. Choir nuns were called Mother, and wore frilled wimples right round their faces coming to a narrow point at the chin, with deep black habits topped by a scapular like an old-fashioned ulster. Lay sisters were called Sister, and had a simpler head-dress, swept off the face, and a grey veil. They did the cleaning and worked in the kitchens; many of them were from France, the Philippines, Austria or Albania, and spoke heavily accented English. Most were middle-aged or older.

After Pope John XXIII's great sweeping reforms of the religious orders, the distinction was swept away and all the nuns wore the same simplified habit and were democratically called Sister. But when I first went to Tunbridge Wells the little lay sisters (they always were little, and generally round) were a cosy and beloved part of the landscape, like so many character-actresses playing the Nurse from *Romeo and Juliet*, or comic cleaning-ladies in an Ealing film. They were very devout, in an untor-mented way, and it was pleasant to meet, along some corridor, an elderly Bretonne mumbling: '*Ô Père Éternel, où est mon* dustpan? So shorry, Mees – *Ah, Jésus, Jésus, je vous aime . . . ici,* good, so!

Saint-Esprit, honneur et gloire . . .' The best of the choir nuns, I think, rather envied them. As St Benedict, father of monastic life, insisted – *Laborare est orare*. But it must be far easier to turn your work into prayer if your work is waxing floors, rather than teaching inattentive children Maths and French, or sorting out disciplinary problems about smuggled bottles of Merrydown cider.

The school had been founded in 1915, with the local canon at the time solemnly reminding the nuns of the new foundation that 'the conversion of this very Protestant town, Tunbridge Wells' was a special charge on them. It had a subtly different atmosphere from the French convent at Rue Royale: it felt more bracing, more like a pioneering outstation.

In Lille, after all, Catholicism was an integral part of the culture, and M. le Maire would be there in Saint-Maurice with everyone else, fondly watching his daughter do her Communion *Solenelle* in a miniature wedding-dress before a vast bourgeois lunch. Whereas in England to be a Catholic was to be outside the establishment, banned from marrying Prince Charles; it was an outlandish, possibly even Irish pursuit. Although some of the nuns and hangers-on of Tunbridge Wells belonged to the upper-crust, Duke-of-Norfolk type of Catholic who rhymed 'Mass' with 'farce', there was still an imperceptible sense that any Catholic convent was a social island.

This sense, I have to admit, was palpably enjoyed by many of the nuns, and mixed with a pride in the ill-funded but energetic growth of their little school over fifty years. They celebrated their sisters' visible achievements over those years: in the teaching block for which lay and choir sisters together had carried breeze-blocks and wheeled barrows in the 1950s, in the memory of Mother Ashton-Case who had carved the stark Calvary on a garden walk called The Way of Peace, lame Mother Fielding who carted sandstone from the hockey pitch to build a rockery and Mother Cardon who, the anniversary booklet proudly reminded us, taught her metalwork group to make the tabernacle doors for the chapel.

Other nuns would return sometimes, leathery and distant-eyed, from extraordinary mission adventures inside Communist China or deep in the Congo; news was relayed to us from the House at Fort Lamy in Tchad, from Poland and Uganda and the Amazon ('where they think nothing of losing a limb in a quarrel!'). The missionary emphasis was on education, especially of girls; and among our own old girls we were told to be proud not only of the myriad 'Good Catholic mothers' the school had produced, but of those who were working their way round America on Greyhound buses or running farms, working 'at terribly important jobs' for the United Nations or writing novels like Jenny Lash. Farther back, there were held up to us such figures as Pauline Gower, one of the pioneer women pilots who ferried aircraft across the Atlantic in the war and always took a mouth-organ, a rosary, and a spanner to knock out panicking passengers.

A certain gawky, gung-ho enthusiasm spread downwards from The Mistress General (a direct translation of the French for headmistress) Mother Wilson. She was an intellectual of powerful repute and piercing eyes behind pebble glasses, a striding, swishing figure who never bothered carrying a bell or a pair of clickers to silence the dining hall, but simply stood tall in the doorway and rang an invisible bell above her head, confident that her presence would always register. Her usual greeting to alarmed Old Girls after years away was always 'How's God?' and she would end a letter 'Three cheers for GOD!' She was a learned and compelling teacher of philosophy who also enjoyed dressing up as a tramp to provide a clue in school treasure hunts; a woman who rose to the challenge of Vatican II derestriction of convent life by taking driving lessons. In these she showed such hot-rod enthusiasm and outbursts of manic prayer that her poor instructor used to be seen getting out of the car at the end of a session to lean on the bonnet, white and shaking, lighting a calming fag (I am not sure how this contributed to the hoped-for conversion of Protestant Tunbridge Wells, but it certainly bucked up his idea of nuns).

In short, a fresh wind blew through this convent, a wind from the whole world; and with all its faults (the faults of almost any girls' school of the day, such as lousy science teaching) it was a breezy and optimistic place to grow up. The eccentric brio of Mother Wilson had much to do with this. While some Catholic children were never allowed to mark Hallowe'en, for instance (and some Christian children still aren't) this Mistress General thought that ghouls and ghosties needed to be mocked, shown where they got off, and chased from the scene by the blinding light of her God and her robust humour.

So we marked Hallowe'en with a gusto unmatched by any other young ladies' boarding school I have ever heard of. The routine was that Mother Wilson would gather the school together before bedtime, ring the invisible bell, and stress in her most convincingly awesome tones (for believe me, she was never in any way a figure of fun) that because of the disruption caused in previous years there was to be no, repeat _no_, attempt to mark this unpleasant and pagan festival. All Saints Day Mass would be celebrated as usual in the morning, white veils please. But any noise after lights out would be dealt with *very severely indeed*.

Then we were packed off to bed in silence. Then, twenty minutes after the younger ones' lights were out, the entire Upper Sixth, dressed as ghosts and witches, would rampage through the dormitories ripping off bedclothes with banshee howls. They would herd us downstairs, shivering and shrieking, into the cellar where the pottery wheels were; lay sisters would serve us cocoa and buns while Mother Wilson told gruesome ghost stories until it was time for the nuns to slip off to Chapel and begin the Great Silence. It is a measure of this woman's character that every Hallowe'en we were convinced by her stern homily that this really *was* the year it all would stop; but that it never did. We were allowed Guy Fawkes bonfires, too, although prudently the Guy was left out in case stricter Catholic parents complained. And we did judo, wrestling on mats with a small, nervous Scotsman without any worry on the nuns' part, or any chaperonage whatsoever.

As for the outside world, we were encouraged to engage with it in what, looking back, seems a pretty carefree way. Comparing notes with other girls' boarding-schools of the period, we convent girls were less chaperoned than they were, not more. On Saturday afternoon we could go downtown on the bus, in threes, to shop at Etam and Richard Shops; only the coffee-bars and pubs were barred to us. Sixth-formers who rebelled against the sloppy science teaching had their petition heard, and were allowed to go and join in better classes in better laboratories at the boys' grammar schoool in town. When our school was organising an Oxfam walk the nuns said calmly that they were not meant to leave the House without special dispensation, so we fifth-formers must sort it all out with the police ourselves. Accordingly we went down and presented ourselves and our route map to a surprised and suspicious Traffic division and were told how to organise parents and helpers into marshalling duties.

Mother Wilson was not above a little civil disobedience, either. When the local authority flatly refused to give us a manned crossing for the day girls who crossed the dangerous Pembury Road, she encouraged the sixth form to take illegal action: we donned lab coats and made our own STOP sign, and ran a lollipop patrol for three days before the police came round. Our Mistress General tranquilly received the inspector in her parlour, and when he came out, slightly shaken, he had agreed to train a group of us as an official, properly costumed and equipped crossing patrol until the authority agreed to pay for a proper one.

This gave us a thrilling sense of real participation in the adult world: my partner Janice and I even managed to take a prisoner. We caught the number of a car that shot past our little flock illegally, reported it, and found ourselves nervously giving evidence against the unfortunate driver in court. To our horror it turned out that he was a probation officer in another Kent court. Mother Wilson thought this tremendously funny and laid a bony hand on our shoulders, shaking with mirth, as she said '*Quis custodet ipsos custodes?* Janice and Libby shall!'

So we were not cut off from the world, not at all. And yet the school was in many ways run as if it were 1935 not 1965. There were many things I recognised from the sister convent in Lille. Mother Wilson had loved the old ways of the French-rooted Sacred Heart as a girl, and saw no reason to discard them. We were still marshalled into lines by a Mistress of Discipline and silenced in the refectory by the use of the old wooden 'clackers', which meant that no nunly voice, technically, ever needed to be raised. We still curtsied to the Mistress General, to Reverend Mother, to visiting bishops and to the portrait of Our Lady on the wall outside the refectory; it is quite an art, curtsying while you are scuttling along a corridor with an armful of files and exercise books. You sort of dip on one step, and rise on the next. It took years to get the habit right out of my blood. Four years after leaving the convent I found myself, nervous in a first job, executing the beginnings of a bob of obeisance when confronted suddenly with the BBC Director-General in a Broadcasting House corridor. I do not think he noticed.

Another familiar rite from Rue Royale surfaced in the prosaic surroundings of Tunbridge Wells, too: we had Notes on a Saturday morning. Once again we wore white socks and white gloves and lined up to receive our cards; I even remembered the colours. Pale blue for Very Good, dark blue for Good, yellow for Fair, white for Mediocre, or the ultimate sanction, No Note and a cold stare from Reverend Mother.

On prize days and at 'Reverend Mother's Wishing' on her festal day things got even more formal: a parterre of flowers lay before the old nun's throne and you had to curtsy, walk round it, curtsy again and take your prize card, then *walk backwards round the parterre, without looking down*, and curtsy again. Only then did you turn your back. There was not inconsiderable terror in walking backwards round a parterre, at fourteen, with all your friends and enemies watching you. Especially if you had not even won a prize, but only gone up to collect a Next in Merit for Geography.

Nor had we any warning: it astonishes me now to see how

schools put out lists of prizewinners before the ceremony, and even rehearse the pupils' arrival on the platform. For us, prizes and the award of prefectorial ribbons – or the witholding of the same – came as a complete surprise on the day, as in the Oscars or a Booker prize dinner. Mother Wilson considered it an important part of our training to be able to accept triumph and disaster in public, without warning, and treat those two impostors with equal grace. She was, for all her own eccentric *joie de vivre*, very keen on graceful behaviour: the one absolutely unbreakable school rule was that anybody who screamed – *ever*, for any reason – would be sent to bed for the rest of the day. Years later, I asked her why this rule was so firm, and whether it was part of the convent Rule. She airily replied that no, it was not: it was just that personally she could not stand the sound of screaming, the bane of girls' schools, and would rather we shouted like boys any day. So we did. We were not supposed to run in corridors, either, but the penalties for this were negligible.

The liturgical year was part of life again now, played out with pageant and tableau, 'wishing' play and liturgy. In summer we spent a long morning gathering rhododendron petals to make patterns on the path for the Host to be carried in the Corpus Christi procession (although we were allowed less than conventional patterns, like the Chinese sign of life). In Lent and Advent we would have a 'practice', in which we tried by non-academic merit and behaviour to win tokens to put onto pictures in the long corridor. Once it was knights in armour, and as I was sticking a tinfoil breastplate on to my knight my less reverent friend Amanda strolled by and said 'I carried Mother Totton's files for her this morning, that has to be worth a codpiece at least'. On the school feast, the Immaculate Conception, we walked a quarter of a mile in procession up stairs and down round the school, each carrying a lighted candle perilously close to the white veil of the girl in front and singing:

Immaculata, Immaculata, ora pro nobis

to a tune which, I was surprised to find years later, was more or less the Tsarist Russian national anthem. And as the liturgical year turned, so did the plainsong we sang each night before supper to the impassive peaceful picture of Mater Admirabilis outside the refectory. The austere rising opening of *Salve Regina* meant that the Christmas term had begun; the triumph of *Regina Caeli, Laetare* greeted us after the Easter holidays. You knew which term and season it was by the tone of each evening's motet.

Music was everywhere, and everywhere tied up with God. In chapel we sang a good deal of Gregorian chant and a fine cross-section of hymns (though few of the old Anglican ones I had once loved). In singing lessons a good half of the music we did was sacred: Britten's *Missa Brevis*, the *War Requiem*, a rousing setting of the Old Hundredth which we performed at the Central Hall in Westminster. Only in the last two years of my time at T.W., when the dull populism of the vernacular mass and 'accessible' hymns was seeping in from the world of parish Catholicism, was this inheritance compromised.

Most of us hated this: if you have learnt, over years, to sing demanding music and read plainsong you do not take kindly to being expected to sing the *Tantum Ergo* at Benediction to the tune of 'Praise my soul, the King of Heaven', and then to find that the hymn which concludes the service is 'Praise my soul, the King of Heaven'. This led to an open revolt against the senior music nun, and a temporary slackening of the march of progress.

These are random memories, spanning four years, to give a general impression of this quirky, archaic, friendly, headlong, good-heartedly libertarian little school. Of course there were morbid oddities as well as endearing ones; some angry old neurotic nuns who came as near as they dared to threatening us with hell, some superstitiously ladylike ones who informed us that if a girl ever crossed her legs or whistled, 'it made the Blessed Virgin cry'; and yes, there were one or two excessively modest ones, like the Mistress of Discipline who banned radios from the bathrooms in the morning because it was not decent for deep, male voices to be heard in a room where a young girl was unclothed. Years later, a *Today* presenter myself, I told John

Timpson this; he was thrilled to think his very voice had once been considered a dark sexual threat to convent girls.

But there was very little of this nonsense; and although it spoils the story rather, I have to admit that dear Mother Totton, after a few days of the radio rule, blushed and laughed and lifted the prohibition.

Perhaps the most beguiling thing, long term, was the eternal monastic counterpoint of flowering spirit and physical parsimony. On the one hand there were emotional and spiritual riches, ornate music and florid ceremony, laughter and palpable fondness in an independent, almost feminist community of women. On the other hand there was the Rule of chaste, obedient poverty: a rule visibly lived out every day in darned habits, small neat writing on cut-up notepaper, and a horror of bragging, untidiness or waste.

Nuns did not eat with us; we never saw them eat. They rarely sat just for comfort or to talk, but stood statuesque in their long robes, not fidgeting from foot to foot nor rubbing an ache or an itch. Black habits made no concesssions to hot summer days, and in cold weather few wore shawls. Thin, tiny Mother Totton used to tell us that 'if you relax and let the cold *in*, you don't mind it'. We knew that their hidden hair was cut unbecomingly short, and noted the youngest nuns' surreptitious fascination with our rollers and lotions. We could test the hardness of the choir-stalls where they knelt early and late to sing Divine Office; and we suspected that when the Great Silence fell at night, their cells were pretty comfortless. Once, when a very old nun died, we went out to the little cemetery where she was buried, in an unadorned and unpicturesque grave, and I thought that perhaps she had a family somewhere in a pretty country churchyard with yews and mossy stones, and how sad it was for her to be buried so far from them, like the soldiers in the war graves of my Flanders childhood. Even after death, the old nun was separated from family and roots, and defined by the holy regiment she had chosen to march in.

More often, we saw the nuns' surges of adoration for visiting babies and realised what they had given up, some of them when they were only a few years older than us. Most of us had a hearty dread of developing 'a vocation' and having to live this life in our turn. We were not steered in the direction of taking the veil, not ever; but a genuine 'vocation', we were told, was as unmistakable and irresistible as measles, and gave you no peace until you capitulated to it. The thought terrified us. Rumours swept around occasionally, by way of the Catholic community of mothers and aunts, that some nun or other in our convent had been 'more or less engaged' before she broke it off to come in, and that the man was still single and heartbroken or – worse – had married another girl and had children. To teenage girls this seemed a very dreadful idea: a perfectly good lover, *wasted!*

Yet – to the best of the nuns, at least – none of the privations mattered and none quashed the spirit. They even found them funny, with a kind of serene gaiety that indicated that whatever we crass, grasping, unformed young things might think, these very adult women considered the world well lost for love of God. A few years later, I called on some of our old school nuns in a different house. Their habits were less formal by then, off the face and showing hair; suddenly I realised how young they had been all the time. One came in, bouncingly, and saw a large, beautiful chocolate box on the table. 'Ooooh!' she said, as any woman would.

The other nun giggled.

'Now, sister,' she said, with a good imitation of the lecturing manner of a visiting Reverend Mother Provincial. 'How long have you been in the religious life? Twenty-two years? Long enough to know that in a convent, a chocolate box *always* contains buttons. Or empty cotton-reels, being Saved for the Missions.' And so it did; and, God knows, it didn't matter.

10. Growing up Slowly

For the next four years, until I was seventeen, school was generally more vivid than home. The family moved to Berne, where Dad worked in a glass Embassy vulgarly known – after a particularly ugly chain of Swiss supermarkets – as *Le Migro Britannique*.

The old city was attractive, with its bears and towers and chiming automaton clocks; the rattling, hooting, romantic night train journeys across Europe were exciting. There was pride for us children in being able to travel unaccompanied except by one another, crossing the quay at Calais to find the train with the right head-code and changing at Basel in the following dawn. Trips to the Alps were magic, and added mountain dawns and snowy distances to my mental library of metaphors for eternity.

On an earthier level, evenings spent minding the British Council library provided me with rudimentary sex education to supplement the shortcomings of basic school biology. Hitherto the only solid information I had was picked up from a dreadful book my friend Rosalind sneaked into school, entitled *Attaining Womanhood*. We were actually far more interested in getting hold of her brother's copy of *Attaining Manhood*, since this was rumoured to be rather more down-to-earth about the plumbing aspect; but even that could not compete with what I found in the library. Among the faded classics and dog-eared Ethel M. Dells was a shelf of begrimed Harold Robbins paperbacks left behind by departing Chancery Guards. Here I could pore undisturbed over clues involving hardening nipples and stirring loins, although the problem with Harold Robbins is that he leaves the questioning young mind with the distinct impression that you have to make a million bucks before you can actually do it.

But otherwise there was nothing for teenagers in Berne; nothing we could be allowed, anyway. Social life was mainly within the British expatriate community and the other diplomatic missions (leavened by the usual extravagantly-titled collection of exiled Poles who gravitated towards my mother). There were evenings of Scottish dancing with children too young for us and parents too old; there were cocktail parties to which we were dragged to brush up our social skills. There were dances, occasionally, with 1950s swing bands and dinner-tables filled with our parents' colleagues. I have a wonderful picture from some newspaper report of the Herr Ambassador's party at some hotel New Year. It shows my father, distinguished and courtly as ever, sitting opposite myself aged about fifteen and bored out of my wits. I am staring stonily at a candle through what must be my sixth glass of wine and I know – I just *know*, looking at the picture – that the band is playing a strict-tempo version of 'Where the Blue of the Night meets the Gold of the Day', that there are still two hellish hours to go before 'Auld Lang Syne', and that I am living in dread that some bastard thirty years too old is going to try and force me to dance.

Rumours were starting to come through, via school, about Swinging Sixties London, and you can tell from the picture that I knew I was missing it all. One year, there were three beautiful Norwegian boys staying in one of the Embassies for two weeks, but I could not yet master enough confident allure to score a hit in such a small target area. The one social consolation of Berne was that I discovered gin-and-tonic.

School, on the other hand, had no boys at all but was socially vital, not to say lightly hysterical. Life in a community of teenage girls is rarely dull or equable. There were fearful dramas, like the affair of the Demon Matron (a story for which the world is not yet prepared) or the rumour of X's pregnancy and abortion in the summer between her Lower and Upper Sixth (a tale never confirmed but never quite denied either: I mention it only in order to say that the abortion was a much, much more shocking and sorrowful matter to the rest of us than the pregnancy and its genesis).

Boys were much talked of, but meanwhile we carried on in the time-honoured fashion of schoolgirls by rehearsing grand passions, secret longings and heartbreaking disappointments on whoever was to hand. It was all quite chaste, because we had not yet taken in the modern notion that every passion must express itself sexually. There were crushes – 'cracks' – on older girls, whose profiles one could adoringly study while singing *Salve Regina* on a cold winter evening before supper. There were passionate alliances and betrayals among classmates, best friends made and discarded, solid happy little gangs formed, and incubi and parasites to be shaken off.

This latter manoeuvre always brought guilt, naturally, because it was made clear to us by the management that being nice to the spotty whining spoilsport of the moment was part of our Christian duty, and not an optional part either. I am always irrationally amazed by the consideration and respect given to individual preference and cliques of friends at modern boarding-schools, when the time comes for house staff to sort out dormitories and cubicles and desks. At Tunbridge Wells, discussions about who would share a room with whom in the following term always seemed to include open, unembarrassed exhortations to charity and to the mortification of one's own desires. (All Catholic children grow up familiar with the idea that discomfort or irritation is to be welcomed, because you can 'offer it up for the Holy Souls in Purgatory'. All my life since, grudgingly but automatically, even in my least devout phases, I seem to have been offering up parking tickets, bad reviews, cloudbursts and verrucae. There is, as yet, no sign of gratitude from the Holy Souls.)

Anyway, groups of friends were not separated or discouraged, but we were made to consider more than our own enjoyment and peace, and confronted by the idea that it would be a greater good if, by sharing with her, we could contribute to the well-being of the most socially dysfunctional member of the class. That, I suppose, is the benchmark of life in a convent school. Without any particularly heavy hand it was just assumed all the time that we were there to become more good and kind, as well as wiser and better-qualified. I wish I could say that my own period of being compulsorily chummed with the difficult one had borne fruit. It didn't, for either of us.

There were black, black periods of teenage angst alleviated only by the support of friends, the patient counsel of Mother Wilson, and the occasional opportunity to bunk off for the weekend with one of the Day Girls and her boyfriend in order to go bowling in a very short skirt and climb into Brands Hatch racetrack without paying. And there were, of course, jokes: when I remember the best of Tunbridge Wells I remember being doubled up with laughter, scooting hysterical with mirth along broad polished corridors, stifling giggles in chapel and in class, and – a favourite pursuit for a time – practising writing cod obituaries for one another's lives in twenty years time. I found one the other day in an old suitcase. It began:

> When her contributions to the musical theatre, astrophysics and clockmaking are considered, it seems tragic that this much-married, unmatchable athlete and famous beauty should primarily be remembered as merely the foremost military historian of our time.

This, I should say, reflected a string of small hilarious defeats in a school play audition, maths O level, cross-country running and history (a subject which, curiously, I loathed).

But at the top of the whole rickety pyramid of life was still God. Actual religious instruction is a bit of a blur; I suspect that as usual with Catholic schools, it became so intricately involved with doctrine and the minutiae of sacramental lore that it lost all impetus. I certainly think I learned more about religion from watching the better nuns and lay-sisters and talking to Mother Wilson than I ever did in RI classes.

On the other hand, to an adolescent permanently drunk on language and rhetoric, the sinewy beauty of liturgy and cere-monial meant ever more. This was given a particular edge of poignancy because the Vatican II reforms were well under way, and much of the old Latinate beauty was rapidly being lost to the banalities of the vernacular Mass and pedestrian parish hymns. The best school job I ever had was assistant sacristan in the big new chapel. There, in a quiet cool-scented side room, with the gentlest of the nuns, I would lay out vestments according to the season, smooth albs, replace candles, refill the censers with grains of incense. Girls, remember, were not yet at this time allowed to serve Mass on the altar, and it was a point of constant irritation to many of us that we – sixteen- or seventeen-year-olds, full of red-hot theological acuity and plainsong skills – were banned from the altar during Mass, and the priest had to bring along some snub-nosed uncomely boy of twelve to ring the bell and pass him things. Still, the new feminism was barely invented in 1967; and even when it was, I do not remember it putting much effort into equal rights for girl altar-servers. And in the sacristy, at least, I could feel for brief half-hours what it might be to be a nun myself.

I liked the adventure of Catechetics, too. After a basic training a group of us volunteers were sent out to local parishes to run a Sunday school after Mass for local children. I hasten to say that although it was called Catechetics, the old red Catechism seemed to have been long since swept away. My beat was Rusthall, a suburban village, where with reasonable success I hauled six or seven resistant brats through some basic stuff about the Lamb of God and Jesus in the Temple, quelled a certain amount of rioting and wriggling, and disabused myself for ever of any idea that I might have a talent for primary school teaching. Once I took them carol-singing, and still bear the mental scars.

Each year we had a silent retreat, starting with a mere weekend and working up to four days. These I enjoyed, thinking dreamy transcendental thoughts to myself and keeping half-sacred, half-secular notebooks; but without warning in the Lower Sixth I started to hate one particular retreat so much that I abruptly broke silence and demanded to go home early. A certain murkiness surrounds the memory of why exactly I had to get out, but the feeling which comes back is of suffocation.

It was too much, too intense, too embarrassing, it cloyed and made me gag. *Deep in thy wounds, Lord, hide and shelter me.* I did not want shelter, I wanted air. Mother Wilson's regular query 'How's God?' became, from that moment on, excruciatingly unanswerable. Although I did not at the time formally renounce belief, something happened during that retreat which made me feel as if any more orthodox Catholicism would asphyxiate me.

The same went for the lay orders which we were invited to join, Angels in the fifth form and Children of Mary in the sixth. I was an 'Angel asp' (aspirant) and briefly an Angel medal-holder; then, being a natural joiner and good-behaver, I aspired and joined the Children of Mary and sat in its solemn holy inner-circle for a few months wearing its socking great silvery medal. I even went out once or twice, I sweat to recall, to do 'good work' in the community, visiting 'poor families' – not to clean their windows but to talk to them about God. I hated it; it gave me the creeps, it was too much, too deeply Catholic, too patronising, too pi.

Perhaps it was genetic, and my Presbyterian forefathers were rising in revolt within me to cast out soupy Papism. I left the Children of Mary and handed in my medal. You were not meant to leave, but Mother Wilson (who I suspect felt rather equivocal herself at times, even a bit Scottish, about such Frenchified manifestations of piety) made no fuss.

The trouble was that whatever real religious sense I had was fast diverging from the sweet dated frilliness of all this. Certainly I preferred my hymns rousing, like my father's stirring in-car renderings of 'Jerusalem', than mystically sentimental. I never quite forgave Mother Brooke for promising that we could have 'Eternal Father Strong to Save' at Benediction one day and then switching it for 'Just as I am' or some similar parish pap. But, as I dimly saw, it was more a matter of idiom than of belief. I had met enough different religious idioms to know the difference. I knew that despite the unfortunate costumes some believers dressed Him in, I believed in God. I also – since a curious moment in my O-level term – had a strong, almost revelatory conviction of being redeemed.

We had been reading, in English class, Milton's 'Hymn on the Morning of Christ's Nativity'. This is a resounding, triumphant piece, with an undercurrent of all the morbidly diabolic imagery which the author deployed more famously in *Paradise Lost*. In the early stanzas the Child lies in a manger, while Nature throws a veil of white over her sinfulness and Peace comes down.

> No war or battle's sound
> Was heard the world around,
>   The idle spear and shield were high up-hung:
> The hooked chariot stood
> Unstained with hostile blood,
>   The trumpet spake not to the armed throng,
> And kings sat still with awful eye,
> As if they surely knew their sovran Lord was by.

In this peaceful night, the stars look on amazed; and the shepherds on the lawn sit innocent, little knowing 'That the mighty Pan was kindly come to live with them below'. As a keen reader of *The Wind in the Willows*, I was particularly glad to have Pan and his pipes subsumed benevolently into the Godhead. Then the stars began to sing:

> Such music (as 'tis said)
> Before was never made,
>   But when of old the sons of morning sung,

Growing up Slowly

While the Creator great
His constellations set,
    And the well-balanced world on hinges hung,
And cast the dark foundations deep,
And bid the welt'ring waves their oozy channel keep.

Singing stars, piercing sweetness, an all-embracing vision of Creation. As passionately as any primitive, I wanted my world well-hung on hinges, ordered and designed and harmonious. The music has such power, says the poet, that if it goes on,

    Time will run back and fetch the age of gold,
And speckled vanity
Will sicken soon, and die,
    And leprous Sin will melt from earthly mould,
And Hell itself will pass away
And leave her dolorous mansions to the peering day.

But the music cannot go that far, not yet; not until the trump of doom, far in the future. At that time, the poet sees a vision of Truth and Justice returning to men, orbed in a rainbow, and Mercy in celestial sheen, clouds streaming from his feet.

    Th' old Dragon under-ground
In straiter limits bound,
    Not half so far casts his usurped sway,
And, wroth to see his kingdom fail,
Swinges the scaly horror of his folded tail.

Adolescents, even those who curtsy to pictures of Our Lady on a regular basis and fold albs and surplices and Offer It Up when they are dropped from the judo team, are volcanically aware of the power of evil. Childhood nightmares of dolorous mansions and scaly horrors have not quite lost their vividness; they blend into an awareness of what is in the daily papers. We had seen John F. Kennedy shot, on television; we had watched the epic

Holy Smoke

BBC history, *The World at War*, through my mother's Polish and Jewish friends I knew people whose homes and lives had been devastated by concentration camps. We were sometimes addressed by missionaries and nuns who had been tortured in frightening, distant edges of the world; closer to home, the newspapers were full of murder. The scaly horror of that folded tail swished across the world, ancient and modern. But in Milton's vision, the clear innocent light of Christmas shone all that into insignificance:

> The oracles are dumb
> No voice or hideous hum
> Runs through the arched roof in words deceiving.
> Apollo from his shrine
> Can no more divine,
> With hollow shriek the steep of Delphos leaving.
> No nightly trance or breathed spell
> Inspires the pale-eyed priest from the prophetic cell.
> And sullen Moloch fled,
> Hath left in shadows dread
> His burning idol all of blackest hue;
> In vain with cymbals' ring
> They call the grisly king,
> In dismal dance about the furnace blue;
> The brutish gods of Nile as fast,
> Isis and Orus, and the dog Anubis, haste.
>
> But see, the Virgin blest
> Hath laid her Babe to rest:
> Time is our tedious song should here have ending,
> Heaven's youngest teemed star,
> Hath fixed her polished car,
> Her sleeping Lord with handmaid lamp attending:
> And all about the courtly stable,
> Bright-harnessed angels sit in order serviceable.

I loved this vision. Looking back now, I can see a powerful reason why it hooked so easily into my imagination. C. S. Lewis, English don that he was, had borrowed heavily and extravagantly from Milton's imagery when he invented the story, from creation to destruction, of Narnia. The clear singing stars, the dragon under-ground, the dolorous caves of Hell laid open to the sweet clean breath of heaven, were familiar from my earliest entranced reading. So were the cruel priesthoods of the composite ancient god Lewis called Tash: and these chimed powerfully with other books I had devoured in foreign solitudes, on long dull train journeys and alone in my French attic. The grisly rites of Rider Haggard's *She* and *King Solomon's Mines*, exotic moments in E. Nesbit, and half-buried childhood memories of my own gave me a strong idea of cruel, murderous priestly castes, blood-dabbled idols, stone knives raised to strike at dawn, unspeakable sacrifices. To have these nightmares swept away by a milky baby, a Virgin, and a cohort of serviceable angels filled as deep a need in me as it would in any medieval peasant.

Then, flicking through the book, I came across other lines on the birth of Christ:

> Given, not lent
> And not withdrawn, once sent.

All at once – and, writing of it, I can see the classroom, know which desk I sat in, can hear the scratching of pens in prep time – I thought: 'Suppose it *was* withdrawn? Suppose it never happened? That there is no redemption, no wiping out of sin, no ultimate haven for the innocent. Suppose we are alone?' There was real panic in the thought, panic that blurs vision and makes the heart hammer.

I suppose that atheists live happily with the idea that humanity can manage on its own, because they do not believe in immortality. The alternative vision which spread before me on that dark winter afternoon was not of men being born, living and dying and ending like beasts, after lives more or less enjoyable according to luck. That would have been depressing enough. But

I believed entirely in life after death, and what frightened me was the thought of consciousness continuing eternally, in unredeemed corrupt pointlessness; the universe, with no ultimate clarifying and ultimate merciful justice, was unthinkable.

But at the desk, turning over the pages of the poetry book, I realised that I did not think it. Not for a moment.

11. Reading

More congenial than religious instruction was Philosophy. On the old Jesuit model, we progressed from some rather half-hearted Psychology to the full gale force of Mother Wilson's philosophy seminars. These followed no particular method that I can discern, but tossed us random snippets of ideas and let us chew them over. Two in particular impressed me enough to slot into my private mental grid of understanding.

The first – which again carried me effortlessly back to *The Last Battle* – was the Platonic theory of archetypes. Everything we see here, every glory, every beauty, every love, is only a faulty reflection of something beyond. Somewhere there exist bright, real, unimaginably beautiful and imperishable truths. I seized on this gratefully. It defined heaven – if you took it that way – in a far more desirable way than any vision of harps and clouds.

It also accounted for the odd sense of frustration which always accompanied a beautiful view: seascape or mountain, city or coral. All my life I had felt this frustration, a conviction of something nearly glimpsed, its robe whisking away round the corner when you turn your head. The best way to dispel that feeling is to get achingly, physically involved in the landscape; if I see a beautiful bay I immediately want to tear off my clothes and swim in it or sail a small boat on it, if I see a mountain I must at least exhaust myself (not a long job) in its foothills, or slither ineptly on its snows on cross-country skis.

Plato's way, however, provides more long-term comfort. I took most joyfully to the idea that there was – and is, and ever will be – something else behind and beyond the coast of West Cork, the dome of San Sofia and the Alps in the dawn. Somewhere there is an ultimate Venice, an archetypal (and probably car-free) London, an unblemished Caribbean. Or, at least, an essence of these things.

The other memory of philosophy classes also has to do with beauty. One afternoon Mother Wilson introduced us to the notion that art or landscape must have three ingredients to be perfectly beautiful (or as perfectly as Plato will let us get). These are *proportio* – a harmonious shape or composition – *integritas*, a quality of being true to itself and its function, and not pretending to something it does not have, and finally *splendor*, an indefinable radiance which links it to its eternal archetype.

We played happily with this idea for the whole session. It explained a great deal. It explained why some technically good pictures or sculptures, especially reproductions, were so lifeless; no *splendor*. It showed why the Taj Mahal was beautiful and a Taj Mahal tea-tray wasn't. It raised craft to a high level, yet not the very highest, and it illuminated a sneaking feeling I had that some of the most modern art we saw, like Warhol and Jackson Pollock and Yoko Ono cutting her clothes off on stage, was cheating. It was trying to go straight for the show-stopping *splendor* by way of a casual eye on the *proportio*, while it utterly bypassed any idea of *integritas*. We were each asked to describe an example of unexpected beauty which had all three ingredients, and I came up with a photo I had taken of the Hamburg dockyard cranes at sunset (we had just moved to Hamburg at the time). They had *proportio*, entirely by accident, the intersecting skeletons of the tower cranes hitting some kind of golden section within my inexpert frame. They had *integritas* because they were real, working cranes, there for a reason. And the *splendor* of them was accidental and God-given: the fine layered sunset behind them. Yet, we all finally agreed, my photograph did not have full beauty: it was just a record of a moment which had it. Whereas another photograph, a black-and-white study of the sea, was itself the full possessor of beauty.

Someone else, with a taste for dance, came up with a question about an execution. Suppose there were a beheading: beautifully done, in an exotic setting, with the most visually harmonious swing of the axe – but it was an unjust and cruel deed. Could it be beautiful? Why not? We decided, collegiately, that it simply lacked *integritas*, because an unjust action could have no integrity. On the other hand the plaster statue of the Virgin in our old chapel had been designed with true belief, full *integritas*, and was made in time-honoured proportions and pose copied off a fine Italian statue. Only being plaster, and somewhat faded and chipped, it lacked *splendor* and always would, so we need not accord it the full status of complete beauty.

These are immature, simplistic thoughts I am recording, but this is a chronicle of immature thoughts. I would not like to admit publicly that I still go round exhibitions like the Royal Academy's *Sensation*, inwardly looking for excuses to hate the stuff by muttering 'where's the bloody *integritas* in half a cow?'

We had a bracing brush with existentialism, too, that being all the rage; Sartre's *Huis Clos* was introduced by Mother Wilson rather than the French teacher and its notion that Hell is Other People was skilfully challenged by the wholly Christian notion that Hell is human self-absorption to the exclusion of God, and therefore a basically voluntary doom. The problem with repentance between the stirrup and the ground, we learnt, was that a truly wicked and God-denying life might actually remove your power of repentance, as it did Pinkie's in *Brighton Rock*. Like the Dwarfs in *The Last Battle*, you might coarsen yourself so far that you were simply not able to see the gates of Heaven opening, but blundered on for ever down the dark narrow path you had always chosen in life.

But Sartre never got my interest in the way that his compatriot, Jean Anouilh, did. A recommendation to read his *Becket* in French before A level led to a brief, violent love affair which took me down to the Tunbridge Wells Public Library week after week to pull out every play he wrote, from *Antigone* to *Pauvre Bitos*, and devour them with confused relish. Especially Antigone and his Joan of Arc play, *L'Alouette*.

Anouilh is ideal for cross, depressive, thwarted teenage girls. Especially, perhaps, in convents where the notion of heroic renunciation is a daily example. His heroines rebel against dull sense and compromise, and live out their principles in a satisfyingly headlong fashion. Not for them the tacky cliché of sexual rebellion, which only leads to worse enslavement. No, they choose *death*. Anouilh's Antigone was my first heroine: a tomboyish, life-loving child newly in love who goes out at dawn to bury her brother Polynices against the king's decree. Then – when King Creon offers to save her and points out that Polynices was a villain and a fraud, and that her cause is nonsense anyway because national peace is only ever achieved by compromise – she still rebels, this time against the idea of calm pragmatic happiness itself:

Happiness . . . ! And what will my happiness be like? What kind of a happy woman will Antigone grow into? What base things will she have to do, day after day, in order to snatch her own little scrap of happiness? Tell me – who will she have to lie to? Smile at? Sell herself to? Who will she have to avert her eyes from, and leave to die? . . . You disgust me, all of you, and your happiness! And your life that has to be loved at any price. You're like dogs fawning on everyone they come across. With just a little hope left every day – if you don't expect too much.

But I want everything, now! And to the full! Or else I decline the offer. I don't want to be sensible, and satisfied with a scrap if I behave myself! I want to be sure of having everything, now, this very day, and it has to be as wonderful as it was when I was little. Otherwise I prefer to die.

Then there was Joan of Arc, to Anouilh another little girl who would not compromise, and rejected all attempts to save her:

Do you see Joan when things have 'adjusted themselves'? Joan set free, perhaps, vegetating at the French Court on her little pension? . . . Joan accepting everything, fat and complacent, Joan doing nothing but eat. Can you see me painted and powdered, trying to look fashionable, getting entangled in her skirts, fussing over her little dog, or trailing a man at her heels?

Joan says no: she has seen something beyond all this, for her life truly began when she rode horseback with a sword in her hand, in breeches, at the head of the King's army with St Michael and glory on her side. I loved Antigone's nihilism, Joan's heroism, and the refusal of either to settle for happiness while – in the words of yet another French heroine – there was one hungry dog left in the street. It was, I suppose, an equivalent frame of mind to that of the anorexic or the reckless teenage motorcyclist; except that I did not actually do anything, only privately dreamed it. All the early tales of martyrdom came back, and caused me to write long impassioned essays on Anouilh which no teacher had actually asked for. It also connected, in a way which at black times threatened to become perilous, with that other despairing proud nihilist female icon of our time, Sylvia Plath. 'Dying is an art. I do it exceptionally well.'

But Tunbridge Wells public library led me along another glowing path. We were allowed to go and forage there on Saturday afternoons, to back up any deficiencies in the school library (which was a bit like an old-fashioned country house library, in which you would never lack for a *Little Dorritt* or *Jungle Book*, but might spend a long time looking for Ramakrishna or Kerouac.) Here I discovered J. D. Salinger. What hooked me was not *Catcher in the Rye*, which we were made to read for English and which I thoroughly detested, considering Holden Caulfield a right little pain in the neck. It was the scattered chronicle, through short stories and *Franny and Zooey* and *Raise High the Roof Beam, Carpenters*, of the Glass family of New York.

Holy Smoke

These stories provided a new lot of ideas, and just as importantly provided an answer to the temptations of priggish nihilism. It says a lot for Salinger that despite my having hated the *Catcher*, and despite my innate prejudice against mouthy Americans with stupid names who smoke their heads off in every scene (see what a grumpy reader I always was) these short brilliant stories got through all my defences. I re-read them constantly for several years for guidance as well as pleasure.

For those not immersed in this particularly 1960s set of stories, a brief guide. Seymour, Buddy, Boo Boo, Franny and Zooey Glass are Jewish-Irish-American New Yorkers, who also have two other non-appearing brothers, Walt (killed in Korea) and Waker (a Catholic priest). All have been prodigies of originality and spiritual vision, prone to seeing God in cups of milk and ashtrays, and were stars of a children's radio Brains Trust through their minority. Seymour is both genius and saint, but marries a shallow unsuitable woman and kills himself in the short story entitled 'A perfect day for Bananafish'. Buddy, a writer, tells most of the stories, and Boo Boo is their relatively normal, extrovert sister. These older ones have been through the experience of wartime service life.

The younger pair are Zooey, a young actor, and Franny his sister, a college girl who at the beginning of her eponymous story is having a kind of breakdown because she finds the strident literary snobbery of her course phoney, despises her lecturers, and finds the contemporary 'clever' poetry to be nothing but 'sort of syntax *droppings*'. Dorm life depresses her, and although she is a gifted actress in summer stock, she has come to despise the shallowness of audience reaction and the pretension of her colleagues. To her uncomprehending boyfriend she says: 'Everything everybody does is so – I don't know, not *wrong*, or even mean, or even stupid necessarily. But just so tiny and meaningless and – sad-making. And the worst part is, if you go bohemian or something crazy like that, you're conforming just as much as everybody else, only in a different way.'

The authentic voice of the student 1960s speaks there: amazing that it was published in 1961. Franny's restlessness is spiritual: she carries around a book which belonged to the dead Seymour, about a pilgrim in Russia who goes from place to place teaching people to say the Jesus Prayer – 'Lord Jesus Christ, have mercy on me' in the repetitive mystical way of the 'Philokalia', over and over again so that the prayer becomes self-active, and gets into your very heartbeat, and you are obeying the biblical dictat to 'pray without cease'. Franny – raised like all her siblings on Seymour and Buddy's enthusiasm for 'Jesus and Buddha and Gautama and all those guys', connects this to the repetitive chanting of Buddhism and the Om of Hinduism, and *The Cloud of Unknowing*, which recommends meditation on the name of God. Franny wants God, very much. She hungers and thirsts for enlightenment. But like any anorexic or Anouilh heroine, she also rejects ordinary life, and lies on the sofa weeping and muttering her prayer in full teenage breakdown mode. The connection with her saintly beloved brother Seymour's suicide is obvious.

Zooey, however, is a few years older and further down the path. As their worried mother tiptoes round the apartment pressing chicken soup on the invalid, he moodily shaves, and contemplates the problem. He sees the origin of her trouble, because he too was drilled in world spirituality by Seymour and Buddy. He is quite funny about it:

'I can't even sit down to a goddam *meal*, to this day, without first saying the Four Great Vows under my breath, and I'll lay any odds you want Franny can't either. They drilled us with such goddam—'

'The four great *what*?' Mrs Glass interrupted, but cautiously.

Zooey put a hand on each side of the washbowl and leaned his chest forward a trifle, his eyes on the general background of enamel. For all his slightness of body, he looked at that moment ready and able to push the washbowl straight through the floor. 'The four great *Vows*' he said and, with rancor, closed his eyes. 'However innumerable beings are, I vow to save them; however inexhaustible the passions are, I vow to extinguish them; however immeasurable the Dharmas are, I vow to master them; however incomparable the Buddha-truth is, I vow to attain it. Yay, team. I know I can do it. Just put me in, coach.'

Their mother thinks Franny should see an analyst: Zooey caustically says that this is the surest way to have her either 'in a nut ward or wandering off into some goddam desert with a burning cross in her hands'. But Zooey berates Franny for her self-indulgence and a sentimentality in her spiritual quest.

> You say your prayer and roll Jesus and St Francis and Seymour and Heidi's grandfather all in one . . . can't you see how sloppily you're looking at things? . . . You take a look round your college campus, and the world, and politics, and one season of summer stock, and you listen to the conversation of a bunch of nitwit college students, and you decide that everything's ego, ego, ego and the only intelligent thing for a girl to do is lie around and shave her head and say the Jesus prayer.

This line does nothing but upset Franny further. The skill of the piece is so great that although nothing happens but their conversation, the drama is held tautly, even frighteningly, for the rest of the book.

Their dilemma – everyone's dilemma – is that the peasant simplicities of the pilgrim book, the simplicities of life which lie at the cultural roots of all Eastern mysticism, are unattainable by moderns who have to live in apartment blocks and fit into the noisy complex societies of the West. It is the very dilemma which, a few years later, drove the hippies to reject mainstream society, and which to this day fuels the flight to the countryside of sandalled, bearded idealists in grimy muslin. It was already, to a 1960s teenager, a visible problem. Remember that we were a horribly favoured generation: nobody had heard of youth unemployment in Britain, university was still just an interesting option rather than a make-or-break life chance, and we did not suffer the agonising fears about unemployment which plague GCSE and A-level students today. So a great deal of our minds was free for hippyish spiritual doubts. Franny's problem, for a spell, was also mine.

Zooey redeems himself. After a fine diatribe against all those who would sentimentalise Christ and use his name to turn away from less enlightened fellow men in shuddering distaste, he tiptoes away from his weeping sister and refreshes himself by sitting in Seymour and Buddy's old room and reading their graffiti.

'I move not without Thy Knowledge!' – Epictetus

'Disciple: Sir, we ought to teach the people that they are doing wrong in worshipping the images and pictures in the temple' –

Ramakrishna: 'That's the way with you Calcutta people: you want to teach and preach. You want to give millions when you are beggars yourselves . . . Do you think God does not know that he is being worshipped in the images and pictures? If a worshipper should make a mistake, do you not think God will know his intent?' – The Gospel of Sri Ramakrishna.

Then he rings up his sister, pretending to be Buddy. Mrs Glass (delightfully described as having been 'cruising in a patrol boat up and down her children's alimentary canals for years') tries the soup on Franny again, and fails. But Zooey, more gently now, apologises for ranting like a minor prophet and makes the book's central statement:

If it's the religious life you want, you ought to know right now that you're missing out on every single goddam religious action that's going on around this house. You don't even have sense enough to drink when somebody brings you a cup of consecrated chicken soup – which is the only kind of chicken soup Bessie ever brings to anybody around this madhouse.

He tells her to stop fussing about the phoneyness and shallowness of the acting world she is rejecting along with her college course and to:

> Do the only thing you can do, the only religious thing. Act. Act for God, if you want to – be God's actress if you want to . . . at least try. There's nothing wrong in trying. You'd better get busy, though, buddy. The goddam sands run out on you everytime you turn round.

He goes further. He reminds her of Seymour making them go on the quiz show as children, even on unwilling evenings, with a trouper's respect for their audience. 'Shine your shoes for the fat lady' he said. Zooey ends:

> I don't care where an actor acts. It can be in summer stock, it can be over a radio, it can be over television, it can be in a goddam Broadway theatre, complete with the most fashionable, most well-fed, most sunburned-looking audience you can imagine. But I'll tell you a terrible secret – Are you listening to me? *There isn't anyone out there who isn't Seymour's Fat Lady*. That includes your Professor Tupper, buddy. There isn't anyone anywhere who isn't Seymour's fat lady. Don't you know that goddam secret yet? And don't you know – *listen* to me now – *don't you know who that fat lady really is?* Ah, buddy. Ah, buddy. It's Christ himself. Christ himself, buddy.

Franny is cured: and all the hip, New York orientalism leads simply and beguilingly back to the Quaker George Fox's vision of how to lead your life, in lines which had been read to us by a visiting Quaker speaker: 'Be patterns, be examples in all countries, places, islands, nations, wherever you come; that your carriage and life may preach among all sorts of people, and to them. Then you will come to walk cheerfully over the world, answering that of God in every one.'

Even the rich sunburned phoneys are Christ, says Zooey. You don't have to join them, but you do have to love them.

I took it in. This had not come from any nun or curriculum; it was less embarrassing and alienating than the version of the same message which came from whispering priests in the confessional. Indeed it happily countermanded some of the more extreme injunctions which came from certain over-anxious priests, injunctions to Flee Bad Company. Avid for experience and new horizons at seventeen, we were anxious not to reject *any* company; the God-in-every-one principle allowed us not only to hang out with them, but love them in an incorruptible Christian way.

This vision was not really devalued by the increasingly weird remainder of the J. D. Salinger canon. I never liked the labyrinthine *Seymour – an Introduction*, which attempts better to explain the enigmatic, suicidal elder brother. I was faintly repelled by the holy, reincarnated Zen master who turns up as the small boy Teddy in the eponymous short story. But in *Franny and Zooey* a curiously perfect synthesis is achieved between holy madness and the need to live a busy, compromised human life.

The ideas in Salinger laid themselves down alongside all the other confused religious baggage I had taken on board. They led me to further grazing in the public library's shelf of oriental mysticism, and for a while, stressed by the prospect of A levels, I found a certain comfort in wandering around murmuring to myself 'Om mani padme hum, the sunrise comes! The dewdrop slips into the shining sea!' Compared to transcendence, what did A levels matter? Or diets, come to that. Or spots.

There were, of course, things in the oriental canon designed to divide the seeker sharply from everything that religion had hitherto meant. If God was in everything and everyone, did it not follow that God *was* everything and everyone, and not a separate blinding Holiness? And more practically, why all the fuss and conflict between Catholic and Protestant down the centuries over transubstantiation of the bread and wine into the true Body and Blood of Christ?

Hours of tedious RI and equally tedious Reformation history had been devoted to this argument, and a degree of rebellion was well overdue. Privately and gleefully I decided that Ramakrishna and Buddha and Seymour Glass and the new frontiers of particle physics made the whole debate pointless. All things were one, and were God. So never mind the sacred moment of the Mass when the host became the true Body: Christ was there already, and had been all along. He was in the bread, the wine, the pew, the vicar, the altar-boy, the sunlight through the window and the distant milk-float hissing along Pembury Road. In the face of such a certainty, what the hell did doctrines of transubstantiation matter? Or whether the priest wore purple or gold, or whether you kissed a Bishop's ring? Why fight amongst brothers, when each of us has God within him? Chair-legs, curtains, friends' faces, bars of music, chapel windows, all used to flare up frequently in those days into unspeakable transcendent versions of themselves. Sometimes cracks appeared between the very paving-stones, from which flowered whole worlds of hope and glory and limitless possibility.

It is curious, looking back, to reflect that I reached all this via Tunbridge Wells public library, while wearing a pleated skirt and striped blouse, a full year before I had really heard anything about San Francisco and the Summer of Love or met a paid-up hippie. It shows how intellectual and religious movements spread their delicate transparent tentacles far and wide a lot earlier than one thinks.

Meanwhile day by day we all knelt, black-veiled, in morning chapel or at dusk in Benediction. Sermons and retreats and Mother Wilson's chummy 'How's God?' meant less and less, yet there were moments of such certainty that it did not matter precisely what I was so certain about: Jesus, Gautama, Buddha, the Shining Sea, or what.

One holiday I had to stay at school over Easter Sunday for some logistical, diplo-travelling reason. It was quite pleasant being alone at school, spoiled by nuns and free to read; it was awe-inspiring to take part in the full Tenebrae service of Good Friday and hold a candle in the nuns' Easter vigil. On the Sunday before Mass, I went out for a walk along the grassy avenue called the Way of Peace. There was a tennis ball in my pocket, and I threw it up in the air, temporarily a child again. I threw it up through shafts of sunlight that slanted through apocalyptic clouds, watched its dampness glitter and threw my soul up after it, higher and higher in great candles of movement. I caught it each time without faltering, and with an utter, confident certainty that I cannot remember ever feeling since.

12. *Forgiving Monsignor Gilbey*

At this point, there will have to be a lowering of the tone and a break in the chronology of these ramblings. If I am to be remotely honest about the hitches which can befall a Catholic upbringing, a chapter must be written which leaps to and fro across the decades in embarrassed agitation, admitting to a shameful and unchristian set of prejudices which coloured my feelings about my Church for much of my growing-up. They are not nice thoughts. Zooey Glass would be very stern about them. Nor are they in the Quaker tradition of finding the God in every one. But at least I know it.

For the moment it is 1967: soon I shall be at Oxford in tempestuous 1968, with student revolution sweeping Europe and all eyes on the USA, where stoned lay saints in drooping cheese-cloth sing 'Masters of War' to acoustic guitars and stuff flowers down gun-barrels. By this stage of my teens I have been long enough back in the UK to realise something which, in diplobrat innocence, I had never before understood: that there is a class system and that it is not fair. I read George Orwell voraciously and repeatedly with very close attention indeed. Bob Dylan sings ceaselessly from my Dansette record player:

> Mothers and fathers of every land,
> Don'criticise what you don't understand,
> Your children are no longer beneath your command,
> For the times they are a-changing . . .

Meanwhile, as one of Mother Wilson's brave little eccentricities, the sixth form have been bidden to a lecture on Marxism given by a man in bright purple gym shoes with a shock of prematurely grey hair, called Mr Gravelle. He sold interested parties a copy of the Communist Manifesto: I still have mine, a pretty little pocket paperback with a cream cover, very like a prayerbook only with Karl Marx's profile instead of IHS or a cross. Again I was made drunk by rhetoric, and blissfully declaimed: '*The proletarians have nothing to lose but their chains. They have a world to win. Workers of the world, unite!*'

With the South African experience still smarting, it made great sense to me. Obviously I had read *Animal Farm*; I knew something of the enslavement of Russia (and more especially of Poland because of my mother's friends). But it was clear that like Christianity, Communism had never been properly tried. Anything could be perverted, couldn't it? And Marx spoke to something deep: '*A spectre is haunting Europe – the spectre of Communism. All the powers of old Europe have entered into a holy alliance to exorcise this spectre: Pope and Tsar, Metternich and Guizot, French Radicals and German police-spies . . .*'

Communist party membership was strictly forbidden, we knew, to Catholics, but Mother Wilson tranquilly trusted us; or else she craftily and quite correctly calculated that an early homoeopathic dose of communism would protect us from proselytising revolutionaries later on. Her own class attitudes were beautifully summed up by the way she was always saying 'I don't care what you do as long as you stay with God and are true to yourselves – you can go and be *shopgirls* in *Woolworths* if you like.' The horror in her voice at the last bit gave her away. Personally, I secretly thought that it would be very romantic to go and be a shop assistant in Woolworths; remember, I had spent a whole year in South Africa sullenly re-reading *John Halifax, Gentleman*, with the passionate and total absorption that only an unhappy child can muster, so I thought it the finest thing in the world to work your own way up, without patronage or unfair advantage, from the most menial level. My professional daydreams were not about swanning in to a professional job from nowhere, but of having my talent spotted while serving as a patient conscientious shelf-stacker, and working my way up.

The following week Mr Gravelle came back to give a talk on anarchism, which he confided fell nearer to his own ideals. I had read enough Sartre and Anouilh to be cosily and homoeo-pathically at home with that, too. Later on I naturally joined the Anarchist Club at Oxford and only gave up because the meetings never, on principle, occurred in the announced time or place.

The solid thing which came out of all this exhilarating teenage fantasy politics was a conviction that indeed, the times *were* a-changing, that hierarchy could no longer be taken for granted, least of all by those at the top of it; and that social justice was a higher ideal than social stability. Cheeky young men and women from Liverpool and the East End were making fortunes, and hairdressers with glottal stops were joshing with the Prime Minister. Sir Alec Douglas-Home had been replaced by Harold Wilson. Even the Vatican seemed to be affected: our nuns suddenly were no longer divided into Mother-in-a-wimple-with-a-book and Sister-in-an-apron-with-a-broom. The rule and the habit had changed, and all were democratically called Sister. I cannot express how difficult it was to force the words 'Sister Wilson' past my teeth.

So at this point I have to confront the painful, uncharitable, almost schismatic fact of the way I felt – and went on feeling, for some years – about the particular clique of Posh English Catholics. *Cart*holicks, they would call themselves, just as they would rhyme Mass with Farce.

Since early days learning the Catechism in Walberswick I had been vaguely aware that there were Catholics like this: tremend-ously grand ones, who came from 'old' Catholic families, stridently claimed kinship with beatified English martyrs, had priests to stay the weekend and kept private chapels where dear Brother Aelfric could say Mass when he came to stay. People who liked to make it very, very clear at every possible opportunity that they were absolutely *not*, in any way, Irish. They longed for an English Pope, and only grudgingly forgave each successive incumbent for being foreign; they considered themselves 'led' in a mysterious way by the Duke of Norfolk – although even at seven I could not quite see why being a Duke in a secular and Protestant hierarchy should make you more of a 'leading' Catholic than any ordained priest from the backstreets of Liverpool. *Bless me, Duke, for I have sinned?* What?

The same irritation arose frequently years later, when I was a presenter on the *Today* programme: I always used to grumble when Norman St John Stevas MP was brought on to comment on some matter concerning Catholics and described as 'a leading RC'. 'Why should he be a leading RC just because he's a toff and a Cabinet Minister?' I would complain loudly in the grumpy dawn office. 'I'm a Catholic and he doesn't lead *me*, thank you.' I would argue that religious systems were entirely different to lay ones – might even be upside-down to them, just as kings used to kneel at the feet of simple Friars to ask a blessing before battle.

Nobody ever listened, any more than they did later on when I complained at news programmes interviewing Ann Widdecombe MP – a Catholic of less than a year's standing – as if she were an authority on whether the erring Bishop of Argyll should be excommunicated. Catholic authority *had* to be detached from secular, didn't it? Otherwise you might as well throw in the towel completely and be an Anglican with Lord Bishops in the House of Lords.

Anyway, these posh Cartholicks were always a bit of a trial to my mother, who was fond of her Irish and plebeian roots but a shade defensive when stared down by the County. In my early childhood they were the ones who affected shock that I was singing 'Hills of the North' down at the village school rather than 'Faith of our Fathers' at some (fee-paying) convent. I myself made a faux-pas at the age of ten by asking the son of one such family, all innocently, apropos a private Mass said in his home by a visiting Jesuit friend of his Mummy's, how any Mass could possibly be 'private'? This was not the result of some precocious theological insight but simply bafflement, because I had only known Mass in churches where anybody could go, and where you were explicitly told to 'offer it up' if a particularly smelly tramp or tone-deaf elderly soprano landed next to you in the pew.

'You,' said the boy (only twelve himself) 'wouldn't understand. You're from a Mixed Marriage, which isn't proper Catholic. Your Dad isn't even a *convert*, is he?'

Foreign postings intervened, and the next time I encountered the tribe of Posh English Catholics was at Tunbridge Wells. Actually, the sister school at Woldingham was their main hangout, but Mother Wilson had been one in her lay youth and socially grand figures still came to call on her. Then, of course, there was Evelyn Waugh with *Brideshead Revisited*, that compellingly hideous blending of spirituality and snobbery which binds up together, all in one reeking bundle, the glamour of tiara-wearing sin with the glamour of Catholic repentance.

This damn book operated like catnip on certain posh Catholics among my schoolmates, but repelled me so much that it almost made me refuse to apply to Oxford. Among my fictional co-religionists I far preferred Graham Greene's whisky-priests to Waugh's precious grandees. I suppose I still do.

So naturally, the notion of ever worshipping in a 'fashionable' church, or having a modish confessor, or using religion to seek out my 'sort' of people, filled me always with a quite disproportionate horror and disgust. This hardened into downright rage when, in early womanhood, I would meet young upper-class Catholic wives who gigglingly confided that they had managed to sidestep the Papal ban on contraception by way of 'this marvellous Jesuit in Farm Street'. They would boast modestly of finding some socialite cleverdick of a sherry-priest who had mastered the knack of talking the dimmest client into thinking she understood a spuriously complicated theology of personal conscience, and could therefore take the Pill *and* Communion and never face the distasteful choice of rebelling against the True Faith or having a child a year.

It disgusted me (and remember, these are unsubtle teenage enragements, faithfully recorded for interest's sake). It was unspeakably vile to know that such Jesuitical intellectual manoeuvrings made it all right for Camilla and Perpetua, who could continue looking adorable in mantillas, while simpler and poorer women in Ireland and Latin America suffered because they had no tame social priest to let them off the terrifying duty of literal obedience.

Not all upper-class Catholics, of course, cheated in this way: many had vast families of Benedicts and Gervases and kept Ampleforth populated. But there was something about their self-assurance, all the same, which for years would infallibly rouse a crazy, bristling, unwholesome hostility in me.

This feeling of my teens and twenties was something almost forgotten, however, until the recent death of Monsignor Alfred Gilbey at 96 and the rash of affectionate obituaries which followed. Reading them transported me straight back to all the impotent fury which I used to feel whenever his name was invoked – and it often was, usually with the word 'marvellous' appended – by just that sort of English Catholic. Although not a member of an 'old family' Gilbey became the embodiment of it all: adored, quoted, lionised by the clique surrounding his thirty-three-year chaplaincy at Cambridge (a mission closed to women, naturally, because he did not believe they should be in the University at all, let alone hearing his exclusive Mass).

Reading the obituaries, noting their fawning tone, I ground my teeth with all the old 1960s schoolgirl feminist hippie-mystical revulsion that came over me at school, and which, to be frank, was a powerful factor in driving me away from the heart of Catholicism. As I have said, I would rather not admit to this hostility; but since this is a chronicle of one person's evolving religious attitudes through a particular period of history, and since it is very much bound up with the atmosphere and the changes of that period, it would be a form of cheating to leave it out.

To these obituaries, then, of Monsignor Gilbey. They spoke mistily of 'the best-dressed priest in England' in breeches, frock-coat, gaiters, broad-brimmed hat and violet gloves. Occasionally, said *The Times*, 'he was known to spend a full hour dressing in the morning . . . more the expression of a love of order and tradition than a vanity'. They pointed out that he had no position in the Catholic hierarchy and had been ordained 'upon his patrimony', as rich men once could, giving allegiance to no bishop and never risking being posted to some parish full of vulgar ordinary people. His mission, they said, was 'narrower' than most, but fell on 'more fertile ground' because he 'moved in the highest circles'. In other words, he only mixed with toffs, right through to adding kudos to their memorial services by getting into his watered-silk soutane and purple pompom biretta and enabling them to have the coveted words in the court report: 'Monsignor Gilbey was robed and in the sanctuary.'

He mainly inhabited London clubland after he left the Cambridge chaplaincy (where, wouldn't you know it, he 'maintained an excellent table and cellar' for his followers). One obituary praised his asceticism, and gave the ludicrous example that in a restaurant he would 'counsel a dinner companion against ordering a certain dish and then choose it for himself as a gentle exercise in self-mortification'. Who needs hair shirts when you can flagellate yourself with an inadequately seasoned *saumon en croûte*?

In his private chapel in the Travellers' Club he drew 'inspiration from valuable furnishings and works of sacred art', inspiration which would in the obituarist's view clearly not have been available from ones that came any cheaper. Reading that, I could only think of those little Maltese lay-sisters at school, pausing in their scrubbing to look reverently up at a cheap plaster statue and murmur 'Jesu!' Monsignor Gilbey opposed women's higher education, all forms of change and ideas of human equality, and considered that the rot set in to the modern world at the French Revolution with the fearful notions of 'Liberty, Equality, Fraternity'. In his last years he was adopted with passion as a mascot by the new fogeyism, the *Spectator* tendency: one wistful mourner wrote that he was 'a living link with a better age', and in another obituary came the astonishing and quite straight-faced claim that his epicurean Cambridge chaplaincy proved his 'ability to attract young men of the "right kind" to Roman Catholicism'.

I am gibbering again, helpless with comic and fruitless rage, even as I copy down these tributes. In penance, I have set myself the task of trying to work out just why all this nonsense has such a powerful emetic effect on me, and why an inoffensive eccentric elderly priest had such impressive power to infuriate.

The first and most obvious reason is that it is not poor dead Monsignor Gilbey at all who drives me crazy, but those who made him their figurehead: the 'right kind of young men', poseurs, nostalgics, Brideshead-junkies, escaped High Anglicans on the run from women priests, and generally creepy misogynist incense-waggers. When they speak of being 'civilised' they mean 'exclusive' – and let us face it, efficient exclusion has always meant that a certain amount of covert savagery is being exercised somewhere along the line. Out of sight.

These people with their country-house attitudes, their substitution of 'civilised values' and the 'art of living' for charity, can do real damage to the name of religion; as much damage as any bent and avaricious US TV evangelist claiming miracle cures and taking telephone credit card donations. Both, disgracefully, appropriate religion to the service of their own worldly concerns. Both are pharisaical.

Of course there must be companies and brotherhoods and sisterhoods, to reinforce shared belief; that is how religions grow. Admittedly it is very hard to draw the line between a genuinely loving and mutually inspiring brotherhood and a poisonous little clique. But drawn it none the less must be. I was never even particularly easy with the hymn we sang at school in Tunbridge Wells, with the chorus:

> Are we not thy chosen soldiers?
> Children of thy Sacred Heart!

Even at fourteen it was easy to work out that the only way we were 'chosen soldiers' was because our parents had chosen to pay a thousand quid a term to send us there. No: cliques and brother-hoods must be examined, and one of the tests is just how welcoming and charitable, how anxious to share the universal good news, is each band of brothers when confronted with the 'wrong sort' of young men.

Or, I suppose, women. Oddly enough, I resent the Gilbeyite attitude to women less than anything else. One obituary spoke of his objection to 'feminism, which Cardinal Manning recog-nised is a solvent of civility beause to put man and woman upon equality is not to elevate woman but to degrade her'. This is nonsense, but not unreasonable nonsense, as it were; not when you allow for history and the man's age (even though it must be admitted that he was only twenty for women's suffrage, and forty-four at the end of the Second World War, a war of Wrens and WRACs; he should not perhaps have been quite so set in his ways). But if you are an Edwardian toff in outlook, it can be argued that in the very narrow social set which is all that an Edwardian toff knows anything about, women (well, the 'right kind of women') were indeed not treated badly at all.

No: the central fault of the Gilbeyites is not that their religious clique excludes women, but that it excludes the majority of human beings. Including those whose labour and suffering enable it to live happily in its clubs.

But I am trying hard, very hard indeed, to take a charitable and understanding attitude to all this because I am middle-aged now, and should have mellowed.

So I grant that you can be a gentleman and a squirearch and possessor of a private chapel and still be genuinely holy. If your religion makes you more careful and just towards your workers and tenants, courteous to all, ready to ignore attacks and insults and return a soft word to those who affront you; if it makes you humane in politics, self-denying in your private life and ready to die for the protection of others, then that religion – however precious and port-stained – is valid and should be honoured. You can be a verray parfit gentil knight. We who mock the reedy pretensions of aristocratic religion should go very carefully, individual by individual, when we judge. The time to point the finger and shout 'hypocrite!' is when we actually catch the possessor of a watered-silk soutane being haughty and unkind to a less classy co-religionist, or visibly oppressing the poor. We should not, as good Catholic teenagers, have allowed ourselves to become alienated from the Church merely by the dispiriting observation that while Anglicans had Bishop Trevor Huddleston taking on apartheid, we had Monsignor Gilbey in a silly hat keeping an enviable cellar.

Perhaps we should be more charitable to the bon-viveur religiasts. Perhaps dreadful Lady Marchmain in *Brideshead* is right when she says that my dear, *of course* a rich man can get through the eye of a needle, because it's miraculous, and that's the lovely thing about the Bible darling – that miracles happen. Leave her in peace, let charity at all costs prevail. Let everybody's motives and private salvation be private and unquestioned by those of us jeering in the pit.

As for the downright infuriatingness of Posh Clique Cartholicks, perhaps they are sent to try the rest and help them on towards salvation. The only proper Christian attitude is to accept the irritation and apparent injustice of it all with joy, and Offer Up the chip on one's shoulder as a mortification.

Yes, of course it is. Monsignor Gilbey, and the few who are like him, gave great pleasure and some inspiration to many people (and never mind what 'sort' they were) over a long life. God rest his soul in peace. I hope the company in heaven is as agreeable as he would like. If not, perhaps, quite as select.

13. Gap, 1968

I would like to recall that I spent my gap summer of 1968 trekking to India in the Beatles' wake to consult the Maharishi Mahesh Yogi, or stoned in San Francisco with flowers in my hair, or marching for Dubček, or plotting in a Montmartre garret with Danny the Red. The truth is that I spent six months working in the Standard Bank in Hamburg and three months as a barmaid in West Cork.

Dad was Consul-General in Hamburg and we lived above the office in the top two floors of an imposing mansion on Harvestehuderweg, which rose like a wedding-cake on the banks of the great Alster lake. My mother was hating diplomatic life by now. Burnt out by a quarter of a century of cocktail parties and Queen's Birthdays, she never wanted to waste another afternoon of her life in small-talk with another silent Japanese military attaché's wife. The peculiar stresses of her way of life were summed up when I asked her once what was the most disgraceful mistake she made in her career as diplo-spouse.

'Well,' she said, 'I once invited the wife of the Number Two at Lloyd's Register of Shipping round to tea before I had invited the wife of the Number One.'

She was not, therefore, well-disposed to parties, preferring whenever possible to zoom exhilaratedly around German prisons with the superb and alarming Sue Ryder trying to spring Polish murderers: poor souls who, traumatised in the aftermath of war, had killed in terror but fallen on the wrong side of the occupying power's merciful discretion. Stirring tales of Lady Ryder's way with intransigent prison authorities would reach me ('That woman' said one governor in a real Black Forest folkloric image of terror, '*has hair on her teeth!*') Such militant, anti-establishment philanthropy from such a Catholic made up in some measure for the continuing disappointment that Bishop Huddleston was an Anglican.

I therefore stood in, quite often, as my father's consort at dip parties. Pretty grim they were: vol-au-vents filled with nothing more than mashed potato, lightly seasoned with paprika and washed not quite all the way down by that hideous German fizzy wine called Sekt.

On the other hand, his contacts in the business community got me a typing job (for, thanks to South Africa, I could still type very fast) filling out Bills of Lading at the Standard Bank in the city centre. I went here daily, with hardly a word of German, and was given my heap of bills to type and a few English letters. It was a very German setting: extremely formal, in that I had to address my immediate deskmate and supervisor, who was all of 18 years old, always as 'Frau Seier' and she would address me as 'Fräulein Purves'.

Each day she taught me a new German proverb to improve my language skills. '*Guten Tag, Fräulein Purves! So – Heute wir sagen – Morgen, Morgen, nur nicht Heute, sagen alle faulen Leute.*' The men in the office all dressed identically in lightweight grey suits, with thin drip-dry white shirts and string vests underneath. On hot days, when the signal went out from the manager that they could take their jackets off, I could see fifty or sixty string vests clearly from where I sat. Once, I went across to London for a fortnight to stay with my schoolfriend Fiona, who was temping in a trendy office in Sheperd Market. These were boom days, when even the most incompetent secretaries could drift from job to job in London and were wooed into firms by ads saying 'Cool chick to work for fab fun boss, great money, great laughs, try us 'n see!' When Fiona called her boss by his Christian name and told him to 'piss off', I nearly fainted with the culture-shock.

Against this prosaic, Germanic, diplomatic background I found opera. The Hamburg Staatsoper had a student queue, quarter price for standby, and at one of the grim parties I met an opera student called Richard who, all platonically, announced his intention of Forming my Taste in opera. He would ring every couple of days with some curt message like 'Tonight – get there by six – it's Domingo's *Trovatore*.' Once he got me to spend five hours of Christmas Day watching *Parsifal*.

Richard tried to sophisticate my taste, and make me appreciate the moderns; but it rapidly became clear that I was a Wagner-wallower and Verdi junkie, irremediably hooked on great swelling emotional cataclysms and noble tragedies. I annoyed him by having a lukewarm response to light opera, even Mozart. All that *Pa-pa-pa-pa-papageno* stuff irked and embarrassed me: I wanted tragedy. All my life since I have kept the addiction to Verdi and Puccini and *Fidelio*, but I lost the taste for Wagner one day in – I think – 1981, when suddenly and without warning at the Royal Opera House I walked out of a performance of *Tannhäuser* feeling sick. Nothing wrong with the performance or the staging: I had just overdosed.

The Verdian tragedies – Leonora pleading at the monastery gate in *Forza del Destino*, Violetta's sacrifice in *Traviata*, a dozen invocations and renunciations and exiled yearnings and noble sorrows – found deep dark echoes within me. Huge, cosmic, cathartic emotions moved me by night and stayed with me, in wisps of remembered music, all day among the bills of lading and the string vests. There were no surtitles, and most of the operas were sung in the original language, so I read synopses avidly in the intervals and groped for meaning in half-understood fragments of each aria, following the emotion perfectly but the sense only vaguely.

Today I like surtitles and libretti; but then, fresh from so many earnest school years of considering the precise meaning of words, I enjoyed the inchoate surge of half-understood scenes of emotion. I had sufficient Latin to pick up a sort of bastardised opera-Italian, which to this day is all I have. On trips to Italy I stumble through the day on wisps of remembered operatics, although '*Pietà de me, mio dio!*' and '*Addio – senza rancor!*' and '*O, l'amor che palpito!*' are really of very little use at the airport car rental desk, (although '*Rittorna vincitor!*' from Aida did enable me to ask for a map for the *Rittorna* to a particularly well-hidden Hertz HQ near Naples airport.)

But I am eternally, and very deeply, grateful to Richard, with whom I lost touch three decades ago. This operatic furniture was something which had been missing from my soul, and those months in Hamburg were profoundly nourishing.

So were the months in County Cork. Five years earlier, battered by Johannesburg, we had taken a short hotel holiday in a village called Schull, looking out towards the Fastnet Rock in the extreme south-west of Ireland. My mother's ancestors had come from Cork, and my eldest brother chose the place at random off the map because the coast looked interesting. And so it is; all of us fell instantly in love with this wild, damp, gentle place and its denizens. It was not yet the fashionable retreat it has since become; my mother, one afternoon, drove down a lane lined with fuchsias and montbretia, saw a farm cottage on sale for £300 and bought it. It was two up, two down, without water, sanitation, or electricity, five busless miles from the village and the coast, and overlooking an active and turbulent pigsty.

In this retreat we camped out for several long summers – my father joining us but staying firmly in the hotel in town – and I am perversely proud to say that we did absolutely nothing to gentrify it. The Elsan remained in the outhouse, the cooking confined to two camping gas burners; and when some wealthy English incomers asked us cosily from their chi-chi holiday home: 'What improvements've you made to yours this year?' I was able to say 'We put the cooker up on two breezeblocks so you don't have to lie on your stomach on the concrete to make toast any more.'

However, as our teens progressed we elder ones rebelled against not being able to get independently into the lively seaside village except by bumming a ride on the churns that went early each day by horse and cart to the creamery on the corner, from where we could hitch the last miles along the main road. The only hope of being in the village was to get jobs; accordingly Mike worked on the trawlers and then in a bar, and I became a waitress at the hotel.

I was a very bad waitress, forever bawled out by Mary-cook for having too short a skirt or taking out egg mayonnaises without any egg on the plate, but it got me a place in the waitresses' bunkhouse out the back. I liked it in the kitchen: haute cuisine (now a bit of a West Cork speciality) had not yet arrived, and there were undemanding occupations like rehydrating Erin brand dried shredded cabbage and carrots, and dodging missiles thrown by Tony from Kerry, the high-spirited washer-up. He used to tell us, with roars of laughter, that he had failed his driving test the first time because when the examiner asked what he would do at a traffic-light he admitted: 'I've never seen a traffic light.'

After a couple of summers of this kind of work I got a much better job, with an attic room of my own thrown in, stocking and minding the bar behind the supermarket over the road. In case you are wondering what all this has to do with a book of religious reminiscence, I should say that of all the formative experiences of my first twenty-one years, one of the most important was being a barmaid.

I was in O'Keeffes all summer for four years running, through the end of school, gap year, and all through University. I came in late June, and sometimes stayed right into cool September when the tourists drifted away and the village drew in on itself again with a sigh of relief. I carried crates, arranged bottles, refilled optics, served, swept, and nipped through to mind the supermarket or help Sheila bone the bacon when things were quiet. Sometimes I had the enviable task of bottling the Midleton whiskey, which arrived in a huge cask with a wicker casing and needed to be put into our own bottles by way of a siphon tube. This enabled me to take fortifying accidental swigs of the smooth Irish, and to fiddle around satisfyingly with labels and corks.

There was an old-fashioned bakery round the back, too, whence Jackie the baker would appear to have his pint and leave a dough-encrusted glass behind.

For the first time in a nomadic and conventual existence, I was right at the heart of an ordinary, proper, homelike community. The bar had a clientele, at that time, which comfortably mixed townspeople, farmers, Cork and Dublin Irish, English visitors and yachtsmen – in different proportions according to the stage the summer had reached. Early and late in the season there were opportunities for slow reflective conversations with the bee-keeper, the bank porter, the draper and ironmonger, and with my colleagues from bar and shop, particularly a remarkable, tiny, hunchbacked wit and indisputable saint called Sheila Hegarty who now – to universal sadness – is dead. In mid-season there was less conversation, just a determined battle to serve shoals of racing yachtsmen waving soggy banknotes, and confront with as much bravery as we could muster the hideous maelstrom of Regatta Day, when the floor beneath the bar staff's feet grew slippery with spillage and we had to throw down sawdust.

Best of all were the times in between, when both groups were in. I, who had never belonged anywhere, liked nothing better than to stand there being as good as local, and solving problems. There were all the usual ones (men really do tell barmaids that their wives don't understand them, it is not a legend) but practical solutions were needed too. Once I was reflectively polishing a glass when a crew came in off a boat, fretting because the skipper had lost a deck shoe overboard and had to leave with the dawn tide. I was able to pour them a drink, calm them down, and introduce them to the owner of the town outfitters, who was sitting at the other end of the bar and willingly opened up the shop for them to buy another pair. For good measure the baker sold them some fresh bread, right there in the bar, and Sheila came through with a pound of bacon from the shop. Another time a crew got a telephone message that their yacht had dragged its anchor in Crookhaven harbour down the coast and was being rescued by fishermen. They had no transport, but another customer casually tossed them his car keys and made a date to meet them for a jar later, when they had secured the yacht.

Sometimes bright-eyed tourists came in with some puzzled question about the lighthouse, or the fishing, and I was able to introduce them to an off-duty lighthousekeeper or fisherman right there at the bar. Sometimes offshore islanders came in on rare visits, gaunt and venerable in their shiny suits, to order mad drinks they had invented in their imaginations during dull winter evenings in their publess redoubts. I particularly remember serving the requested 'lager and raspberry', and 'whiskey and Lucozade with a dash of lime'.

In the other corner of the bar might be some of the early pioneers of hip English tourism in West Cork: the journalist Vincent Mulchrone, a television producer reminiscing about his glory days on the *Tonight* programme, or Alastair Miller, governor of Parkhurst prison, who became a great friend. I remember Sheila telling me, on one of my first bar shifts, to serve him quickly and respect the poor man's feelings because 'He's had a telegram, I t'ink his prisoners are rioting again'.

One year, as the region's fashionable status began to rise, Jim the owner introduced a team under a fashionable London restaurateur to start a restaurant in the barn at the back. So in addition to locals and family tourists I had the company of a group of Kensington exquisites: rake-thin nervy girls in crop-tops and their manager, a languidly beautiful Adonis. He and I circled one another warily for a few days, competing over ice ('I *need* it in the cocktail bar, Libby *darling*, and you *don't*'). Then one night after closing time we emptied a bottle of Midleton together and became firm friends. He is still in the trade, and even now from time to time at some book-launch party in London Charles glides past with a high-class trayful of canapés, and winks and murmurs '*Hullo*, Liberty-belle!' And I spill my drink in delight and lose all interest in the surrounding glitterati as we reminisce in furtive mutters about old days by the Atlantic shore.

I would not wish to be sentimental about rural Irish religion:

too many people have difficult memories of its failures of human sympathy. Among those I knew, and know now, there are both good priests and bad, happy Catholics and bitter ones, generous-hearted ecumenicals and bitter bigots. Yet there was, in those late 1960s and early 1970s, still a satisfying wholeness about life there, or at least the surfaces of life. When a funeral passed, we traders all pulled down our shutters and closed out of respect. At the Saturday dance, the priest stood outside with the Gardai, and inside the hall it was considered very rude indeed for any girl to refuse a dance with any man or vice versa. On Sunday, the pubs did not open until after the main service. Each evening at six the Angelus bell rang out, in reality and on RTE, and unselfconsciously, many people crossed themselves. When somebody died it was – and still is – natural in that good place to say 'God rest him!' and talk gently, fondly, reminiscently about the dead without Anglo-Saxon embarrassment.

But for me, it was not explicit Catholicism that mattered during those long happy summers in the bar. It was something made easy by the prevailing kindliness of the place, and perhaps by the great empty rocky beautiful spaces around us, wild spaces which bring human beings closer to one another. It was something closer to the Salinger vision: the determination to perceive something wonderful and transcendent in everybody who came into the bar, to serve them and soothe them and connect with them and *answer that of God in every one*. I really wanted to give my fellow human beings their pints and whiskies and ginger ales and crab sandwiches in a spirit of nothing less than love. Sometimes, I managed it. Sometimes it was almost frighteningly easy. Especially when I was slightly drunk myself.

It probably also helped when, as was inevitable at the age of eighteen, I was hopelessly, desperately, manically and quite unproductively thwarted in love. This happened more than once during those late teenage summers, and on each occasion the best recourse was either a thundering, passionate bout of Verdi (when in Hamburg) or (when in Ireland) an extra-long stint behind the bar, loving my neighbour with indiscriminate, slightly over-wrought, goldenheartedly bosomy intensity.

Just as the best barmaids have done, down all the ages.

14. *Sex and the* Sensus Fidelium

Of course, the whole business of falling in love was newer to me than it would be to most modern eighteen-year-olds. Convent schools and foreign postings do not make for much of a social life, and a great deal of it had been conducted purely in theory. Groups of schoolfriends would conduct endless, worried, preoccupied seminars about what love *should* be, what it *might* be, what each partner ought to expect from the other, and so forth. Even weekends out with the day girls in their paradise of independence did not help much. Inconclusive snogging sessions at parties with boys whose faces you could hardly see made very little contribution to the whole conundrum.

The least helpful guidance of all came in the convent sex education lessons. These, loosely disguised as part of 'Psychology' were conducted by a middle-aged, intelligent, sternly bespectacled mathematics teacher nun who quite obviously had not the faintest idea about sexuality. And why should she have, poor woman? She had discarded and renounced it, joyfully, for a greater vision when she was too young and from too pious a family to have got anywhere near the stuff.

Her session on Christian marriage practices, which followed hard on a display of rather faded and discouraging cross-sections of human plumbing, was a *tour de force* of exquisite embarrassment. First of all there was a contretemps between her and my good friend Rosalind, who as a day girl was rather more experienced. Sister X started by explaining that there was a difference between 'fun kissing, and *passion* kissing' . . . Rosalind observed aloud that in her experience, passion kissing *was* fun. She was sent from the room, and therefore blessedly enabled to miss the next bit: Sister X's disastrous attempt to paint a picture of the Catholic Couple at Bedtime:

'The Catholic Wife will go up to the bedroom first . . . perhaps taking up the cocoa for both of them . . . undress and put on her nightgown and get into bed. Meanwhile the Catholic Husband will lock up the doors and fit the fireguard . . .' (and, presumably, put out the Catholic Cat). 'Then he goes upstairs and gets into his Night Things . . . and then they can say their prayers together . . . um . . . and then . . . um . . . the Act of Love Takes Place.'

At which point she glanced down nervously at the cross-sectional diagram of sperm canals and uteri, leaning discarded against the leg of her desk.

Twenty-five teenage girls sat before her, longing for the earth to swallow them up. We preferred the *Gone with the Wind* model, where the husband storms in, indulges in a bit of verbal abuse, picks up his wife in his arms and runs up the stairs. And the next thing you know it is morning, with the ravished bride humming contentedly and rearranging her ruffles. No cocoa involved at any stage.

Contraception, however, was a hot issue, and not discussed nearly enough within the school. It was, perhaps, too early: it was in July of 1968, when I had left for the Irish bar, that the Pope finally pronounced in the encyclical *Humanae Vitae* that all artificial contraception was wrong and must never be practised by the world's Catholics (530 million and growing).

This perpetuated the situation which condemned Catholic women to play Vatican Roulette with their fertile cycles. In the immortal words of H. L. Mencken, one might enrol mathematics to avoid pregnancy, 'but not yet physics or chemistry'.

It is difficult now to convey how hard a message this was for the Catholic schoolgirls of 1968, setting out on adult life. A great many church leaders had expected a relaxation of the rule, and that the ban would fade into the past like the medieval church ruling against usury or the strict ban on meat in Lent. Some had even hoped that the Church would take an easier line with members who wanted to marry previously divorced people. All such liberals were disappointed.

I venture to say that it was harder for my generation than for any other to accept the ruling. It gave us no tolerable future to look forward to, as with A levels behind us we stepped out into wider fields to confront the World, the Flesh, the Devil and the Rolling Stones. Yet we were not the rebel convent-girls of male fantasy, anxious to make up for years of white-veiled innocence by creating sexual mayhem. Many of us were just earnest teenagers, wanting to be good and save the world. We might look trollopy in our miniskirts and sooty black false eyelashes, we might be a bit queasy about the Little Flower of Lisieux and (in my case) renegade from the Children of Mary; yet the sweetness and idealism and spirituality of the Church still echoed through our lives like plainsong. Throwing off Catholicism, and indeed Christianity, was not necessarily part of the agenda.

But we had lives to lead in a modern world, and *Humanae Vitae* was a hard slap in the face. Theologically the ruling was obscure and unconvincing, redolent of a sort of resigned fatalism and contempt for prudence and self-reliance which was not preached by the church in any other area. Practically, it was plain disastrous. An idealistic girl can accept all sorts of difficult demands: celibacy outside marriage, chastity within it, the absolute impossibility of abortion or divorce. But this was the final straw. It was an uncompromising, uncharitable edict that made all practical birth control a grave sin: even inside marriage, even after many children. The 'rhythm method' – to which most of us owed a sibling or two or three – was the only option. It did not work at all reliably (although science has made it more reliable today). It gave a very short safe period indeed, and virtually none at all for those with uneven cycles. It became clear that a great deal of sexual abstinence would be required of us and our future partners, and that the legendary 'Catholic

Husband' of Sister X's lecture might as well put himself out with the cat, while he was at it.

It was not just that it did not fit in with the times. Religion does not have to follow fashions in thought. The frustrating thing was that it did not fit in with what we had been taught to think about sex, either. Our nuns, remember, had not taught us prurient disgust and horror of it; we were plainly told, year after year, that the real reason you did not squander and debase sex was that it was a holy and sublime act of love, inseparable from the serious commitment of marriage.

Yet now we were told, effectively, that even in marriage a very strict rationing would apply to this hallowed and sublime act of love. If, indeed, love could ever be found: in a mainly non-Catholic nation we were told either to stay single, or find ourselves husbands who would accept either perpetual pregnancy or perpetual abstinence. We knew that the law of averages meant that many of us would marry outside the faith if we married at all; nobody gave us any clue as to how we could break such news to our consorts.

Nor did the new age of opportunities and dignity for women much incline us to the lives we had seen Catholic women leading: either managing very large families or else (rather more often) having to stay away from the communion rail until the menopause, with all the old biddies in the church nudging one another and guessing why. One young married woman I knew admitted to taking occasional 'holidays' from her state of sin during the seven days that she did not take the Pill: she would pop the last one of the cycle into her mouth as she approached the confessional, get shriven, then go to communion on that Sunday, before the next card of pills was due to start. She admitted that this was probably not valid, since she was benefiting from the crime even when not taking the tablets, but it was the kind of depressing little compromise that became all too common among simple-hearted Catholic women.

Of course, some women felt otherwise. They gallantly embraced what the splendid Mrs Victoria Gillick has called 'the great adventure'. While the rest of us were rebelling, quietly or noisily, against that particular diktat of *Humanae Vitae* she was marrying her Gordon, and later said robustly: 'We would not have given tuppence for the idea of sterilizing our healthy young bodies with chemicals and bits of wire and rubber.' She told me once that there were two approaches to family life: either you were the kind of person who primly sends out formal invitations with RSVP on them, and makes individual mousses in ramekins; or else you declared open house and pot luck out of a great big pan, and caroused with whoever turned up. Since my attitude to entertaining has always been closer to the second option, I was charmed by this; and I still think that Mrs Gillick (mother of ten extremely nice children) is a bit of a heroine in her way.

But it was not, thirty years ago, my way; and I do not see why it should be the only one. Neither theologically nor emotionally – and certainly not practically – was it possible to accept that contraception was a sin to be ranked with other grave sins that barred you from the communion rail: adultery, cruelty, theft. Ours was not a merely selfish rebellion, either: thinking of rural Ireland and devout Latin America a slow-burning anger rose on behalf of women pushed, by a male priestly hierarchy, into the front line. What did the infallible blasted celibate Pope know of Irishwomen who saved up their meagre housekeeping money so that their husbands could be made drunk enough on Saturday to forgo their 'rights' and the risk of yet another baby? Of mothers bearing child after child in countries with minimal medical care, who died young and exhausted? Of the lifelong sadness and humility of those who broke the rules and went through life believing themselves sinners? Often women took all the sin upon themselves: the Irish nurse who first fitted me for a diaphragm in the early 1970s assured me that it was undetectable by making the startling confession: 'I used it myself for thirty years before my husband died, God rest him. Every Sunday morning he would pray to St Joseph to keep his family small enough for him to support decently. And every Saturday night I would put in me ol' cap. He never knew.'

I wrote about this twenty-five years later, in 1993, in *The Times*, because the encyclical *Veritatis Splendor* had just explicitly reiterated the ban. I was replying to a coquettish article by an editor of the *Catholic Herald*, who wrote :

> Latins regard the speed limit on their roads as an ideal to be aimed at – but have never seriously thought that they should obey it to the letter. For 25 years, liberals within the Catholic Church have adopted the same approach to the Church's teaching on birth control.

I replied:

> In which case, to hell with them. A church cannot afford the kind of double standards in which a smug chattering-class bends the rules by sophistry, while simple and faithful people are flatly told that contraception is a grave sin. But it happens: all over the world honest Catholics either hold to the rule and suffer, or break it and grieve for their wickedness. It is monstrous. It also torpedoes many other teachings. Catholicism rightly resists the trivialisation of sexuality and birth; there is a deeply humane case to be made against abortion. But the ban on contraception devalues by association everything else the Church says about sex. It is an indefensible own goal, and for 25 years it has blighted the Catholic marriage bed with dishonesty and bewilderment, sophistry and subtle corruption. At 18 I wanted none of it, and I still do not.

The result was a flood of letters from Catholics of every hue: some outraged, some confused, many expressing a real hurt and anguish which reflected my own. Only a few were hostile: the priest who sneered that contraception 'merely enabled you young women to build careers and bank balances', and another who accused me of being a latter-day Aleister Crowley ('Do what thou wilt shall be all of the law'). Several clearly disliked every aspect of sex and thought all women Jezebels.

Outrageously, a Jesuit priest wrote that he could explain why my objection contained 'eight debatable presuppositions' and announced that he would give me absolution for using contraception 'without firm purpose of amendment, either'. Nudge, nudge, wink, wink. I threw the letter in the bin with fury. Had I not said, and clearly, that I wanted no such cheating absolution?

There was one thoughtful letter from a Catholic doctor which expressed the dilemma which the Pill has put us all into this past quarter-century: 'On the one hand are the appalling effects of separating childbearing and children from procreative activity. On the other, the terrible effects of excessive procreation.'

Others said that the danger of contraception is that it enables men to think they can enjoy sex without responsibility, and that this leads to a degradation both of women and of love. With that I more or less agree. But the great majority of the letters were simply full of pain, and of a thwarted desire to lead possible lives and at the same time remain honestly within the Church.

'Most of us', said one, 'remain inside dishonestly. I wish to God that everyone who feels as you and I do would leave the Church now, publicly, without guilt, so that they could see the empty pews and understand what they have done to our faith.'

And a middle-aged Catholic woman asked for 'an hour, just one hour, with His Holiness, to tell him the strain and unhappiness caused to faithful simple souls trying desperately to stick to the rules.'

A missionary worker in Latin America wrote of 'twisted solutions rejected by honest people, and encyclicals which make careful human beings feel ashamed'.

Doctors wrote, mothers wrote, apostate priests wrote, decent men wrote with a kind of shame. One spoke of the 'purgatory' of his past married life and said: 'The dreadful rhythm method is about as far from the spirit of our Lord Jesus Christ as it is possible to get.' Another remembered the day he and his wife lost their second child from a genetic disease, when they had been warned to have no more 'And we could not embrace that night and fully show our continuing love, because the calendar said no.'

One layman wrote impassionedly of a forgotten doctrine, the '*sensus fidelium*', or infallibility of the faithful. Despite assurances from his Benedictine brother-in-law that the Faithful are only infallible when they agree entirely with the Pope, this correspondent concluded bravely: 'When millions of well-intentioned laypeople are thinking the same way, surely the Holy Spirit cannot be entirely absent from their collective mind?'

All in all, it was strangely comforting to find that the old rage of 1968 still lives, in some hearts at least. Depressingly though, few Western Catholics grumble loudly about the contraception rule today: which has to be fair proof that most of them quietly ignore it. Look at the low birth rate in devout Italy and Ireland, and observe how very often, as an Irish friend puts it: 'God's will seems to provide for two conveniently spaced children.' Priests who take confession must be quietly turning a blind eye to all this, or else turning a clever phrase to avoid it.

How deeply this corrupts and vitiates this Church's general standing, and its ability to take a moral lead in sexual matters, is something every onlooker must privately judge. At any rate, in 1968 this one issue threw up the most important barrier between me and the church I grew up in. It was not an immediate personal issue: I was not married and stayed a long time chaste. I did not break with the old church over a prescription packet, but over a principle. I dug in my heels. That, after all, was part of what it had taught me all these years.

15. Oxford

One of the advantages of being a Catholic is that at least you know when you have stopped. Stopped 'practising', that is: since it is a formally enjoined minimum duty to go to Mass every Sunday and take the sacraments at Easter, the first Sunday that you choose not to go to Mass is a day you can mark on the calendar. Something ends, or at least visibly pauses. The Mass rule is actually a very helpful one: it focuses the mind on what you are doing, in a way which is unknown to most English Protestants. I rather envied my compeers who could drift vaguely around for years thinking of themselves as Church, or Chapel, or 'C-of-E-I-suppose', without ever making a firm decision one way or the other.

When I first went to Oxford in the autumn of 1968, I heard Mass weekly at the Catholic chaplaincy. During that time my rage over *Humanae Vitae* was brewing, and I was further incensed about a particularly blatant example of a well-connected European Catholic family who had gained a suspiciously easy annulment of marriage on obscure grounds (another scandalous cheat which, from time to time, mars the Church).

So I did not go either to Confession or Communion. The atmosphere at the Catholic chaplaincy was not especially welcoming or stimulating, and the one contact I had with the Sacred Heart nuns (who ran a house in Oxford) was brief and unsatisfactory. On the occasion when my old headmistress, Sister Wilson, visited that convent and came to call on my tutor at St

Anne's I went to tea, but was in no good state. I behaved with enough eccentricity to cause a certain amount of speculation between her and my tutor as to whether I was Cracking Up.

In fact, it was just bad timing: a cosmic joke. I had arrived at the tea-party fresh from an unexpected scene. One of my new friends, a lively and funny girl from St Hilda's, had poleaxed me by announcing with deadly sincerity that she was a) a lesbian and b) in love with me.

Anyone's first homosexual pass is always a shock, I suppose. I had known that she was a long way farther down the free-wheeling late-1960s primrose path than I was, and had tranquilly accepted it. Nearly everyone I knew in Oxford was more sexually experienced than me, and curiously this did not bother me very much. I never could understand the frenzy which overcame other virgins of the period to 'get rid of it'. Some thought it a kind of duty to do so, in order to 'move on'. That idea seemed to me as unkindly rigid as the previous generation's insistence on Keeping Yourself Pure. Nor was I particularly convinced by a friend's depressing revelation that losing your virginity 'knocked the nonsense out of you'. I quite liked the nonsense in me, my clouds of glory.

What mainly plunged me into shock when the pass was made – on the eve of Preliminary Examinations and the day of this Sister Wilson visit – was sympathy for the monstrous unfairness which seemed to have been visited on my poor friend. I was very naive, and lesbian inclinations seemed to me something very bizarre and probably very rare. I could not bear to think of clever, brave, honest Ros going through her whole life suffering thwarted love. I had suffered enough of that myself to be horrified on her behalf, and was genuinely sorry that returning her passion was out of the question. Indeed I suddenly realised how certain young men must have felt when I had mooned over them uninvited.

Secondly, I felt vertiginously unsettled. All of a sudden, the half of the human race in front of which one could casually undress was no longer safe. The miniskirt and skinnyrib sweater had only recently landed on the planet, and all of us girls at the time were constantly being told to beware of inadvertently provoking ungovernable male passions. To start worrying about ungovernable female ones as well seemed too much to bear. The great horror of women at the time was being regarded as what Women's Lib called a 'sex object', and the idea of being one to women as well was unspeakable.

So I was not at all receptive to nunly chat of the How's-God type that day, and a certain estrangement ensued. It was after that that I stopped bothering with Sunday Mass.

The focus of spiritual and moral energy, in any case, had moved far away from the banal vernacular devotions and nervy tea-parties of the chaplaincy. It is fashionable now to sneer, with lofty hindsight, at the revolutions of 1968 and after, but if you were young and in love with the human race that was a period when genuine passion and excitement were in the air, heady as hawthorn-blossom. We were angry about Vietnam (the pictures of Vietnamese victims reminded me very much of the gentle Thais of my infancy). We were angry about Martin Luther King's death and the shooting of Rudi Dutschke in Germany. We were behind the US black athletes who were boycotting the Mexico City games in protest at the all-white teams from South Africa. We were inspired by Melina Mercouri's fiery speeches against the Greek junta – *Eleuthera y thanatos!* – Freedom or death! We stood in silent vigil in St Giles' over the death of Jan Palach, who made himself a human torch of protest as the Soviet tanks rolled into Prague. The walls of Balliol and All Souls' began to sprout graffiti inspired by the ones which had appeared in the previous spring in Paris:

Open the gates of the universities, the schools and all other prisons
Hang the last capitalist with the entrails of the last bureaucrat!
Be realistic – demand the impossible!
Property is theft
God is dead – signed Nietzsche

Although under this last, a wit would always inscribe:

So is Nietzsche – signed, God.

In Oxford – rather anticlimactically – students occupied the Examination Schools in a hazy protest against the discovery that the University kept files on all of us. The Foreign Secretary Michael Stewart was booed out of the Oxford Union for not condemning the US in Cambodia. When Enoch Powell was due to speak there, months after his 'Tiber foaming with much blood' speech, more violent street disruption ensued, organised by ORSS – the Oxford Revolutionary Socialist Students, under the ubiquitous Tariq Ali.

I was not by any means at the heart of all this. You will not find me in the history books or even the press cuttings. I joined nothing political, and confined myself to the frivolous debates at the Oxford Union ('This House would do its own thing'). But revolution was in the air that we all breathed, and it affected everyone in some way. I was in the Union when Stewart was shouted down: it was my first experience of a mob, and I hated it. I loved argument and wanted him argued with: I did not really understand what was happening in the far East or why, and wanted to be informed. The sight of the staid little man's bowed, balding head as he was strongarmed from the debating chamber amid ritual booing and spitting reminded me too vividly of the Two Minutes' Hate in *1984* to be comfortable.

When Powell was coming, a group of us tried to persuade ORSS that the best demonstration would be to assemble all the black and Asian students and citizens we could, and silently line his path from the railway station with alternate black and white faces, standing together and all smiling broadly. It would have been a lovely, mocking photo-opportunity but ORSS would have none of it, preferring to shriek and throw things and thump the roof of his car. So we peaceful ones stayed away.

In this atmosphere (which, I should say, gradually faded during my three years in the University city) there were several routes of escape taken by those who did not enjoy ORSS, were irritated by the patriarchal airs of its male leaders and thought the sit-ins silly. You could discard it all with a flounce and join the OUCA, the Conservatives. Or you could line up with the Trades Union tendency based at Ruskin, the working men's college, and sing the Harry Pollitt song:

> Harry went to heaven
> Saw St Peter with his keys
> Said 'Can I speak to Comrade God
> I'm Harry Pollitt please . . .'

Or your refuge could be the Young Liberals, whose idol, young David Steel, came frequently to speak. Most intelligently of all, you could be like the admirable Paul Cavadino, who still runs NACRO, and take the line of concentrating your desire to change the world into enlightened, patient philanthropy – a direction where it might actually succeed. If I had been a better and more mature person I would have involved myself with Christian Aid, with the rapidly burgeoning Oxfam, with CAFOD.

But I did none of these things. My only social work was a couple of terms later on when – inspired by Orwell's account of his life among the tramps and Sally Trench's book *Bury Me in My Boots*, I signed on to help at the Simon Community shelter down near Oxford station. I spent many strangely contented evenings here, doing chores like ironing the damp sheets dry, washing up, and chatting to assorted down-and-outs, mostly men. My barmaid experience stood me in good stead, as did a continuing covert determination to connect with 'that of God in everyone'. I made some short-term friends (they were forever moving on) whose stories of misfortune or perversity ballasted me against letting my own life drift in an overly Bridesheady direction.

Mostly, though, I joined drama groups and made comedy speeches at the Union and amused myself by being a parlour pinko and baiting stern young Conservatives like Ann Widdecombe and my friend Stephen Milligan. I also fell in love with a succession of men who turned out to be gay, or otherwise involved, or just plain terrified by my earnest virginal idealism about human relations. Some very nice men did fall for me, but they were never the right ones. There was one very near miss, a chap who pursued me determinedly for a term; but at the very moment when I realised how wonderful he was and what a resource of happiness I had been wasting, he gave up the chase and fell into the clutches of somebody else. Luckily it was the end of a summer term, and almost time to go back to Ireland and work off the grief behind the bar again.

Meanwhile, the women's movement crept into our common consciousness. Women's Lib, as it was then called without contumely or irony, became part of the landscape. The magazine *Black Dwarf* published a moving and prophetic appeal not for a battle but for 'a new kind of humanity' for both men and women, based on loving equality and an end to women's 'assumption of secondariness'. I remember that phrase particularly, because it made me realise that I *had* always assumed myself to be secondary, although not necessarily to men.

Our set model, after all, had always been the Virgin Mary: 'Behold the handmaid of the Lord', she said, and was much given to pondering things quietly in her heart and meekly accepting snubs from her twelve-year-old son when he said he must be 'about his Father's business'. Yes, yes: I know perfectly well that theology can explain and reconcile Mary's passivity with a decent respect for women's potential. But none the less her example, as portrayed to us at school, did create a sense of chronic secondariness.

Whether or not my left-over Mariolatry was to blame, there was a shrillness about much of the Women's Lib agitprop with which I was uneasy. I liked the dungarees and the cheekiness, but could never get entirely comfortable with political lesbianism, or with people who were prepared to go around carrying banners demanding 'Women's right to abortion, nurseries, contraception, orgasm'. As a bluff Lancashire friend, a miner's son, remarked: 'Apart from anything else, isn't that the wrong order?'

Germaine Greer came to speak at a hall in Jericho, near the canal, and I went along with friends of friends, one of whom was a bland young American called Bill Clinton. My chief memory is of Ms Greer's passionate contempt for us 'pampered' white middle-class Oxford girls, and her description of the plight of working-class girls and how grim it was that they were so unrespected in what she vaguely referred to as 'the North'. She said she had heard young men in this 'North' saying that they could do without even the sexual services of women, because 'a wank is as good as a fuck any day'. The reason I remember this is that I did not know the word 'wank', and had to ask my neighbour what it meant. Alas, it was not Bill Clinton I asked (he was two seats down the row) or I could have been dining out on the story to this day.

I only once went on a Women's Lib rally: a march to Reclaim the Night, in around 1971. That was entirely wonderful. The idea was that street rape attacks were not women's problem to solve, but men's: women should not *have* to stay indoors, take expensive taxis, recruit male minders and avoid dark alleys. This is something I passionately believed then, and still do. We banged saucepans and carried flaming torches and chanted 'Whatever we wear, wherever we go, yes means yes and no means no', and young men on street corners looked deeply uncomfortable.

Hardening within me, through all this, was a far more private kind of feminism. It seemed to me that for a lot of my women friends, the new freewheeling attitude to sex was just another kind of slavery. The Pill had lifted the dread of pregnancy, sure; but the lifting of that dread from the shoulders of immature men had made some of them, if possible, even more callous and inconsiderate than before. It was perfectly obvious that even the most promiscuous and apparently carefree girls took sex much harder, much more emotionally, than their partners. It was even more obvious that promiscuous men – often revolutionary men, officially devoted to human dignity – refused to accept this and gave their sleeping partners no dignity at all.

Some pairs of true lovebirds did match up, and stay matched, and care for one another as full human beings in sickness and health; but they were the exception. There was a prevailing atmosphere of female sadness and insecurity. Dylan sang 'It ain't me, babe', and a hundred moody guitarists strummed the male need to be a free spirit on the open road, not chained down by any woman. The male peacocks (very brightly coloured they were by 1970, with hair flowing and cool purple shirts and snakeskin boots) preened and strutted; their females like the pea-hen grew drooping and draggled, armed neither with the dignity of motherhood nor the privileges of purity. I knew at least four attempted suicides by girls my own age, and not one of them had anything to do with exam pressure.

After the Pill and before AIDS, some men's seduction lines were extraordinarily frank about the way they now felt about us as a no-strings, zipless sexual convenience. 'Don't be so *selfish*' they would say indignantly. And 'You're just *scared*. You have to overcome that' and 'It's no use to *you*. Anyway, you need to make sure you're not *frigid*, so you can get it sorted out before it wrecks your life'. One Irish boy, mistakenly interpreting my continued virtue as religiously motivated, reassured me as he lunged: 'Sure, it's all right between Catholics. It would be a mortal sin, now, for you to go to bed wit' a Protestant, because he could never confess and get absolution. But between Catholics . . .' The phenomenon now known as 'date rape', and which lands young men in court, was then rarely complained of. It was part of almost every girl's experience to wake in the morning with a hangover and a sense of guilty regret, and to blame herself for 'sending out the wrong signals'. As if men were trains, helpless to restrain themselves as they hurtled across the points.

All in all, when I look at teenage girls of all classes now I am relieved to note a certain toughness and sense of self-worth which we, the experimental pill generation, notably lacked. Of course, some had it more than others, and definitely more than me. I might have been a virgin, but in many other ways I was one of Nature's doormats. I remember a violent row in a Chaucer tutorial over the Decameron story of Patient Griselda, the wife who promised obedience to her husband and was bitterly tested by him – insulted, banished, her children taken and apparently killed, forced to work for years as a menial, asked to prepare wedding clothes for his new wife. Chaucer called her:

> *This flour of wyfly pacience*
> *That neither by hir wordes ne hir face*
> *Biforn the folk, ne eek in hir absence,*
> *Ne shewed she that hir was doon offence.*

Eventually Griselda is praised for her humility and raised again to dignity, the test passed. The story is generally seen by medievalists as a fable, imaging the relationship of the Christian with a God who hides himself and tests our faith.

The row occurred because my tutorial partners (and from clues in the text Chaucer himself) thought it an outrageous story and the King in question a thoroughgoing bastard. I, on the other hand, perversely argued that since Griselda had made a promise to obey, she was doing right. The King might be wrong; but if she had reneged her vows and told him where he got off, that would have been a broken vow. Two wrongs could not make a right. There was something of the uncompromising Anouilh heroine's unreason in my interpretation of her.

I was a born debater, and do not think I entirely believed what I was saying, but it was not entirely done for mischief. I had a certain masochistic streak and genuinely put a high value on stoical, rock-like endurance: 'If' was a favourite poem, and I had always rather liked the Book of Job. This tendency to stoicism, and to accept the impossibility of fulfilling the highest yearnings, was something which did me few favours where men were concerned over the next few years. But perhaps it was all part of the enduring and ineradicable religious outlook I still bore: like the apostate Shelley's translating of human love into:

> The desire of the moth for the star
> Of the night for the morrow
> The devotion to something afar
> From the sphere of our sorrow.

Still, if it did impede my ability to conduct a sensible, human liaison with a human object of desire, I dare say it serves me right. If I had stayed a faithful Catholic I would presumably never have made the mistake of confusing fallible human love with the Divine, and certainly not have been so prone to see so dangerously *much* of God in any individual man.

Apart from the Griselda row, political and social conundrums rarely intruded into the tutorials and seminars of the English School. Here I found almost unalloyed joy. The old Oxford English course was about to change for ever, losing much of its emphasis on the early roots of languge and literature on this island. I was lucky enough to be one of the last to undergo the old regime, because if ever a course was designed for me, this was it. From Grendel to *Great Expectations* everything in my mental landscape found an echo there, even sometimes an explanation.

There was barely anything from the twentieth century, which was fine by me; not because I saw no value in my own century but because it was so readily available and easy to read that it seemed a waste of time to study it the way we did Milton or Herbertson or Fielding. The strong component of Anglo-Saxon and Middle English was something I knew was coming, and loved straight away. Some of my contemporaries had not been so well-informed at school about the nature of the Oxford course, and were outraged when they arrived, full of eagerness to confront cutting-edge literature, and found themselves sat down to learn by heart the Lord's Prayer in Old English. *FaeÐer ure, Þu Þe eart on heofonum, swa Þin nama gehalgod, gewurÞa Þin willa on eorÞan swa swa on heofonum . . .*

I plunged into it, relishing the connection between old language and new, between the childhood prayer and the new age that was beginning. I loved *Beowulf*, and *The Seafarer*, was intoxicated by the noble rhythms of the old tongue, and spent hours voluntarily translating them into iambic pentameter. I still hated Latin, but got myself through Book I of the *Aeneid* (the final hurdle, disposed of at Prelims) with the help of an infamous little word-for-word crib entitled *Kelly's Keys to the Classics*, whose tortured English precisely reflected the word-order of the Latin, and needed only to be learnt parrot-fashion in order to pass any likely lump of translation. Learning parrot-fashion was a useful skill left over from all those *Fables de La Fontaine* I had been made to learn nightly in Lille when I was eleven.

A proper religious education proved to be an enormous asset with the rest of the curriculum. C. S. Lewis used to tell his students that they were lucky to have a believing Christian like him to teach Milton and Donne and George Herbert, and I was immediately in tune with the theology, because I had so recently lived it. There was another aspect to that as well, not noted by Lewis: having smarted at church rules and been outraged by church hypocrisies myself, I was better able to understand the anticlerical fury of rebels like Shelley and Blake. Fellow-students from religion-free progressive schools had a noticeably different, prevailingly baffled reaction to some of the devotional history that wound through our literary course. It was as if, by going through so many kinds of religious education, I had been given the key to a thousand years of the history of thought and emotion.

It helped me immensely, whether through *Paradise Lost* or the Middle English text entitled *Hali Meidenhad*, with its frisson of sexual loathing and terror of all things carnal ('Marriage is but a net, spread to catch the sinner as he hurtles towards Hell').

My Zennish phase helped too: often I got quite carried away with the intoxicating sense of the interconnectedness of things. I wanted the truths within literature as much as the forms it came clothed in, preferring to argue with the author personally than to trace the development of his or her style. One tutorial partner and I were separated when we began, as the tutor drily said, to 'write essays against one another'. She was a dour clever critical girl from Lancashire, and it came to a head when the subject was 'Trace the development of Adam and Eve through the first two books of *Paradise Lost*'. Her essay began: 'The development of Adam and Eve through the first two books of *Paradise Lost* may well be represented by means of a graph.'

Mine began: 'All here is sorrow' says Buddha in the first of the Four Noble Truths; but adds – 'because of our desires.' Adam and Eve . . .'

Both of us were gently rebuked: she for clumping literality, and I for high-flown waffle. Gradually I managed to tame the waffle, or at least to support each wild theory in turn with chapter and verse. My excellent tutor, Dorothy Bednarowska, in succeeding terms called in all sorts of swops and favours through-out the University so I got taught by some of the greatest names of the day: Hugo Dyson, Lord David Cecil, John Jones. My first Anglo-Saxon teacher, in the term he died, was Professor C. L. Wrenn himself, and there were lectures by Dame Helen Gardner, Christopher Tolkien, and John Carey. Jewels were cast before me, and for once I knew it and was grateful. During those years, it is fair to say that classic English literature – with its depths of feeling and expression, nobility and humour, passion and truth – replaced most of the elements of religion in my life, and kept my keel level through a late and not always easy adolescence.

If church-going did not figure much during those years, none the less the old matrix, the basic Christian model of the universe, remained like a skeleton inside all my personal and political attitudes. I could not be persuaded about the usefulness of violence against non-combatants, or believe that the shout 'Liberty or death!' could include anyone's death but one's own. I did not want to hang the last king with the entrails of the last priest, or the last capitalist with the last bureaucrat's, because there was 'that of God in everyone'. Above all, I was comforted through the worst doubts about humanity and the darkest, messiest, most confused tangles of love by a belief in what I can only call ultimate justice.

Oxford

I know I felt this, because I found it in my notebook for that last year at Oxford, together with some very bad poems which will never see the light of day. The statement of belief ran: 'Two sure things. Whatever disasters happen. Firstly, it is sure that there will be a reckoning : at the end of all days, all good things will be weighed and given their due, and all bad things recognised and rejected. Secondly, honest love is never wasted.'

I remember writing that last sentence, and why. Things were rather bad at the time, and moreover I had just finished Hardy's *The Woodlanders*, with its magnificent last words, a declaration of abiding love for Giles' memory, spoken by the despised and bereaved Marty South (they left it out of the recent film, wouldn't you know it).

What I had decided, firmly and from deep within, that honest love may be deceived or ridiculed or ignored, but is not wasted. Rejected, yes; mocked, probably; but not, *sub specie aeternitatis*, wasted. In the eye of eternity good things endure and evil does not and that is the beginning and end of it. *All shall be well, and all manner of thing shall be well.*

Whatever it was in my mixed and confused education which gave me that conviction, I am very grateful to it. Without it I might not have made it as far as 1972.

16. Doors of Perception

I was depressive, and I saw things. Looking back with 1990s hindsight and what is now common knowledge about brain chemistry and manic depressive illness, it is perfectly clear that as an undergraduate I could have done with more hard physical exercise, a less eccentric diet, a bit of reassurance, an occasional bout of the kind of pills that were not yet invented, and a few sessions with a sensible psychiatrist.

As it was, our generation had to make do with poetry, politics, black coffee, talking all night, prevailing sexual chaos and ever more available supplies of hash and LSD. Oh, and a pretty terrible college psychiatrist: I was sent to him once after an incident when I walked into the dining-hall in St Anne's and clearly saw a human skull grinning up at me from the middle of the floor just beneath the serving hatch. I screamed. The shrink rather bad-temperedly asked a few set questions about how I got on with my father (pretty well, actually) and then told me about a patient of his who had set fire to himself the week before. I suppose this may have been some sort of well-calculated shock therapy, but at the time I interpreted it as a boast. *I've got far more extreme cases than you, little girl.*

I also felt a kind of protective fury on behalf of more vulnerably suicidal patients than myself – as I have said, I had already known attempted suicides, and our generation was dangerously obsessed with Sylvia Plath. It seemed to me that this man might one day say something like that to someone worse off than me, with disastrous results. This reflection in turn made me realise that I could not be all that crazy if I was fit to worry about crazier patients, so I discharged myself from his lackadaisical care into a private programme of whiskey-drinking (I had generous supplies at knockdown prices from the American PX stores in Celle, near Hamburg, one of the better diplomatic perks)

The problem was that quite apart from ordinary bouts of Byronic teenage depression, I was increasingly prone – without benefit of drugs – to sudden sharp visions and perceptions more normally reported from takers of LSD trips and heavy cannabis smokers. Quite suddenly, in the middle of a prosaic task, either I would black out for a moment and return not knowing how long it had been or where I had got to; or else, more frequently, some material object close by would take on a huge and awesome significance. It could be anything: a fold of skirt, a gleam of sunlight, the shine on an old bicycle saddle, a prospect of Great Tom tower. Usually it pierced me with sudden joy: the object would seem to have a preternatural energy and beauty and significance, so that I glimpsed through the crack in reality the same thing I had seen as a child among mountains or pagodas or fires on the high veld or shafts of light through stained glass. I would see the impossible archetype, the *splendor* of fullest beauty, Wordsworth's 'Light that never was on land or sea', Blake's 'world in a grain of sand'.

That was fine. I supposed that it was pretty common, which it may well be among adolescents. Sometimes, however, in periods of depression the heightened and otherworldly significance of objects was terrible. The skull on the dining-hall floor was the only occasion when anything actually changed shape (it was a cleaner's bucket) but mainly the object stayed the same but became a conduit into a world of purest horror: stench, corruption, illimitable echoing blackness. I would find myself staring in helpless terror at a paperclip or a sliver of green soap. Forces of chaos, anarchy and destruction leered and threatened from innocent sash windows and parked Ford Anglias.

Less often, words could do it: I could be exalted for days by a small clutch of words, but once fled a tutorial in horror because some turn of phrase in a Victorian poem had convinced me that all my brothers were dead. I should say in passing that this form of intense suggestibility to verbal cues is definitely not uncommon in young women: I was very cheered to read in Nancy Mitford's autobiographical *The Pursuit of Love* how Linda would burst into floods of tears even at the sight of a match or a teasing sister's significant glance at a matchbox, all because of a nonsense verse:

> A little houseless match
> It has no house, no thatch
> It lives alone, it makes no moan
> That little houseless match.

And the poet, my own friend the late Sally Purcell, once burst into floods of inconsolable grief when somebody mentioned Lostwithiel and a companion jokingly remarked 'Ah, poor lost Withiel – never come home again!' As in the Mitford story, some cosmic archetypal sorrow used the nonsense as a gateway, and momentarily felled her with its universal grief. It still happens. Think of some of those young faces in the Mall during Diana Week.

Anyway, this tendency to switch suddenly from ordinary life into visions of glory or doom was something which ran strong in me during those years. A useful side- effect was that it kept me off drugs, which were getting easier to find by the day. Oxford's drugs of choice were pot (marijuana) and LSD, the lysergic acid beloved of Dr Timothy Leary and other US prophets of 'tripping'. I was offered both, reasonably often, and urged to sample their ability to make you perceive the world anew. I held back: I had a strong, fearful suspicion that this could be bad news for me. When I was seeing glories I needed no enhancement of them, and when things went the other way the very thought of intensifying the vision was too frightening to entertain.

As it happened, in my final term I discovered this prudence to have been entirely well-judged. Some wicked fool spiked my drink at a party with what must have been LSD: the resulting bout of terrified hallucinations wrecked several other people's evening beside my own. It took days to recover any kind of balance.

I made some tentative sense of all this by way of Salinger again: the saintly visionary Seymour Glass, after all, was in the habit of raking through old ashtrays with a beatific expression, as if he expected 'to find Christ curled up cherubically in the centre'. I was not sure, though, whether he saw the Christ there with his own eyes, as in traditional visions, or whether (more likely) he just got high on the quintessential *Istigkeit* of fag-ends. But it was another book entirely, to which I am eternally grateful, which properly helped me to understand what was going on in my head and to reconcile it with what I already knew of religious experience.

It was casually recommended by a tutor, when the conversation turned to the LSD culture and the swirly 'psychedelic' art and design then flowing from it. This academic gently pointed out to us that nothing is all that new, and that Aldous Huxley, familiar to us from *Brave New World*, had written two essays in the mid-1950s about his experiments with peyotl, the Mexican sacred cactus drug which LSD mimics. The first was *The Doors of Perception*, the second *Heaven and Hell*. The former became a bit of a cult bible for hippies, and indeed it is after that book that the group The Doors named themselves.

When I went down to Blackwell's to flick through the paperback I was drawn to it immediately by his use as superscription of a line I had already drawn comfort from, William Blake's: 'If the doors of perception were cleansed everything would appear to man as it is, infinite.'

Aldous Huxley was the perfect interpreter between old and new perceptions: a literary intellectual with a strong bent for science, a native Christian with a curiosity about Far Eastern mysticism, a civilised historian who did not shrink from the odder vagaries of the human mind, past and present (he also wrote *The*

Devils of Loudun, on which the film about sexual religious hysteria in seventeenth-century France was based). Other accounts of mescalin and LSD trips bored and irritated me: they were sloppy and self-indulgent and as tediously 'oh, wow, like, man' vague as any of my friends got after a few drags at a joint. Huxley, however, is diamond-clear about what went on: he saw no swirling visions or landscapes, nothing remotely like a drama or a parable, just what I had intermittently and momentarily seen: the transformation of real things on the desk into miracles:

> I was not looking now at a flower arrangement, I was seeing what Adam had seen on the morning of his creation – the miracle, moment by moment, of naked existence . . . *Istigkeit* – wasn't that the word Meister Eckhart liked to use? 'Is-ness'. The Being of Platonic philosophy – except that Plato seems to have made the grotesque mistake of separating Being from becoming and identifying it with the mathematical abstraction of the Idea. He could never, poor fellow, have seen a bunch of flowers shining with their own inner light and all but quivering under the pressure of the significance with which they were charged; could never have perceived that what rose and iris and carnation so intensely signified was nothing more, and nothing less, than what they were – a transience that was yet eternal life, a perpetual perishing that was at the same time pure Being, a bundle of minute, unique particulars in which, by some unspeakable and yet self-evident paradox, was to be seen the divine source of all existence.

He looks at books, at tables, at curtains and furniture bursting with a 'sacramental vision of reality'. Folds in his trouser-legs hold the keys to the universe and a bamboo chair-leg is 'St Michael and all angels'. Specific effects of the mescalin – brighter colours, for example – are secondary to this intensified perception of the unity and mystery of all things. The excitement of reading about this was, to me, immense: *I knew what he meant.* I had felt it, in short undrugged bursts of excitement, for most of my life. I had seen it – though I have a poor eye for fine arts – in some of the paintings where Huxley identifies it: in Van Gogh and Vermeer and Rembrandt. I had been taught about the way that the great contemplatives found it, and read about its presence in the Far Eastern religions. Huxley's exposition reassured me, especially about that dewdrop that slips in to the shining sea. I had always, I realised, worried about its loss of identity. In the vision which Huxley analyses and teases out of the mystical experience of history, the dewdrop remains utterly itself, the very essence of dewdropness, while at the same time uniting itself to the shining sea.

It linked back, also, to the struggle in the Salinger stories between the mundane and the eternal. Huxley says:

> From the records of religion and the surviving monuments of poetry and the plastic arts it is plain that at most times and in most places, men have attached more importance to the inscape than to objective existence, have felt that what they saw with their eyes shut possessed a spiritually higher significance than what they saw with their eyes open. The reason? Familiarity breeds contempt.

He sees this as a problem to solve, and regrets the Christian tradition of striving for a perfection that turns its back on 'the world' in which we all have to live. He quotes Lalemant's phrase, from the seventeenth century, 'We should feel wonder for nothing at all in Nature, except only the Incarnation of Christ' and sees that this way lies madness. Zen Buddhists and Taoists, to him as to so many other Western thinkers in the second half of this century, had a better way. Creation's beauty and significance is the Dharma-body of the Buddha: the Godhead itself, or part of it.

Saints' visions, drugtakers' visions, and the visions of madmen are, he sees, close. And they can all go bad. Schizophrenics have a grey wilderness to live in, and a hell too, as well as the occasional vision of heaven, and so do we all. His own 'trip' included panic:

Confronted by a chair which looked like the Last Judgement – or, to be more accurate, by a Last Judgement which after a long time and with considerable difficulty I recognised as a chair – I found myself all at once on the brink of panic. This, I suddenly felt, was going too far. Too far, even though the going was into intenser beauty, deeper significance . . . Following Boehme and William Law, we may say that, by unregenerate souls, the divine Light at its full blaze can be apprehended only as a burning, purgatorial fire.

Full circle: back to the dwarfs in Narnia, shrinking back in horror from the good food they are given because all they can smell is stinking stable-litter. I was also much struck by Huxley's evidence that throughout art and visionary experience and the accounts of schizophrenic agonies, Hell has been associated with 'pressure and constriction . . . a body that seems to grow progressively more dense, more tightly packed . . . Dante's sinners are buried in mud, shut up in the trunks of trees, frozen solid in blocks of ice, crushed beneath stones'. All to do with the liver, apparently, and chemically explicable; which was satisfying to know, since ever since the childhood hepatitis, every fever I had had involved a curious phase when the sheets and bedding seem impossibly thick and heavy, my fingers vast as salamis, my tongue and lips and eyelids inches thick, my body dense.

Not that a chemical explanation – either for perceptions of heaven or hell – in any way devalued the experience itself. I was as happy as Huxley was to brush aside those whose philosophy accepts only the 'spiritual'.

God, they will insist, is a spirit and is to be worshipped in spirit. Therefore an experience which is chemically conditioned cannot be an experience of the divine. But, in one way or another, *all* our experiences are chemically conditioned, and if we imagine that some of them are purely 'spiritual', or 'intellectual' or 'aesthetic', it is merely because we have never troubled to investigate the internal chemical environment at the moment of their occurrence.

Like Huxley himself, I saw unity in the different levels of transcendent experience, and accepted that humanity would always need what he calls these Doors in the Wall, so they were not to be feared but understood and used. Alcohol, he observed, can be a door; so can dope of various kinds. He wishes that Christianity were more tolerant of chemical aids to meditation, to stimulate the urge to worship and bring it to the assistance of the Will. For only in some people will 'the candle of vision' ever burn spontaneously.

In the second essay, *Heaven and Hell*, he tracks some of the drugless ways in which religions have tried to stimulate transcendental awareness and visit 'the antipodes of the mind'. There is sensory deprivation, as in hermit caverns (or, today, isolation tanks). There is fasting, and self-flagellation, bringing on surges of adrenalin and histamine; there are fireworks and stained glass, evoking the bright colours seen by visionaries and mescalin trippers: jewels and gilding in religious art, frescoes and reliquaries and mosaics; fireworks and pageantry and the fans and curlicues that surround both Popes and Chinese emperors. The Reformation frowned on these, preferring to give supremacy to the printed word; but other routes to mental release, a release from rationality, endured. The mild carbon dioxide poisoning brought on by yogic breathing or continuous chanting or singing, for one: and had I not felt this, in the convent chapel at dusk singing long, long lines of plainsong? *Lumen ad revelationem Gentium . . .*

'It is a matter of historical record', writes Huxley, dry and elegant and serious, 'that most contemplatives worked systematically to modify their body chemistry, with a view to creating the internal conditions favourable to spiritual insight.' He sees this as a disabling of the 'cerebral reducing valve' which normally prevents us, practical animals, from allowing the visionary universe to flood in.

When they were not starving themselves into low blood sugar and a vitamin deficiency, or beating themselves into intoxication by histamine, adrenalin and decomposed protein, they were cultivating insomnia and praying for long periods in uncomfortable positions, in order to create the psycho-physical symptoms of stress. In the intervals they sang interminable psalms, thus increasing the amount of carbon dioxide in the lungs and the blood-stream, or, if they were Orientals, they did breathing exercises to accomplish the same purpose.

Huxley could have concluded, as atheist cynics do, that all these religious people down the ages were kidding themselves, and that nothing exists out there beyond the puddles of chemicals in our brains. He could have decided with the hippies and the ravers that we might as well use the drugs and the disco-lights for pure recreation: tune in, turn on, drop out, as we said in 1970.

He did not: the conviction I drew from the book was that the wonders of visionary experience are as real as the earthly Antipodes and that the drugs or practices which have the power briefly to clear the doors of perception are only a useful tool on a far longer path to enlightenment. For me, these clear, steady essays were both revelation and comfort. They made some sense of the cracks that so often appeared in the stage-set of reality and left me free to believe or not, but with less terror. Huxley explained Teresa of Avila and the Guru Maharaji and *son et lumière* and why so many of my friends – deprived of a heavy-duty religious education full of plainsong and fasting before Mass – spent earnest hours cross-legged chanting '*Hare Krishna*'. He not only staunched my own panic at the attacks of sudden significance which assaulted me, but helped me to understand and respect Blake, and Coleridge, and Wordsworth, whose reality very often cracked into clouds of glory (I still see his best sonnet 'The world is too much with us', as a lament for the efficiency of the 'cerebral reducing valve' of modernity, which stops us seeing eternity on the shore).

Doors of Perception

Even as I write a new set of scientists in Pennsylvania has wired up some monks and nuns of various sects to map what goes on in their brains; first results suggest that they got technically a bit farther than Aldous Huxley but philosophically, they are at the same spot exactly. For even if measurable aberrations of the brain cause men and women to see God, you can argue that God made the brain that way for this very purpose. Anyway, Huxley's little book continues, to this day, to ensure that no manifestation whatsoever of the New Age – not crystals, not joss-sticks, not isolation tanks – has the power to surprise me. It puts the mirror-balls and Barnum showmanship of the Nine o'Clock Service and the 'Planetary Mass' into a historic frame of reference. It puts visions in their place, which is not above the smoke and fret of ordinary endeavours to do practical good, but alongside them.

That I did learn at Oxford. It only took the briefest contemplation of hippie patriarchs being foul to their concubines, or constant pot-smokers too comatose to care about the liveliness of politics, to make it obvious that visions and perceptions, however fine, will never be enough.

17. Work

The last university year was spent in a shared house by the Oxford canal, and when the summer term ended I volunteered to stay on and pack up the tenancy while I waited for my *viva voce* exam. I lived on the £100 my tutor, Dorothy Bednarowska, paid me to catalogue her library ('Don't think of getting work in some café, my dear, I wouldn't *trust* you as a waitress'). So happy hours were spent browsing and fiddling in the intoxicating scent of old books, occasionally uttering a plaintive cry of 'Do you want Machiavelli classifying as a Foreigner or an Influence?'

For love I worked on the new-fledged BBC Radio Oxford, compiling a five-minute slot called *Tourist Trap*, instituted because the Programme Organiser had a weird theory that American visitors would all tune in, by habit, to the nearest bit of FM. With a partner, William Horsley (who later became an alarmingly eminent Far East correspondent – would that I had treated him with more respect) I zapped around the city recording church bells, haunting museums, combing James Morris's *Oxford* for good curiosities, pestering vicars and curators to do something involving sound effects, and getting overexcited about such small historical anecdotes as the spread of the Oxford Ragwort. The naturalist Bobart brought the yellow plant home from Sicily as a rarity in (I think) the eighteenth century, and put it in the Botanical Gardens. It climbed the wall, nipped along the verges, found the first railway cutting sometime in the 1850s or so and was thereafter spread all across the nation, a noxious weed, its seeds floating happily on the warm huff-huff of the Great Western Railway's pistons.

For some reason I loved to know this, much as I had wasted hours in my Finals term trying to trace the legend of the Barnacle Goose through the Bodleian's resources. Barnacle Goose: an Arctic migrant, never seen nesting in British waters and therefore suspected for centuries of having grown from the very heart of the sea, hatching from the feathery innards of a goose-barnacle under the bow of ships at sea. I found poems and pictures and references and a splendid Papal instruction that the faithful must not, repeat not, classify this bird as a fish and therefore feel free to eat it in Lent.

The radio work suited me well: I was in a mood to collect reverberant trivia, for I was at the time in no very good state emotionally. Evidence of the world's wideness and diversity and long endurance was a counterweight to private, short-term confusion. T. H. White's Merlyn, in another cult book of the time *The Sword in the Stone*, had offered the only clue to finding life tolerable: I wrote the passage out and it has remained a favourite for years:

The best thing for being sad is to learn something. That is the only thing that never fails. You may grow old and trembling in your anatomies, you may lie awake at night listening to the disorder of your veins, you may miss your only love, you may see the world about you devastated by evil lunatics, or know your honour trampled in the sewers of baser minds.

There is only one thing for it then – to learn. Learn why the world wags and what wags it. That is the only thing which the mind can never exhaust, never alienate, never be tortured by, never fear or distrust and never dream of regretting. Look at what a lot of things there are to learn . . . astronomy in a lifetime, natural history in three, literature in six. And then, after you have exhausted a milliard lifetimes in biology and medicine and theo-criticism and geography and history and economics – why, you can start to make a cartwheel out of the appropriate wood, or spend fifty years learning to begin to learn to beat your adversary and fencing. After that you can start on mathematics, until it is time to learn to plough.

The research for *Tourist Trap* provided the comfort of learning things, topped by the equal comfort of passing them on *con brio* to presumably interested fellow-creatures. It set the final seal on my relationship with Oxford. Near the end of that month of summer limbo, I was buying a cup of coffee in the High Street with my gown draped over my arm. I had just come from the viva in which the examiners – to my shock and shattered delight – had told me that I had a First. I had not expected this after a year of emotional turmoil and ragged concentration, and it was all the sweeter because I knew that in several of my papers I had opposed prevailing critical fashion and taken my own line, with what had felt like a certain kamikaze eloquence. Therefore the message that the examiners seemed to be giving me was not the shallow pleasure of 'Aren't you clever?' but the far deeper, more necessary one of 'Yes, your views and beliefs are worth considering. Your thoughts are valid.'

These days it is fashionable to make all students, at all levels above infancy, believe from the outset that their views are valid. This was not so in 1971; one spent a lot of time feeling shifty and stupid, especially if female. Much of that long-held sense of 'secondariness' passed away from me on that hot Oxford day.

Anyway, as I queued for my coffee on the way home a pair of middle-aged American tourists said to me 'Hey – d' you belong ta this place?' and I said 'Yes. I do. Totally.'

I meant it, and realised that until this moment I had never particularly belonged anywhere. To cap this most glorious of days the Americans were sufficiently satisfied of my authenticity to pay me £25 – a princely sum – to lead them on a tour of central Oxford and tell them all the quirky stories I had picked up doing the radio programme. I belonged: by the end of that dusty shimmering afternoon I was transcendently in love with the city and the university, with the past and the future, the pleasant Americans and the entire human race. I told them the ragwort story and picked them a flower from a wall in New College Lane. The wife pressed it to her heart and said: 'Oxford ragwort – from the ancient walls of Noo College. I shall keep it always.'

I picked a clump of the stinking stuff myself, and wore it behind my ear for the rest of the day.

And that was it. Having found how to belong, I went away. On my last day in the hot city our neighbour Michael Black, a monumental sculptor in every sense of the word, rowed me and my trunk to the railway station in his double-sculling skiff and gravely saw me off. I had sold my scholar's gown and my Shorter Oxford Dictionary to get the fare to Ireland for a final summer behind the bar. Altogether, it was one of those rare moments in life when a rite of passage feels like one: properly ceremonial and aesthetically complete.

In the autumn, after a spell as temporary telex operator in the Gordon's Gin HQ in Islington, cheerfully dispatching incorrect orders for Pimms to the Stranraer Cash and Carry, I took up my first official job and became a BBC studio manager trainee. It was a technical job in the main, and there had been some suggestion that I was the kind of student who ought to apply instead for a News traineeship. I did not want to. For one thing the News trainees spent a lot of time in television, and I was in love with radio. I liked its ease and immediacy and its total dependence on the word and the nuances and emotions of the voice. For another, I hungered to learn something practical and technical after the cerebral years; to be a kind of barmaid again, pulling faders instead of pumps and optics, and looking after producers and broadcasters instead of drinkers. I wanted to be in a team. On the first day of our course, we were taught to 'line up' tape machines and issued with screwdrivers, and a tough Cockney engineering instructor said: 'Get this straight – you may all have first class degrees in higher intellectual god-knows-what, but if I ever catch you on duty without your screwdriver, God help you.'

That was supposed to frighten us and take us down a peg, but it made me very happy. I was sick to the back teeth of intellectuals (for reasons too teeth-grindingly personal to go into) and had temporarily discarded most other reading in favour of Nevil Shute books. These – still great favourites – are generally about practical, straightforward, good-hearted people with smears of oil on their cheeks, maintaining aeroplanes and motorboats for the benefit of humanity. They are willing, but not eager, to give up their lives for others' benefit, they conduct their love affairs with simple honesty and – in *Round the Bend* – depart into a mystical, Zen-cum-Benedictine sense that work well done is the truest form of prayer. I kept my screwdriver and tape editing kit with me even off duty, as a talisman. I wanted to be practical, and make things work, to put jackplugs in the right hole and catch the Greenwich Time Signal neatly in the upturned cup of the round black fader. I wanted to help programmes to go out on time and to earn my place in an ordered universe. There had been too much disorder and fey impracticality, that past year. The tight timing and careful order of broadcasting, the transmitter-breaks and network junctions and precise razor-blade editing of the BBC suited me wonderfully. *Laborare est orare*. To this day I am obscurely uplifted, even brought to a momentary sniff of tears, by the sight of a studio jackfield.

After six months' training I opted to work at Bush House, home of the BBC World Service and its galaxy of foreign language services. Things in private life were still dark grey, and I lived in fairly cheerless bedsitters; so there was immense comfort in belonging to the big antheap on the Strand which never closed day or night, and where the shift system ensured that you could walk in to the Studio Managers' common room at any time of night and find somebody to lend you your taxi fare home.

The 'sections', the foreign language broadcasters, were a delight; over the months of working on their transmissions day and night one came to feel part of a global village, pausing to chat with Thais and Bulgarians, Vietnamese and Russians and soulful dark-eyed Latin American lechers whose flowery compliments followed us girls through our night shifts with a not unpleasant thrill of menace ('Any more of that, Julio, and I'll play your bloody signature tune back to front'). The canteen food was infinitely better at Bush House too: they would never have got away with serving what other canteens called 'curry' or 'paella' to real Indians and real Spaniards.

The shifts were strange and gruelling: one day 10 till 6, the next 12 till 8, the next 2 till 10, and so on until you reached a full night-shift, a few days off and a new beginning. At intervals there was a fortnight of float-shifts when you might be called in any time. This effectively dislocated any social life, virtually abolished weekends, and confused everybody's sleep patterns. I took to seeing cracks in the universe again, and on one occasion a ghost walked into a studio behind me at 3 a.m., with a creak and hiss of the pneumatic door mechanism. I assumed it was the Duty chief, but when it put its hands on my shoulders and said 'You OK?', I turned round and nobody was there. It was not particularly worrying. I told a colleague about it at my break, and he said that he had once hallucinated a large tabby cat lying across the controls in front of him, and felt its fur tickling his fingers when he tried to open a fader to play the *English by Radio* signature tune. That was on a night shift, too.

As a studio manager you served all the main cultures of the world: snatches of music, of prayer, of wisdom, of news, of belief, all rippled past your busy fingers and alert ears. For me, faint childhood echoes were forever being stirred. The Koran wailed through the dawn Arabic transmission, deep-throated Orthodox monks sang the creed from glistening black 78 rpm records for the Greeks, 'Imperial Echoes' crashed triumphantly from the Radio Newsreel record, and the Japanese news magazine was introduced (inscrutably) with a smooth orchestral rendering of the sea song 'Admiral Benbow'. Sometimes, inexplicably early for his transmission, some strong-faced exile from the Iron Curtain bloc would sit down and talk a little about the enslavement of his country and their dreams of freedom from the Soviet yoke. Once a friend, fresh from voluntary work in a troubled zone of Burundi, came to supper with me in the canteen and when I pointed out to her the newsreaders whose voices she had heard out in the Bush, she almost cried. 'They were the only voices we could trust, anywhere.'

Sometimes, alone in a studio waiting for a broadcaster to sprint in late with script in hand, I would open the fader which gave, to each live desk, a direct feed of the BBC microphone inside the tower of Big Ben. If you wound up all the levels on the desk as far as they would go, you could clearly hear the distant roar of London traffic on Westminster Bridge, and sometimes a bird singing. It was at once immensely romantic and prosaically reassuring. I liked the sense of being in a city, in a web of humanity, with fuggy warmth and casual nourishing comradeship. I liked getting the No. 11 bus home to Pimlico in the early morning after a night shift, and joshing with the conductor (we Bush girls always knew what we looked like: on good days bus conductors mistook us for tarts on the way home, on bad days for office cleaners).

If my most intensely personal relationships were failing disastrously, I could at least replace them with a million less personal ones. *That of God in every one.* Only once, sleepless and crazy at the last twist of the knife in the bad affair, did I stand at the eighth-floor windows in the small hours and briefly consider kicking them in and stepping out. What held me back was not ethics or religion nor even a sense of family (families are very shadowy when you are twenty-two and far from home). It was simply the thought of some poor honest devil of a commissionaire or policeman having to scrape me up, and then go home to his own family and his own troubles. Come to think of it, perhaps it was religious after all. I turned my back on the window, commandeered an empty studio, and lay on the floor for a bit playing Cat Stevens's 'Wild World' very loud.

By and large though, Bush was a good time. I almost belonged;

to this day, if I scuttle into a BBC studio and find one of my old shift running the desk, we greet one another with little jumps and squeaks of pleasure. But the following year I applied for a job back on Radio Oxford, and once again plunged into affection and curiosity about a city and community. For the radio and for the beginnings of my written journalism I climbed up cranes and down sewers, travelled on racing-pigeon lorries to release swirls of dusty birds in the dawn on a cliff-top, learnt about speedway and greyhounds and city councils and chimney-sweeping and blanket-weaving and stonemasonry: anything practical and craftsmanlike. Sometimes I played record requests '*for Dottie and Edna and Jim and Sean and all the kids especially Kimmie, who's just had a birthday, yay Kimmie, double figures! – oh, and everyone down at the Queens', and Moll and Dolly and Big Mal and of course Sinatra the cat*'. It made me feel temporarily part of a huge, phantom extended family all across the two counties. Sometimes there was evidence that they felt the same way, for local radio audiences are warm and like their mini-celebrities; I got invited to open the annual show of the Morris Motors Athletic and Social Club Cage Birds Section, or a fairground modellers competition, and felt honoured to be asked. I particularly liked working at Christmas, waking up the transmitter on my own at dawn, playing church bells off a tape and wishing well to anybody who happened to be alone enough to need a local radio station on Christmas morning.

And so it went on: growing up, growing happier, taking good turnings and bad ones, marrying, having children, rusticating, being a working mother and all the rest of it. This is not a book about a career, but about growing up; so the narrative, I think, should more or less stop right here. The last part of this book will become far more general, far more objective. Which feels right, because quite frankly, even in an age of non-stop therapy for all it befits adults to be more objective and less obsessed with their own development than adolescents and children. It is a quarter of a century now since I began, tentatively, to consider myself more or less grown-up; of course there are changes and miniature conversions, and always will be, but by the time you are twenty-five the important foundations of thought and belief are laid down. Their outlines will show through every action until death; and, no doubt, beyond it.

So the rest can go unchronicled for the moment. There is no space here – nor would it be kind or decorous – to give a blow-by-blow account of a media career, still less of marriage and childbearing. This is no time to chart the slow comfortable wearing-down of those sharp early passions into the pragmatic dogged kindnesses of family life and the jerky, uneven slog of earning a freelance living. It is far more fun, anyway, to express these things in novels.

But I will record one things which surfaced in mid-career, and connected me straight back to this brooding religious youth. Its enduring result is that I do not allow myself enmity. Ever.

The media world is a curious one: on the one hand it can be an extraordinarily sentimental, marshmallow environment of cooingly supportive networks and the kind of mutual admiration for which the best epithet is the *Private Eye* term 'luvvie'. On the other hand, it is shot through with jagged streaks of enmity and sourness and spite. X mocks Y's book or takes issue with Z's column; reputations are inflated and then cruelly knifed; jobs are offered and un-offered, poached and undermined. Individuals from inside and outside the trade are – with consummate skill and elegance – held up to public ridicule and exposure; if they are within the trade they are expected either to put up with it because 'that's the game', or else to maintain long-term committed feuds for the entertainment of everybody else.

I have been inside all this: I think that almost everyone in the business has been. I have mocked and been mocked, and been tempted to neurotic journalists' rage against any number of assorted bastards, bitches, ignorant creeps, malevolent interviewers, snide reviewers, treacherous editors, etc. I have traded insults, scored points, brooded obsessively on rivals and coveted my neighbour's byline. This mindset reached a peak at one stage, a difficult career juncture about ten years back; although I dare say the seething devil within me was efficiently hidden beneath the usual façade of lovable mid-market jollity

But at a definite point, and a definitely religious moment (on the bowsprit of the Brixham sailing trawler *Lorne Leader* just off Ardnamurchan Point, if you must know) I gave it all up. No more enmities, no more resentment: all men and women are my brothers and sisters.

It dawned on me that if the starry vision of the cosmos that formed around me in my youth means anything at all, it means not only that I have a political duty to humanity at large, but that it is wrong ever to engage with any human being on other than a fully human level. Nobody is a caricature or a write-off or a waste of space. I am not perfect, nor holy, nor particularly nice; but I have more or less tried since that moment to accept that principle. Even when it makes me feel weak and stupid.

So if I mock or caricature you in print over some public matter, and you ring me up to berate me, I will not hide. I will talk, even on occasion apologise. *Per contra*, if you are horrible to me, or about me, and it hurts, I will not nurse a grudge. It may take some energy to stifle it, but I shall. If you write me mad hate letters, a worryingly popular amusement among consumers of British journalism, I will try to think mildly of you. If you think this is a god-awful book and review it with such deadly skill that I burst into tears over the Sunday papers, I shall forgive you.

I have to, out of sheer self-interest. There is no choice. Because of the essential harmony of all creation my relationship with everything else – from the ocean sunset to my own children – would be damaged and diminished by any smear of malice towards anyone. If you burgle my house or harm my family, I will seek justice as keenly as anybody, but I will also fight tooth and nail against any impulse to hate you. And if I succeed, that will be a direct legacy of every proper piece of Christianity that I ever encountered during the first twenty years of life. *Blessed are the meek;* but oh, it takes a lot of strength to be meek.

So much for autobiography. The only other important thing which happened to me in early adulthood is that I began to go to sea on small yachts, a small-ad crew for anybody who would have me. This fulfilled an unformed desire which had nagged me for most of my life, ever since the long liner journeys of childhood and 'They that go down to the sea in ships'.

But I have written enough about the sea elsewhere, and it is such an embarrassingly obvious metaphor for endeavour and eternity and a quest into the unknown that it is hardly worth going into. Suffice to say that the sea cured, for years, my tendency to depression. Rolling down the trade wind in mid-Atlantic, with the belt of Orion glittering ahead, high between the spreaders, or watching a brass cabin lamp swinging on a wild night off Barra lighthouse, it is hard to be depressed. Scared, yes; cold and wet and tired and doubtful; but always elated, always awed, always knowing that the next landfall is worth staying afloat for. As usual, although I was trying to kick the habit, a tag of poetry would surface at the beginning of even the simplest journey to Cherbourg or Calais. Nearly always it was Louis MacNeice: 'Our end is Life. Put out to sea'.

18. The Rock and the Rubble

I am walking along the main street in Glastonbury, microphone in hand, trailed by the producer Colin Parks. It is a millennium project: we are engaged on the grandiose task of tracing the footprints of Christianity on every aspect of British culture over the last thousand years. Colin is a man of encyclopaedic reading and religious curiosity, a temporary escapee from the Radio Newsroom who has hurled himself into the project with a force and rigour which both alarms and inspires the other producer and myself. It alarms us because there is no way that we can use a quarter of his research or taped interviews in six forty-five-minute programmes. It inspires us because we are learning so much, making such unexpected connections, and diving into a shared cultural and emotional history.

We have called it *Mysterious Ways*, although originally its title was the one which I have annexed for this book, *Holy Smoke*. The image which inspired us was of a thousand years of incense still twisting and curling around our national psyche, potent but unacknowledged, both enriching and fuddling. If there had been no Christianity everything about Britain (and much about the world) would be unrecognisably different. We have done our share of peering at rood-screens, but the most important footprints are the invisible ones. The 28,487 parish churches and a pride of cathedrals are the least of it.

Quartering the nation, we dug out eminences and mavericks, historians and holinesses, two cardinals, the Archbishop of

173

Canterbury and Tony Benn. We unravelled legacies beyond our wildest hopes, as weird, unexpected strands of continuity over ten centuries emerged in politics, law, arts, science, education, sex, literature, music. We investigated Speaker's Prayers at the House of Commons, the malodorous affair of the rancid Coronation Oil, and the influence of Moses' tablets on the development of British compensation law. We found Bishop Odo killing with a blunt mace in the eleventh century because bishops may not shed blood, and Bishop Winnington Ingram in 1915 urging soldiers to kill 'good Germans as well as bad'. We drew direct lines from medieval church carvings of bawdy gossips to Vera Duckworth of *Coronation Street*, from Charles Wesley's lyrical clarity to Britpop, from monastic choirs to party politics.

We acknowledged the Christian gift to sanitation, literacy, station architecture, P. D. James and P. G. Wodehouse, and the harm it sometimes did to science, social justice and sexuality. We saw it operate in one place as social cement, in another as social gelignite. We grew damp-eyed over the discovery in an Australian bookshop of a newspaper cutting about the persecution of the Nonconformist scientist Priestley, a fragment of anger folded, saved, and carried defiantly to a new life two hundred years ago by some transported dissenter.

It was a heady journey, half footslogging and half intense reading, and we each came to odd private conclusions. One of my pet theories was that the British disease of romantic nostalgia, all the way to John Major's bicycling old maids, can be laid squarely at the door of the Reformation: a traumatic moment when landscape, loyalties and rituals were rudely kicked to pieces and the nation never got over it. We all exulted in the frequent moments of throwback, when the curl of the old incense touched the most materialistic corners of the modern age. We relished the period in the 1960s when the history of seventeenth-century Scottish Covenanters directly caused Lord Beaverbrook to run a newspaper campaign in the *Scottish Daily Express* railing against the threat of the 'piskies' invading the Scottish church with bishops. His editor Ian McColl, elderly now but still fervent, told us with piping, righteous indignation, how the Beaver dictated down the telephone from Canada the headline JEHOVAH HAS TRIUMPHED, THE PEOPLE ARE SET FREE!

We reviewed a host of clergymen: bone-idle and corrupt, holy and visionary; there were worldlings and eccentrics and plotters and knaves and saints and doughty pragmatists like the Revd Charles Kingsley who used to ride the lanes with huge stone bottles of antiseptic mouthwash on his saddle forcing the parishioners to gargle.

Finally, just as we were carving the vast unwieldy programmes into shape, the mourning for Diana, Princess of Wales proved three of our points before our very eyes. First, that pre-Reformation instincts for devotion never actually went away; second, that huge emotions still require huge cathedrals; and third, that the things we do in them – down to thumping a rock piano and loudly applauding an angry Earl – are always up for change. As medieval shrines of flowers built themselves overnight down the Mall, we saw how the power of past instinct can surge back any time and knock the present off its feet.

Power, indeed, was the running theme: emotional power wielded by the religion which, for good and ill, long held the only keys to transcendence, ritual, inspiration and consolation. To me it was a particularly enlightening journey, as during it I began to trace the parallel workings of that emotional power in my own life, from the pre-Reformation glow of childhood to the more sparse, dour, enduring philosophies which came to be needed later. The same kind of process has befallen the culture at large: our very language is impossible to imagine without the prayer-book heritage: in the programme entitled *Ceremonies* it became apparent how liturgy, which affected me so powerfully from earliest years, has affected all European culture in parallel. The outward spread of religious mannerisms into every kind of art is easy enough to explain: there is an intensity, a richness and flying beauty of metaphor and musical rhythm which writers, composers and architects alike seem to find only when trying to express the unseen and illimitable. Why else does Parliament echo a Gothic cathedral, or every pop composer feel himself incomplete before he has attempted a Requiem?

Christian footprints? By the end we had mapped craters, mountains, slag-heaps, rivers, roads, whole tracts of landscape still ineradicably marked by something which most people would claim that they hardly believe.

And today, in Glastonbury High Street, we are somewhere near the end of that process, trying to tackle the most elusive inheritance of all: individual belief. The reason for being here is to try and explore the significance of the New Age cults, and how they both relate to the Christian inheritance and threaten it. In front of us is the scatty chaos of late twentieth-century mix-'n-match belief, from Feng Shui furniture arranging to confident announcements of the return of King Arthur aboard the Hale-Bopp comet. I walk up the street. Here is *Man, Myth and Magic*, where Native American feathers lie next to a Buddha with a crystal in its fist; here, beyond the dry-cleaners, is a bookshop full of titles like *The Laying on of Stones*, *Celtic Tree Oracles*, *The Arthurian Tarot* and *Angels Today*.

I wander into the Maitreya Dharma Centre, where chimes tinkle incessantly and smiling Phil the manager tinkles too: 'It's a synthesis between all those different religions laid down through centuries . . . our founder is the Incarnate Buddha of our time . . . magnetic therapy, aligning the etheric body's energetic system . . . pure laboratory-grown quartz crystal with this copper coil in a right-hand spin which generates what in physics is called the Schumann wave . . .' Still they can't quite do without the Christian heritage: being near Glastonbury Abbey, he says, is an important part of the 'synthesis' because of Joseph of Arimathea coming there after the Crucifixion. But on the way out I note that Krishna, Gautama, Adam, Jesus, White Eagle, Sananda and King Arthur are all on the same list, in that order, and are all deemed to be the same chap as this Maitreya. Up the road in the Abbey ruins the curator, an amiably peppery ex-officer, talks about the day when he woke up to find a pyramid of copper piping in the Lady-Chapel, and how difficult it was as a Christian and a handyman to resist the temptation to keep the piping rather than return it.

Not everybody worries about the lunatic fringe, and not every Christian is insecure enough to bother condemning it A few miles away at Downside, Dom Aelred Watkin, the modern-day titular Abbot and great scholar of medieval monasticism relates, with snuffling giggles, how he persuaded the Church authorities to accept money from rich American spiritualists to help with the excavation.

'These ladies were very keen on Automatic Writing, and their spooks would tell them "Dig ye down here and ye shall find ye ruins." Well, dear me, you can't dig anywhere in Glastonbury without finding ruins, so the spooks were always right! But I think I was right to take their money, don't you? We needed it for the excavation.'

Now, though, at the gates of the exposed and numinous ruins, ever more spooky barbarians gather. Beyond the Gothic Image café and the shop full of black candles and the healing centre and someone selling 'holy rose-petal essence' we find more of the earnest New Agers, seeking this and that and all very disgruntled with the idea of what C. S. Lewis called Mere Christianity. It lacked glamour.

'I was taught other people's thoughts and they didn't hold water and my understanding of the new age process is about letting go of beliefs taught from outside so you can find a clean space inside . . .'

'As I change, my beliefs change. Beliefs are a limiting factor, they stop you from moving on. They keep people disempowered from finding their true self . . . if something's dry, I drop it.'

'I just sort of use beliefs as a structure then when I outgrow that structure I use something else. I'm like, into the Grail just now, but also Buddha.'

None of them see any problem in treating belief as a private therapy, a smart new cladding for their thought, a spiritual entertainment to be changed as effortlessly as slotting in a new video. Not 'Firmly I Believe and Truly', and certainly not 'Faith of Our Fathers'. Subjective feeling is supreme. Near a poster for chi-sonics and a tantric self-healing group and a Goddess Workshop a dreamy, slow-moving man says 'We are just bundles of energy. Vibrating. Crystals are spiritual magnifying glasses, reflecting back the aspects of ourselves that we need.' G. K. Chesterton was right: if a society stops believing in religion, it doesn't believe in nothing, but in *everything*.

How did we get here? Is it full circle, back to medievalism? We ask the eminent historian Eamon Duffy whether – as some austere Protestants claim – the cacophony of superstition at modern Glastonbury is a genuine parallel to the gaudy corrupt pre-Reformation world which was swept away on the indignation of reformers five hundred years ago?

No, he says, not at all: this is different. Before the Reformation, quaint though some of the superstitions might be, there was a genuine coherence in them. All spiritual power flowed from the one God, the Incarnation, the Crucifix and the Mass. High and low beliefs were held together, so that you could draw a straight line from St Thomas Aquinas to the blessing of ploughs, from the most daring speculations about the nature of God to prayers to St Anthony for the tantony-pig, the runt of the litter. Pagan superstitions were rolled up in religious practice, as at Christmas and Easter, but they were still corralled within the disciplined coherence of Christian theology: God is one, omnipotent, omniscient, omnipresent; He gave us free will and we abused it; His son took on humanity in order to redeem all wickedness; He promises eternal life and joy to those who accept that redemption and love Him and their neighbour.

Soaked in Christian history, with the tinkling of the New Agers still in my ears, I invent a metaphor for what has happened to Belief.

I see it before the Reformation as one great solid rock: massive, sheltering, immobile; a bit crumbly round the edges, perhaps, a bit encrusted with lichen and strange life-forms, and prone to release showers of woodlice and pale nasty creatures when you try to move it on. Some of the nastier woodlice even get to be Borgia Popes. But all the same, it is one big rock, and upon it can be built a church.

Then come the reformers: austere Wycliffes and Luthers, disgusted at the lichen and the woodlice. They split the rock with one great blow. Others follow them, sculptors of religion, striking it into still more pieces; but still each remains recognisable as a chip off the old Christian block.

But the twentieth century comes, and just as the inhabitants of all these variously-shaped lumps of belief are thinking about moving back together, cementing themselves with ecumenism and rejoicing in their common Christ, there is a flurry of new blows. There is war, industrial revolution, material prosperity, unimaginably fast travel, instant communication, and a sudden heady influx of world beliefs and world drugs. The fractured rock is suddenly pulverised into far smaller pieces, until there seems to be nothing but rubble and whirling, choking dust: instead of the great Rock a million small incoherent beliefs: blue plastic pyramids, spirit writing, crystals, copper wire, drugs, all of them fit only to be peddled to people who know they need something invisible in their lives, but not what.

It is not a perfect metaphor. The rock, churchmen say, is still there, just hidden by the clouds of dust and seeming to lie up too steep and hard a path for soft modern sensibilities. Other church-men have gone out to meet the New Agers on their own terms, offering showy hysterical services with mirror-balls and rock music, or charismatic outbreaks of tongues, or instant 'healing' before an audience of thousands in return for emotional public declarations of conversion.

But all have to admit what any of us can see: that the last quarter of the twentieth century has seen a sharper decline in Christianity, both devotional and cultural, than any moment in the millennium. In the early 1970s, on Radio Oxford, I was shocked to visit a school where seven-year-olds – Anglo-Saxon by parentage – did not know the figures in a picture of the

Christmas crib ('Whosat lady with the donkey?'). Today it is a commonplace for adults not to know what Easter celebrates, or the name of 'the little man' on their ornamental crucifix, or who was the Madonna before Madonna was.

In a sense, this matters less than the situation of children who are dutifully taught comparative religion at school but never introduced personally to the concept of sacredness. Bright multicultural chatter or the kind of RE which vaguely equates Jesus with Nelson Mandela is not much help to children who have never been taught to 'be still, then, and know that I am God'.

This was brought home to me in 1993 when there was a particularly silly little row in the press over a school in Lewisham which was alleged to have dropped its Nativity play under the pressure of multicultural guidelines about giving equal precedence to all religious festivals. It transpired that the guideline was not intended to be taken so literally, and they got the tea-towels on the children's heads after all. But after a couple of days irritable brooding on the coverage of this, I worked out what it was that was riling me. It was because, from their statements, both sides in the debate on religious multiculturalism seemed to show an equal ignorance, if not contempt, for the actual significance of the symbols they bandied about.

In the tea-towel Nativity play faction we had the harmless but fatuous sentimentality of the kind of adult who never goes near a church or utters a Christian sentiment from one year's end to another, but regards it as a right to sniffle nostalgically at the sight of children singing 'lickel donkey' and brandishing toy lambs at Christmas. Meanwhile in the multiculturally PC faction we had earnest people who talk of an 'understanding of each other's religions and cultures' as if the two were precisely the same, and who pat themselves on the back for knowing when Diwali and Eid are; yet most of them would be hideously embarrassed at the idea that there might actually *be* a real Deity. Religion, to them, is not an imperative or a vocation or a revelation of joy which gives the universe meaning. It is on the same level as cookery or costume or any other manifestation of 'ethnicity'.

Of course there is no harm in having a Nativity play if you are not a true believer; the symbols belong to us all, and canny fishers of souls know that conversions can happen at such moments, just as they do at funerals, when what you have thought was empty traditionalism suddenly and blessedly fills with real, private meaning for some onlookers. And of course it is seemly for even the most harassed and agnostic playleaders to show decent reverence for the symbols while the play is being put on; you do not drop the infant Jesus doll on its head or swear at it.

But if by chance the Nativity play is taught and directed by believing adults, with a real sense of sacredness and awe and the significance of religious tradition, then the paradox is that those adults are actually teaching their charges far more about the essence of Hinduism, Islam and the rest than about Christianity. Unless his mentors are very bigoted indeed, a child who has been taught to respect one religion as true is far less likely to despise another. Over the *Satanic Verses* affair I met some genuinely upset Muslim women who actually wept as they spoke to me; it was a Catholic education which made me able to empathise with their shock, rather than dismissing them as superstitious or bigoted or oversensitive. Because I grew up with nuns, especially those lay sisters with their simple kindly faith, I knew that blasphemy does create real shock: not an offended, uppity sort of shock but more the sensation you would get if somebody called your mother a whore, or drew obscenely on your baby's photograph.

Religions are not interchangeable, but a sense of reverence is. This is why, in celebrating Christmas (or Easter, or just Sunday) properly with children, you do more for inter-faith understanding than you would with any amount of self-important academic footling around explaining multi-ethnic symbols which none of you believe in. Equally, an Islamic or Sikh child brought up to give reverence to its faith probably understands the crib and the

Nativity play a lot better than any modish council official sketching out 'guidelines'.

This sense of reverence being interchangeable does not mean that doctrine does not matter. It does. Doctrine forms a bridge between a sense of worship – which is programmed into us all, and can take the most unhealthy forms if left alone – and a code of ethical behaviour. And in the realm of behaviour, despite all the world faiths and new variants on offer in this age of buffet-counter religion, nothing quite matches up to the basic tenets of Christianity.

It combines humility and a sense of sin with confidence in redemption and glory. It places love of one's neighbour at the centre. Not tolerance, not approval, not judgment: love. It forbids the things which do worst harm, such as vengeance, treachery, resentment, self-importance, and casting stones at sinners. It cannot, without ugly distortion, be tamed to the cause of any self-interested human faction. As Dean Inge said, it is a revolu-tionary idealism which estranges revolutionaries by its idealism and conservatives by its drastic revaluation of earthly goods.

It can be understood by a child, sometimes better than by an adult; yet its central mystery and paradox can fuel a lifetime's contemplation. And sometimes the sharpest shafts of under-standing and appreciation of what it is come from unbelievers. Matthew Parris, the commentator, often proclaims his lack of belief but once said, contemplating what Christianity preaches, that he cannot understand how those who *do* believe all this stuff none the less manage to carry on their lives exactly as he does. If he did believe it, he observed, he would have to think of nothing else, to live no other way, and to proclaim the good news day and night.

Which is more or less what Christians were told to do, two thousand years ago.

19. Against All Reason: Encounters with Faith

The months working on *Mysterious Ways*, a potted history of all our beliefs, were the genesis of this book, which is about the growth of my own. If ever anybody had a heavy-duty, industrial-grade religious education I did; none of the basic cultural Christian stuff is missing. I can read Milton and Donne without confusion, spot the difference between a reliquary and a taber-nacle, and know who is who in quattrocento paintings. Moreover, I have had my share of moments when the Christian faith and its surrounding paraphernalia have bestowed a sense of transcendent, more than emotional understanding and gratitude, and when I have known with a high and joyful certainty that Julian of Norwich is right, and that we may 'Go gladly and gaily, because of His love'.

But reflecting on it, I had to admit that in justice I should apply the same caveat to myself and my feelings about Giotto and Julian and Bunyan and Durham Cathedral, as I do to the shimmering New Age prophets, doped hippies, spiritual tourists and assorted frenzied holy-rollers that I instinctively mistrust. If one thing unites crystal-gazers, huckster TV evangelists and High Church heritage-aesthetes, it is the elevation of religious *feeling* above dull plodding religious duty. If you bristle with mistrust at the self-indulgence of Glastonbury wire-twisters, you should extend that mistrust to emotional revival meetings where you are urged to 'Let Jesus be your friend' and to 'bear witness' on stage – but never told that when the meeting is over you should go home and be nicer to your family, not to mention your enemies at the office.

Although the mystical, contemplative experience is inseparable from religion, all Christian ages have seen warnings against letting it stand alone, independent of virtuous behaviour. As one convent chaplain instructed his nursing nuns, you must be a Martha abroad and a contemplative Mary only at home. St Paul tartly observes that without charity, speaking with the tongues of men and angels is no better than a tooting trumpet or tinkling cymbals. Of Faith, Hope, and Charity, he put the latter first. St Teresa of Avila, unnervingly full of contemplative rapture herself up on the high battlements of her Interior Castle, none the less severely told her sisters: 'Contemplation is a gift of God which is *not* necessary for salvation nor for earning our eternal reward, nor will anyone require you to possess it'.

St Gregory said that the Citadel of Contemplation was reached only via the Field of Labour. The favourite Christian saint of legend has not, by and large, been the one found hovering in divine levitation, hypnotised by devotion and marked by stigmata. He – or she – is more likely found giving a cloak to a beggar, being whipped for helping the outcast, or stepping forward to die in another's place.

On the other hand, 'right doing springs from right being', and to the Christian any purely secular attempt to do good by one's neighbour without the support of divine strength, is unthinkably arrogant and impracticable. For one thing, if you do not believe in the individual immortal soul it is almost inevitable that your grand rational scheme for doing good will lead to the painless and convenient eradication of those whose presence does not fit your scheme. Christianity certainly must take its share of blame for tyrannies and inquisitions, but most countries which have attempted to put a purely rational order on society have ended up perpetrating far worse horrors. The Paris revolutionaries of 1968 wrote on walls 'How can anybody think clearly in the shadow of a steeple?', but when Stalins and Ceaucescus have knocked down the steeples, they have built far wickeder structures. The medieval picture of a king kneeling to confess to a humble friar still has a resonance today. There must be a higher Authority than authority; lose sight of that and everything falls apart.

Yet to turn it all round again, good social behaviour can never be the whole of Christianity. An infuriating tendency of the last fifteen years or so has been the appropriation of religion by governments to act as handy spiritual sticking-plaster for our myriad social ills. 'Teach them right and wrong in RE lessons! Do Assembly!' is the constant cry of Education Secretaries, as if school prayers were a sure cure for ram-raiding.

There are two problems with this. One is that to think most school RE will make children behave is as stupid as thinking that TV football will make them fit. The other problem with the notion of religion-as-behaviour is that it gives the impression that Christianity aims low. It boils it down to the commandments on stealing, killing, adultery, lying, and honouring your father and mother. It enjoins the obviously sensible commands to be kind and well-socialised, and ignores the great and mysterious demand that we worship the invisible and speak its name with reverence. It fails to acknowledge that if you really believe, that belief will alter everything; and that much of it will lead you down paths which social science and biological determinism will find counter-intuitive, if not plain barking mad. As Harold Macmillan once plaintively said: 'If you don't believe in God, all you have to believe in is decency. Decency is very good. Better decent than indecent. But I don't think it's enough.'

The full, horrifying, exhilarating truth is that if you actually look at the tenets of Christianity they tell you that good behaviour is only the baseline, the launching pad, the *sine qua non*. The point at which Christianity takes off and begins to glow is when it does become counter-intuitive and downright troublesome in worldly terms. There are some very disturbing, subversive instructions there: '*sell all thou hast and give to the poor . . . turn the other cheek . . . judge not, that ye shall not be judged . . .*

blessed are the meek . . . lay not up treasures upon earth . . . consider the lilies of the field . . .'

These are not sensible injunctions, fit for a Lord Chesterfield letter or a newspaper leader column. They sit uneasily in a society convinced that decent people are those who own property and are constantly busy, getting and spending. They sound odd in a time when every group bristles with awareness of its 'rights' and is determined to stand on them and sue for compensation at the slightest, even accidental, tap to its cheek.

They sit uneasily, too, with the tough landlording policies over the years of the Church Commissioners in England, with the arrogant obduracy of feuding clerics in the great cathedrals, with the wealth of the Vatican, with the argument against priestly celibacy which focuses on the 'natural right' to a married life, with the snobberies and snarlings of different layers of Catholic and Anglo-Catholic spokesmen, and with the fact that more and more clergymen are joining trade unions and speaking without a blush of their 'job security' and 'career structures'. The ultimate absurdity came a couple of years back in a House of Lords debate, when speakers deplored the poverty of clergy not because it is unkind to clergy but because 'these days, people don't listen to paupers'. Lord Morris spoke with distaste of priests who had to drive around in 'old bangers'.

Who, with any sense of absurdity, did not laugh aloud at that, prior to banging their head on the wall in frustration? What on earth happened to the ragged figure with the burning eyes, crying the name of the Lord in the wilderness? Where are the hermits in their cells, dispensing kindness? The joyful Franciscans bidden by St Francis to 'carry nothing for the journey, neither a knapsack nor a purse, nor bread nor money, but whatever house they enter let them first say "peace to this house" '? These days we would have the police round and get them cleared away as a rabble of New Age travellers. As for the tradition of mild-eyed saints who keep destabilising the economy by setting their slaves free and breaching health and safety guidelines by kissing lepers, it has long since given way to a more modern culture of Lord

Bishops in ermine and Cardinals in Mercedes cars and bickering Synods and socialite congregations. Where have all the extreme Christians gone? Where are the world-denying gestures and divine unreasonableness which clearly draw the lines between believers and the rest?

When these do appear, we are rattled. In a brief *cause célèbre* of the 1990s the Scottish Cardinal Thomas Winning caused uproar with a piece of literal Christianity. He believed profoundly enough in the Catholic teaching on the sanctity of the unborn life to make a compassionate public offer to all young women considering abortion, promising any kind of help in his power to support them in a decision to have the baby. To read the barracking in the national press the next day you would have thought he had called for a return of the rack and thumbscrew for heretics. 'A shameful bribe', they said, and the National Abortion Campaign asked whether he thought women could be bought? He was accused of making women feel guilty, and in the *Evening Standard* it was decried as 'political posturing at its most transparent'.

Yet what the Cardinal said was simple and rather touching: he condemned any idea of violence or embarrassing people, distanced himself from aggressive pro-life tactics but gently invited those with unwanted pregnancies to ask for help:

> Whatever worries or care you may have in this regard, we will help you. If you want help to cope with raising the baby on your own, we will help you. If you want to discuss adoption of your unborn child, we will help you. We will help find you somewhere to have your baby surrounded by support and encouragement.

Other voices cried shame on him, since his Church in Scotland is notoriously poor; where would the money come from for this help? But a priest is not an accountant, and *Dominus providebit*. If the offer did cause endless administrative and financial headaches, and still does, then so what? Provided that the Cardinal himself is willing to be less comfortable for his principles than most (and he had already given up his official car for one of the old bangers so reviled by Lord Morris in the C of E context) he had every reason to do it.

Or take the Vicar of Sundon. He became my Christian pin-up of the week for a while in 1995, when he attracted the contumely of the national press by 'insulting' his parishioners in his newsletter. All that the Revd Stephen Pullan actually said was that 95 per cent of them, poor church attenders, 'live out their sordid little lives without any reference to God'.

Tactless, maybe, but I was charmed. He was just doing a bit of proper ecclesiastical thundering, trying to shake the parish awake. I looked up 'sordid' and its definitions were very satisfying in this context – 'base, mean, ignoble, coarse, inferior, squalid, selfish and influenced only by mercenery considerations'. Well, what else is modern life, without worship, eh? We pore anxiously over lifestyle journalism, scheme to get a few extra years' life then fret about whether we will enjoy them; from our Gradgrind approach to education as solely a means to get 'qualifications' and earn more, we pass to an anxious adult obsession with money, thence to an old age when we become not wise tribal chiefs, leading the young towards a unified and glorious vision of creation, but worrisome 'pensioners' – defined once again by our income. Sordid, or what? There are, of course, routes into more transcendent feeling – love, parenthood, fine art, travel to less sordid cultures than our own. Some try to struggle out by getting involved in quick-fix cults or practices, or passionate sentimentality about animals. But by and large, life without any religion comes, pretty quickly, to meet all the conditions of that dictionary definition. Sordid. Why shouldn't a vicar say so? Provided, of course, that he also asks himself why his church – as do most churches – never seems to occur to the great majority as a sensible route out of the sordidness trap.

But those who attempt or profess a headlong, passionate, fully committed Christianity generally get reviled. It is almost a benchmark. Some of them take it with fine carefree scorn, like

Victoria Gillick: I shall never forget her saying to me, apropos the rubbishing she took about her stand over contraception and about her ten children:'The world is just so tight and organised and dull. Paganism is always like that, you know: a narrow, fear-ridden society living in a dark forest, with acquisitive anxious values. A society that doesn't know its Maker is a lonely one, and things like AIDS can panic it completely. I know that we are all children of God, and this gives you a place in the cosmos and a faith in the future.' There are areas where Mrs Gillick makes me gulp and flinch, as any sensible secular modern woman would, especially one who is still at odds with her cradle Church over the matter of contraception; but another part of me is forever standing in salute to the Gillicks. We need them.

Others take the incomprehension of the secular world with a deliberate (possibly slightly artful) simplicity. Take the late Mother Teresa of Calcutta, who dismayed her followers in Britain by forbidding them to raise funds. Once, questioned by a reporter who accused her of being publicity-hungry 'or else why are you doing this interview' the infuriating saint said with a radiant smile: 'To help you, because you asked, and it is your job.' This uncontemporary attitude, coupled with her perfectly Christian belief that there is an actual value in suffering, enraged critics like Christopher Hitchens who wrote and broadcast blistering attacks on her. It cannot help their blood pressure to know that without doubt Mother Teresa will have forgiven them instantly, rejoiced in having the humiliation to Offer Up, and prayed for her detractors' souls.

There are endless other examples: down the years in journalism, and mainly outside religious programmes, I have found people whose attitude and answers stay in my mind, hooked like burrs, simply because they do stand outside the sordidness of everyday values, taking their orders from another world. They are reminders that Christianity must not be sensible: it marches to a different drum, it goes the extra mile. It is more than philanthropy and more than unbalanced brain chemistry: it is that Wordsworthian light that never was on land or sea.

In an age of lifestyle and image, it barely cares where it is. On the Glastonbury visit Dom Aelred Watkin, shortly before his death in 1997, sat in his sandals and robe in a chilly stone-flagged room at Downside and remembered the moment of his conversion as the discovery of the utter unimportance of the whole world:

> When I was young, I was a complete unbeliever . . . I just went through the motions and disliked priests more than I can tell you. But in one moment – I hardly like to tell you this, it sounds so absurd – in one moment, I was looking at a picture in a book by someone I utterly despised, a picture of a tomb which I thought was hideous – oh, everything was against it. And I suddenly saw as in a moment that the next world was so much more real than this world you simply couldn't put the two together, however hard you tried.

As the conversation wore on, he talked about his sense of kinship with earlier Abbots, or some of them, and how faith in an eternal God annihilates history. Talking of medieval figures and their writings he stood beside them across the gulf of centuries, entirely kin and comfortable. 'Each Christian is in a sense para-historic, or whatever you'd call it,' he said tranquilly. 'Eternity lies outside history, although it touches it.'

The same dizzy familiarity with eternity and tradition marked Father Llewellyn, with whom I sat in the reconstructed cell of the anchorite Julian of Norwich.

'Now, I'm going to shock you. One thing she says which I like very much is that God cannot forgive us our sins. Now, I've shocked you! But you see – I cannot come into this room because I am already here, God cannot forgive us our sins because he already has. Yet there was a time when I *did* come into this room – but there was no time when God had not already forgiven us our sins.'

As the gentle old priest talked, marvellingly, about Julian's vision of the comfort of God we read a passage from her book:

Once in my imagination I was taken down to the bed of the sea, and saw there green hills and dales that seemed to be clothed with moss, seaweed and stones. And I understood that if a person firmly belives that God is always with man, then even if he is thrown into the depths of the sea, he will be preserved in body and soul and will enjoy greater solace and comfort than all this world can offer.

While we read this, there was a middle-aged man, slightly unkempt, moving around by the altar collecting candles and scraping up wax and muttering to himself. His movements were jerky, but I thought perhaps he was some harmless, slightly troubled figure employed by the nuns at the Julian centre as a sacristan. Slowly, however, he moved closer and began interrupting the conversation, at first inconsequentially and then more determined and coherent. 'There's evil here. There's been a bit of trouble. Do you see that? Cat's hairs, feathers, candles. Satanists been at work here. I've had my work cut out to deal with it all.'

We ended the interview and went outside. Father Llewellyn had to leave, but we asked the nun in charge whether she knew the disturbed man. She did not. 'It's a city centre, a lot of people walk around.' The chapel was due to be locked, but he would not leave. My BBC colleague and I did not like to leave her alone with the man and stood irresolute, wondering what to do. He came out.

'I have a knife,' he said. We stiffened. He brandished it.

'I scrape off the wax. Satanists.' Then he turned to us. 'There's evil, Satan, everywhere' he said. 'I want you to repeat after me, Jesus is the Lord God. Go on, say it.' Colin demurred. 'Say it!' Colin said it, rather sulkily. The man turned away, jerkier now, waving the little knife. 'I've been fighting now since January the third, and I grow stronger every day. Stronger for the end.'

Wandering mental patients, some of them schizophrenic, are a sad feature of British city centres today. The nun told us, resignedly, that they get a lot of the 'poor souls', who are attracted to the mystery and peace of churches. She was calm and gentle with him, but I went up to the bookshop and rang the police, who came quickly. No sooner had he been quietly persuaded off the premises, knife and all, followed by a kindly 'Bless you' from the nun, than another older man weaved up to us.

'DO YOU BELIEVE IN THE CHRIST JESUS?' he shouted. 'Alleluia!'

'Oh, I know him,' said one of the sisters. 'He comes by quite often to see us, don't you, Billy?'

Her calmness shamed us, but it seemed to me as we drove off that Julian's spirit lived on. At the bottom of this ocean too, on the terrifying sea-bed of urban insanity and insecurity, the unprotected nuns felt solace and comfort Even in the sad mad city centres of the 1990s, all shall be well, and all manner of thing shall be well.

We half-believers or unbelievers are often shamed into silence by the gay tranquillity of those who act – against reason and prudence – as if they were entirely armed by a God who is beyond death. Sally Trench, whose book *Bury Me in My Boots* sent me down to iron the dossers' sheets at the Simon hostel years before, surfaced again with a project for reclaiming teenagers excluded from school. She cut through the red tape and taught them in her own house, alone. The interview was about her tactics, not her beliefs, but at one stage in the interview I asked why after a series of injuries and rebuffs she carried on. 'I'm a Christian' she said briskly. 'These kids need someone to help them. It's obvious. I don't understand how people *don't* help.'

Even more unforgettable was Jackie Pullinger, a radical young Christian musician who set off across the world with a Quixotic naïveté to find where she was called to work. She lighted upon Hong Kong's walled city of Kowloon, the 'City of darkness', before that unspeakable slum was pulled down in 1989. In this place of misery, of violence, of prostitutes from ten to seventy years old, of almost universal drug addiction and Triad gangs she walked the dark alleys like a Victorian philanthropist seeing 'another city in its place, ablaze with light. It was my dream. No more crying, no more death or pain.'

Her first tactic was to walk up to a gangster and say 'Jesus loves you'. He just seemed bored, so she began handing out tracts, but the addicts just rolled up her papers and used them to inhale heroin off their scraps of tinfoil, 'chasing the dragon'. So she got a teaching job outside, and used her earnings to start a youth club for young Triads who were unwelcome elsewhere. They sneered that she was 'cracked about Jesus' but came. From these beginnings grew a remarkable mission of rehabilitation, which culminated when she brought a group of her Bible students, reformed addicts, to London.

I was wary when I met her: born-again Christians and speakers in tongues had raised my hackles before with their Bible-centred earnestness. But the evidence of her work won me over, and more than that, I liked the Humpty Dumpty inversion of commonsense which marked her brand of Christianity.

'I don't understand why most people try to organise the bricks and mortar and staff first, before the relationships. We begin with the love. The money? Oh, we pray for it. We don't fund-raise.'

I sense a score of experienced aid workers casting their eyes up to heaven and groaning at this, but Pullinger has the right to do it her way. She was gently sceptical about telethons and institutional, commercial charities in a Western world where we have all trained ourselves to ignore blank-eyed figures squatting in cardboard boxes on cold winter nights. 'I pray for people that they may not be able to sleep at night because of the man in the cardboard box. The awfulness comes when you think you don't need to consider him because someone else is, or because society is.'

She looked at me gently, this skinny straw-haired flame of a woman, when I asked her about the sacrifice she has made.

'No sacrifice. That's dumb. I have more fun than most people. People are always telling me to take it easy or I'll burn out, but a couple of years later it always turns out that they've burned out themselves, and I haven't. The Bible doesn't say anything about looking after yourself, does it?'

Unreasonable, incomprehensible in the world's terms, infuriating, glorious. Christian, all the way.

I cannot forget other faces too, looking at me with those clear happy eyes: the imprisoned Russian poet Irina Ratushinskaya, remembering how she carved her poems in soap and learned them, and felt the prayers of those who remembered her like a solid warm wall of comfort. I remember the late Bishop of Liverpool, Derek Worlock, talking about a relic he had once prayed before, in a time of great trouble, and how it reached out towards him; and an evangelical convert explaining, with hesitant modesty, how a poster on a railway station changed his life. I remember other moments, more personal, when a few minutes face-to-face with somebody brought me almost harshly face-to-face with the glorious irrationality of faith. And always, the mark of them was that they brought me back to humanity, as much or more than they brought me to the idea of God. Back I would come, from whatever resentful spiteful hostile media ratpack mind-set I had fallen into, and with rueful reluctance return to the search for divinity in every difficult bastard I had to deal with that day.

Although sometimes, obviously, it was with the muttered motto my mother taught me. 'God put us here on earth to help others. What he put the others here for, God only knows.'

The idea of the gloriousness of unreasonable faith, unreasonable hope and unreasonable charity was finally solidified in my mind by the uproar over the Bishop of Argyll, Roderick Wright. It was a sad story, and its shockingness unfolded by tantalising stages. At first there were rumours of a woman, but his Cardinal and colleagues spoke anxiously about the possibility that he was upset or in trouble. Then the woman was confirmed as a reality, and still there was a reluctance to condemn. Then his teenage son – by another woman – revealed himself and the hopeful Catholic voices on the radio from Scotland still tried to understand and forgive. Only when he sold his story to a newspaper did the word 'betrayal' reluctantly get used. The gentleness of the Church response caused a lot of huffing anger from those who leap to condemn; I found myself, an exiled unpractising Catholic, strangely moved by their anxiety to forgive, to recall, to kindle again the faith in one confused man's heart. I could not resist the joint statement from Cardinal Winning and his archbishop, both stunned as mullets, their church humiliated, their judgment questioned in every newspaper, thoroughly at bay but still trying. They deplored the sale of Bishop Roddy's story but added: 'We are glad to note, however, that he appears to be well.' Considering that Catholic convert MPs were by that time using the word *excommunication*, this was mildness itself. But what really came home to me was a tragically daft statement from the Bishop himself, in his hideout.

'There is a difference between cold logic and love, and this was becoming love.'

That was the clue. In a fit of passion, sitting in an Irish cottage with my own long hinterland of failed Catholicism behind me, I wrote for *The Times*:

> Try again, bishop: think it through, take a cold bath, work it out. If your Church, your vocation, had come to represent no more than cold logic, easily outshone by faulty human love, then you lost the plot and the faith long ago. Religion is not cold logic: it is a greater love or it is nothing at all.
>
> And that is the serious thing, the only important thing. Never mind any number of embarrassed cardinals, furious colleagues, sermons about Judas, debate about celibacy. When a church becomes nothing but 'cold logic' to one of its bishops, the problem is all his own.

A greater love, or nothing at all. High, glorious unreason and a love beyond love. Intellect alone won't do, any more than visions will. The centre of Christianity remains, and always will, a mystery. *The* Mystery.

20. Where I Begunne

Christmas is coming. I have a lot to do, because almost by accident, I am a collector of cribs. I have Nativity scenes, in plaster and wood and clay and tin and silver-paper and pipe-cleaners and paper and ebony and olivewood and wire and wax, from all over the world. There are about a hundred and fifty of them in the attic, from matchbox size to great sprawling Provençal *santon* villages and a Neapolitan mountain with soppy angels and a towering *Szopka* from Poland, based on Cracow Cathedral with the Holy Family in the main door.

The Andean Jesus is swaddled tightly and laid by a fire by his Indian parents; the Chilean is standing upright, being fed from a spoon; the Peruvian villagers beneath the stable are clearly drunk; the Rwandan figures have an impala among them, the Romanians have subdivided the manger so that the ox can still eat while the Baby takes one end, the Bangladeshi ones have a waterbuffalo. This year's discovery – gloatingly welcome to a mother – is of the Byzantine icon tradition in which the Virgin is not kneeling uncomfortably on the hard stable floor but reclining while others look after the baby at her side. At the other extreme, this year it is my earnest intention to get hold of something I have heard of but never seen, a *clockwork* crib from Barcelona.

There is a contemporary set, too, which I commissioned, bit by bit, and set under a railway arch: Mary is a hippie, Joseph a Rasta, and among the visitors are tramps and drunks and High

Court judges and Robert Maxwell and Lady Thatcher and Peter Mandelson, because every year on principle we commission a popular hate-figure to add. Quite unironically, just on the principle that anybody may stand around the Crib, and that nobody shall ever be excluded from Christmas through antipathy or quarrel.

The cribs are not valuable, not really; but their numbers and variety have come to mean a lot. They range from the simply beautiful via the solemnly magnificent to the unspeakably kitsch, and therefore betray a lot about humanity and a little about divinity.

I must get them down from the attic again, in a messy conglomeration of boxes and bundles, because they no longer really belong to me. Ever since the early days, when people were giving them to me for fun and I was collecting out of anthropological interest and to amuse my children, I have held exhibitions.

At first they were in the house, and we gave everyone a glass of mulled wine and a gingerbread, lit them entirely with candles and twice, in a particularly gung-ho mood, organised a Nativity play in the damp farmyard, with real sheep and cows. It made money for Save the Children, but more than that it made a quiet, reflective last Sunday before Christmas. We, and whoever came, could escape for a while the frenzied world of shopping, and look with innocent eyes at a hundred ways a craftsman might portray new life and new hope in a stable.

Then the collection outgrew the house, and we dropped the exhibition for one year, and felt dreadful: as if Christmas were missing on one cylinder. The next year we regrouped, used a local gallery and kept it going for a whole week. Finally we invaded the Round Chapel at Norwich Cathedral, with the wholehearted support of the Dean and an inexhaustible supply of wardens volunteered by Christian Aid in the city.

Now, for the second year, a van to Norwich must be hired (rather larger, because of the Neapolitan crib and my determination to hang the pictures as well this time and set out the cardboard theatre-cribs too). Dozens of sets must be assembled, with the usual panics and some swearing when the Child Jesus goes missing, or Joseph's head proves to have fallen off, or somebody mixes up the black Tanzanian ebony with the equally black Bengali clay set and starts an argument about whose ass is whose. It must be done. It has become an Observance; part theatrical, part anthropological, sentimental if you care to take it that way, but inescapably devotional.

While I was putting them up last year (it took all day) a sour kind of Cathedral lady visitor came up to me and said:

'You aren't leaving them here? even with a warden? Surely!'

'Yes, I am.'

'They'll be broken. Vandalised. People will steal the figures. Children. *Boys*. You can't trust anybody these days.'

'I've never had a breakage or a theft. Ever. In ten years, most of them in my own house.'

'You should have glass in front of them.'

'No. I don't want them under glass. I want them alive and close to people. Don't worry.'

She walked away, shoes squeaking with disapproval. I wanted to say all sorts of things, starting with 'Look, lady, if you can't put a crib up in a bloody *Cathedral*, we might as well all give up.' But I bit my tongue and turned back to my hundred families, a hundred baby Incarnations representing what Milton saw: the Virgin and the Baby and the moment of rest and wonder.

> And all around the courtly stable
> Bright-harnessed angels sit in order serviceable.

This is not a novel, so it has no tidy end. I cannot say that I am back where I was as a child. Who can? Nor am I thoroughly back in step with the Catholic Church.

But sometimes, the best metaphor for the way it is seems to be Donne's compasses, with the firm centre and the wandering arc. Even if it wasn't supposed to be one of his religious poems.

Where I Begunne

So wilt thou be to mee, who must
Like th'other foot, obliquely runne
Thy firmnes makes my circle just
And makes mee end, where I begunne.

Bibliography

Anouilh, J. L., *Antigone*, translated by Lewis Galantine (Methuen Drama, 1994)
   "   "   *L'Alouette*, translated by Christopher Fry (Methuen, 1986)

A Catechism of Christian Doctrine (Catholic Truth Society 1889, latest edition 1997)

Huxley, A., *The Doors of Perception* and *Heaven and Hell* (Flamingo, 1994)

Lewis, C. S., *The Magician's Nephew* (Collins, 1989)
   "   "   *The Silver Chair* (Lions, 1990)
   "   "   *The Last Battle* (Collins, 1989)

Milton, J., *Hymn on the Morning of Christ's Nativity* (Folio Press, 1987)

Mitford, N., *The Pursuit of Love* (The Folio Society, 1991)

Salinger, J. D., *Franny and Zooey* (Penguin, 1994 and Heinemann, 1994)

White, T. H., *The Sword in the Stone* (Collins, 1977)